大考英文聽力
搶分秘笈

主編 政大英文系 **陳超明** 教授

編著 **TOEIC** *900!* 工作團隊

目錄

A

看圖辨義 ……… 27

B

對答 ……… 103

C

D

聽力技巧三部曲

　　學習英文，學生們反應最大的困難在於聽和說，然而如果聽不懂，說的能力也會受影響，因為這兩者同是屬於對於語言聲音的認知與表達。雖然讀跟寫是對文字的理解運用較相關，但其實學習語文是一體的，聽不懂英文也會減緩學習英文的效率。 傳統對於聽力的練習都是鼓勵不斷聆聽，這樣能培養英文語感跟掌握語句的節奏。但這種方式進步速度太慢，這裡我們要以系統性學習的方法，分為三部提供挑戰英文聽力的方向。

第一部　單字與句型

　　聽不懂英文的困擾，包括三種：第一是聽不懂英文單字，因為聽到字音，卻無法與字的意義連結在一起，而且認識的單字太少；第二是聽不懂句子，尤其當句子比較長的時候；第三是當字句都可能聽懂，卻一時之間找不到重點資訊，這點我們到第三篇再仔細分析。

1. 單字

A・認識的單字太少

　　因為認識的字不多，所以聽到的時候都反應不過來。 其實一般日常生活用到的單字大約兩到三千字，也就是國中三年跟高中一半的單字量，不算很多，本書中出現的單字大部份都屬於這類基本單字，把他們記熟就可以應付大部份的生活所需。

B・那麼如何掌握單字呢？

　　一定要透過聲音去學單字，首先聆聽單字的發音，再複誦。不只如此，為了要長久記憶這些單字的音和意，最好錄下自己唸出的單字，放出來反複聆聽與念誦，聽自己的聲音會比較印象深刻。記住音的同時也要記住涵義。注意該單字出現於文章中的場合與用法，並能自己用這個單字多造一些句子。

C・注意不同時態

　　在依照上述方法記憶單字的音和意時，也不要只聆聽與背誦單字的原型，因為實際運用的時候大都不是原來的形式。記名詞時也要多唸它的複數用法；記動詞時同時也要唸出它的各種時態。

綜合上述掌握單字的方法，看以下這段範例：

David and Emily <u>exercise</u> regularly. They often <u>jog</u> on the <u>weekends</u>. Whenever they run, they wear <u>shorts</u> or <u>warm-up suits</u> and <u>put on</u> <u>running shoes</u> to protect their feet. Sometimes Emily <u>wears</u> <u>earphones</u> and <u>listens to</u> <u>music</u> while <u>running</u>. If you go to the <u>park</u> this weekend, you'll probably see them <u>jogging</u> together.
（David 和 Emily 有規律地運動。他們常在周末去慢跑。每當他們去慢跑，他們穿短褲、保暖衣物，而且會穿上慢跑鞋以保護他們的腳。有時候 Emily 會在跑步時帶耳機來聽音樂。如果你這個週末去公園，你可能會看到他們一起慢跑。）

以上每個字都是基本日常生活必備，熟悉這些單字，盡管有一些可能沒聽清楚也能猜出大概含意。
名詞：weekend 週末、shorts 短褲、warm-up suits 保暖衣物、running shoes 慢跑鞋、feet (foot 單數) 腳、earphones 耳機、music 音樂、park 公園。
動詞：exercise 運動、jog (jogging) 慢跑、run (running) 跑步、wear (wears) 穿、put on 穿上、protect 保護、listen to (listens) 聽、go 去、see 看。
注意單字在文章中出現時的不同形式，在唸的時候也要同時多唸它們的各種形式，在聽到時才不會慌亂。如：weekend/weekends，run/running 等等。

2. 句了

會導致聽不懂句子的可能性分為以下四種：

A · 重讀

◎英文字和中文字不同，一個字裡可能有多個音節，而且每個字在句中的輕重音都不一樣，重音不同會影響字的意思，也會造成語句的誤解。首先，大多數字都是第一個音節加重音，如上一例子中的 exercise 運動、regularly 規律地；而 protect 保護 就是屬於重音在第二音節的字。

◎有些字動詞名詞拼法相同但念法的重音不同。如：increase（增加）、contract（合約）、 survey（調查）等等，這些字重音在前為名詞，重音在後為動詞。

◎再者，在句子中，是內容字的發音比功能性的字重讀。掌握句子含意的名詞和動詞是內容字；而助動詞、介系詞、連接詞等則是功能字。形容詞和副詞則依照影響句意的程度決定是否為內容字而加重讀。

以上段文章為例，列出的名詞和動詞都是內容字，還有專有名詞如他們的名字。這些字在唸文章時要稍微加重音。其他沒有畫線的字則是功能字。這篇文章中的副詞 regularly、probably、often、sometimes 等等並不會影響文章句意太多，所以不需要加重去讀。

◎有時不是內容字但若要強調時也會加重音，否定的字 not 尤其多見。

I'm not sure.（我不確定。）強調「不」確定，not 要加重音。

B · 語調

英文句子因為字和句都會有高低起伏，不習慣的情形下就無法輕易理解。原則上直述句語氣往下降，問句往上，驚嘆短句重音在前。但根據句子的長短也會有調整。

◎直述句：語氣是越往後越下沉，如果句子較長，會先在句子中間停頓處略略先往上，之後再下降。

She wants to travel and aid people in need.

（她想要旅遊並幫助窮困的人。）

這句話的語調在中間 and 之前會有點上揚，然後再往下降。

◎問句：是非疑問句句尾語氣往上，長問句會先往下，句尾再往上揚。附加疑問句也是如此。但如果是 5W1H 的問句主要是要詢問資訊，句尾往上的語調就不明顯，而改成是句首的疑問詞加重音強調。

Should we take classes to learn how to use it?

（我們是否應該上課學習如何使用它？）

這個是非疑問句較長，所以前面語調沒有向上，直到後面片語 how to use it 才往上揚。

What does the man mean?（這男人所指的是什麼？）

疑問詞的問句中，句首疑問詞 what 加重音強調，句尾沒有語調向上。

◎驚嘆句：這種句子通常不長，所以語調沒有起伏，而是在句首加重音。

That's great!（真棒！）

此驚嘆句只有兩個字，句首 that's 加重音，great 是重點所以也重音。

C · 停頓

雖然每個人說話的節奏不同，但大都會根據句子的結構以及語句含意切分句子，稍做停頓。了解停頓點可以方便聽者找到重點，同時也能讓說話者換氣呼吸。停頓的情形可以分為以下幾種：

◎重要關鍵字或訊息前

Welcome to the opening day of this year's baseball season here at Sparrow Stadium.

（歡迎來到 Sparrow 球場觀看本棒球季的開場賽。）

opening day 球季開始的第一天，這是這句話所要強調的重點，所以在之前要稍微停頓，提醒聽者注意。

◎主要子句與附屬子句之間

As you can see from the picture below, / volleyball players must try to return the ball across the net.

（如你在下方圖片所見，排球選手必須試圖將球打回過網。）

As 開頭的子句和 volleyball players 帶頭的主要子句之間，必須停頓。

◎句子組成結構之間

分為主詞、動詞、受詞、片語等，中間都會停頓

Our scheduled arrival time / for Ellis County Airport / will be delayed a bit / as the area is experiencing heavy thunderstorms.

（我們預定抵達 Ellis County 機場的時間將延遲，因為該地區有大雷雨。）

主詞 / 片語 / 動詞 / 子句 。這句話可以根據結構分成四部份，最後面的子句也可以再區分，但因為該子句不長所以應該可以一口氣說完。以結構分段停頓是大原則，每個人的說話速度跟習慣也可能省略一兩停頓點，或是慢慢說話而增加多些停頓。

◎連接詞之間：常用的如 and、but、or

Her mother said she needs clothes / and that's what I'm going to buy.

（她媽媽說她需要衣服，所以我正要去買。）

◎眾多選項之間：超過兩個的選項之間會用逗點隔開，也就是停頓的時機

Iris learns to play a variety of sports such as baseball, basketball, tennis, and volleyball.

（Iris 學習很多種運動，如棒球、籃球、網球、和排球。）

除了連接詞 and 之前要停頓外，每個項目之間都要稍微停頓。

D．省略與連音

母語人士口語上的省略和連音最容易讓人聽不懂。以下列出一些最常見的情況，多練習唸就比較能抓住音感進而了解聽懂。

◎ Be 動 詞 與 助 動 詞：am、are、is、was、were、will、do、does、did、would、have、has 和 had 等等會省略並與前面或後面的字連音。

◎ 代名詞：I、you、he、she、we、they、it，所有格代名詞 my、yours、his、her、our、their、its，以及受格代名詞 me、you、him、her、us、them。

◎ 介系詞：最常見的是 to (tu, da)、for (fer, fe) 和 of (u, a)。

◎ 連接詞 ：常用的有 and (n)、or (er)、或 because (cause)。

◎ 其他情形：字尾是 ing (in)、字首是 h（不發音）、can 和 can't (kin, kant)、want to (wanna) 和 go to (gonna) 等等。

通常口語聊天對話都會有連音的情況，以下將可能省略和連音的部份劃線：

M：Have you finished your New Year's shopping, yet?

W：Not quite. I'm still having trouble trying to decide what to buy my niece.
　　　　　 I'm　　　 havin'　　　 tryin'tu　　　 whatu

M：How about something for home entertainment?
　　　　　　　　　　　　　 fe

M：I thought about that, and it's a good idea. Still, I'm thinking about
　　　　　　　　　　　　　 it's　　　　　　　　　 I'm thinkin'

something to wear.
　　　　　 tu

M：I used to hate it when I got clothes for a New Year's present.
　　 useda　　　　　　　　　　　　　　　　 fe

W：That's because you were a boy. It's different for girls.
　　 That's　 'cause　 you're　　　 It's

M: Oh, yeah. I forgot.

W: The problem is: what kind of clothes do you buy for a 16-year-old girl?
　　　　　　　　　　　　　　 a　　　　　 du　 fer

M: Clothes are too hard to choose. I would play it safe and just buy some
jewelry.　　　　　　　　　　　　　　 I'd　　　　　　　 'n

口語省略很生活化，規則其實也時常更動，主要大方向為上述所提，可以多看英語發音的電影或影集來模仿學習。

　　學習英文多年，在實際運用的場合卻聽不懂別人說的英文，這是台灣學生常有的困擾，這主要是因為缺乏情境學習（Situated Learning）的緣故。情境學習不是要背單字跟句法，而是要將自己融入實際的場景，訓練習慣某些情境，捉住語言表現的模式，接收情境下要給的資訊。了解並熟悉情境，就能預先對可能出現的資訊單字有心理準備，就算當場漏聽了一些字句，也能依照上下文快速掌握重點。

　　學習英文可以是無時無刻的，記得要養成習慣多聆聽並吸收周遭的生活英文。以下列出一些大考常出現，我們生活周遭也常會遇到的情境對話來練習，包括：餐飲、購物、居家、交通、校園、休閒等等，以下列了六種情境作練習：

1・餐飲

　　在餐飲方面的情境最常出現的就是討論出外用餐的對話，可能是朋友間討論去吃何種料理，或是在餐廳裡與服務生點菜的對話。這類型的對話中需要較多關於食物的專有名稱，但因為點菜時會有菜單，聽者只要具備基本餐點的單字就可以。

　　常出現於該情境的字可能是：restaurant 餐廳、café 小餐館、dine / dining 用餐、order 點餐、delicious 美味的等等。也會有很多餐點種類如牛排（steak），vegetarian cuisine 素食，fast food 速食、curry 咖哩、breakfast/ lunch/ dinner 早 / 午 / 晚餐。各國料理如：Japanese 日式、Chinese 中式、Italian 義式、French 法式等等。

範例：

M：The guidebook recommends we go to Antonio's if we want Italian.

W：That's fine with me, unless you want to get <u>Chinese</u> or order some <u>room service.</u>

M：I'm not really in the mood for Chinese, and I want to <u>go out</u> tonight.

　　根據對話中的關鍵字 Italian 義式、Chinese 中式、room service 客房服務、go out 出去，雖然對話中沒有明顯提到 eat 吃，或是其他與食物相關的字，我們仍是可以猜到這是篇要討論出外用餐的對話。考題中也會有題目或情境介紹，預先閱讀可以幫助了解情境以及要掌握的方向。如：

（情境介紹）When people go out for dinner, they usually discuss what they want to eat before deciding where to go. 當人們出外吃晚餐，通常會先討論要去哪裡吃。

（題目）Where are they likely to have dinner? 他們可能會去哪裡吃晚餐？

2・購物

購物的情境種類繁多，各類名詞都有可能會出現，在情境對話或圖片辨義中要注意的不是產品的專有名詞，而是一些通用的名詞如 item 品項、store ∕ shop 商店、price 價格、sale 出售或特價、shopper 購物者、fitting room 試衣間、credit card 信用卡、check 支票、cash 現金、register 收銀機以及一些基本商品名稱；動詞如：buy, shop, purchase 購買、browse 瀏覽、pick out 挑選、try on 試穿、check 核對、付款 pay 等等。

範例：

Vicky and Vera usually go to the department stores to buy new clothes. They browse through the items on the sales racks, pick out the pieces they like, and try them on in the fitting room. Being smart shoppers, they always check the prices to make sure the clothes are priced reasonably.

熟悉情境會出現的字彙後，就能輕易進入狀況，接著不論考題是圖片、問答、或短文，都能馬上找到重點。再看一個 announcement 訊息廣播：

Attention, shoppers. D.B.Mathews will be closing in 20 minutes. Please bring the clothes you wish to purchase to the nearest register. Registers are located on every floor. We accept cash, checks, all major credit cards and, of course, the D. B. Mathews charge card. We will be open tomorrow from 10:00 a.m. until 8:00 p.m. as usual.

Where is the announcement being heard? 這則廣播會哪裡聽到？
a）in a theater （在戲院）
b）in an office （在辦公室）
c）in a clothing store （在服飾店）
d）in a museum （在博物館）

光是聽懂關鍵字（如：shoppers, clothes, purchase, cash, checks 等）就可

以知道這則廣播的地點是商場類，答案選 clothing store，若是要問其他資訊，先看題目是要問時間或地點等等，一般只要熟悉情境，心理上不慌亂就較能聽到重點。

3・居家

　　居家生活的日常用語比較不會用短文的形式出題，較多圖片或生活對話。出現的情境有很多種，圖片題會需要知道動詞以及連接的受詞 planting flowers 種花、cleaning the rooms 清潔房間、mopping the floor 拖地、sweeping the floor 掃地、wiping the tables 擦拭桌子、cooking 料理、fixing 修理、taking out the trash 倒垃圾、watching TV 看電視等等，圖片中尤其多使用現在分詞；而對話題比較多名詞，如：kitchen 廚房、花園等各種家裡環境，以及 battery 電池、bulb 燈泡、pipe 水管、plumber 水管工人、gas 瓦斯、washing machine 洗衣機等等家庭生活用品。

　　範例：
Sam is his mother's best helper. Whenever she is busy, she can always count on Sam to lend an extra hand. At home, Sam sweeps the floor, takes out the trash, and cleans the rooms. Today, Sam's mother has to go to the grocery store to buy soy sauce and some eggs while food is cooking on the stove.
（grocery store 雜貨店、soy sauce 醬油、stove 爐）

　　居家生活也容易出現家人的稱呼，再加上一些生活上的字，馬上就能理解狀況，接著就注意問題中要把握的重點。這裡的關鍵字是 keep an eye on the stove 注意爐火，因為前面介紹有提到 help 幫助，進入情境就不會被其他句子混淆答題。

Would you come keep an eye on the stove for me? 可以請你幫我顧爐火嗎？
　　a）Yes, I put a pot on the stove. 是的，我把鍋子放在火爐上。
　　b）I'll be right there. 我馬上就來。
　　c）I see what you mean. 我懂你的意思。
　　d）Where would you like me to put it? 你要我把它放在哪兒？

交通工具相關的題型用字很固定，首先必須熟記各種交通工具的名稱，再者是相對應的動詞，對於圖片題和簡短對話，熟悉常用的動詞名詞即可。若是短文，也都有固定型態，多以廣播公告為主，飛機上內容較多變，公車、捷運、客運、火車或船則大同小異。

名詞：car 車、bus / coach 公車、train 火車、rapid transit / subway 捷運、ferry 渡輪、taxi 計程車、airplane 飛機、passenger 乘客、seat 座椅、handrail 扶手、cabin 客艙、carriage 等等。

動詞：driving 駕駛、taking 搭乘、getting on 上車、getting off 下車、waiting 等待、waving 揮手、holding on 緊握、taking off 起飛、landing 降落著陸、boarding 乘上 (飛機 / 船 / 車) 等等，常用現在分詞 +ing。

範例：

Charles takes <u>public transportation</u> whenever he can. During the week he takes the <u>bus</u> to work, and on the weekends he makes day trips by <u>train</u> and <u>rapid transit system</u>. Taking public transportation is safe and convenient. Charles is happy that he can save money and help protect the environment by not <u>driving a car</u>.

情境介紹舉了很多大眾交通工具 public transportation 的字，在聽的時候就可以先預想題目中將會提到的字。如看到下面圖片就可以馬上聯想到上下車等動作。

Look at the picture. What are they doing? 請看圖片，他們在做什麼？
a) The passengers are getting off the bus. （這些乘客在下公車。）
b) The passengers are waiting for the bus. （這些乘客在等公車。）
c) The passengers are waving to the bus. （這些乘客在揮手招公車。）
d) The passengers are getting on the bus. （這些乘客在上公車。）

至於其它交通工具，例如飛機機艙內的廣播，會再多一些關於天氣狀態的資訊，請參看後面篇章：

May I have your attention, please? This is your captain speaking. Our scheduled arrival time for Ellis County Airport will be delayed a bit as the area is experiencing heavy thunderstorms.

請注意，以下是機長廣播，我們預計抵達 Ellis County 機場的時間將會延遲，因為該地區有大雷雨。

5. 校園

校園生活的題型融合了生活對話和課業討論、考試演講等等。授課內容的短文可能會有一些專有名詞，比較難聽懂，技巧在於先看題目所問為何，預先掌握方向，聽的時候要很注意細節。

範例：

Theresa and Victor received the <u>results</u> of a <u>qualification test</u> they took recently. The test is considered difficult because many people had to take it several times before they <u>passed</u>. Theresa was very pleased with her <u>score</u>. When Victor came to congratulate her, Theresa told him about the <u>preparation guidebook</u> she used and how she managed her time beforehand.

這段情境介紹是針對校園最常出現的考試話題，result 結果、qualification test 資格考試、preparation 準備、guidebook 指南書籍、score 分數，動詞最常出現的就是 take 拿取 / 參加、pass 通過。其他常出現於校園的關鍵名詞如 textbook 課本、course 課程、class 課堂、seminar 講座、 midterm / final exam 期中 / 期末考試、lab 研究 / 實驗室、library 圖書館、teacher 老師、speaker 演講者、professor 教授、assistant 助教 / 助理、paper 書面報告，以及一些科目的專有名稱。動詞有 study 研讀、analyze 分析、 research 研究與 report 報告（這兩個字是動詞名詞唸法相同）。

M：How did you ever do it? Some people take it five or six times before they pass.

W：I had a good preparation guidebook and I studied every day for two weeks beforehand.

M：That's great. Congratulations. You're sure to get a good job.

　　接續上面情境，對話中描述兩人討論如何準備考試，以及恭喜對方通過考試。要先看題目是針對哪部份提問，在聽的時候加強注意。

6 · 休閒

　　休閒娛樂種類繁多，出現在圖片題以測驗名詞地點和動作為主，對話題多以預約購票為主，以考題問句做重點掌握。另外，各種景點遊樂設施會有各式的短文公告，這類則以提醒開放時間和注意事項為主。

範例：

Look at the picture. Where are the tourists? 看圖片，這些觀光客在哪裡？

a）The tourists are gathered at the square. （這些觀光客聚集在廣場。）

b）The tourists are getting on the bus. （這些觀光客在上公車。）

c）The tourists are in front of the skyscrapers.
　　（這些觀光客在摩天大樓前方。）

d）The tourists are lining up. （這些觀光客在排隊。）

　　由上述的選項可知，動詞和名詞是必須要注意的關鍵重點。動詞和名詞的搭配也很重要，如：seeing a movie 看電影、visiting a museum 參觀博物館、climbing mountains 爬山、taking pictures 照相、having a picnic 野餐、having some drinks 喝飲料、choosing souvenirs 選紀念品等等。

　　短文廣播一定要先看題目，確定問題是針對地點、數字、或是原因，再仔細聆聽：

Ladies and gentlemen, welcome to the Clairmont Theater. Tonight's performance will be presented in four acts, with a short intermission. Filming or photography is not allowed during the performance. Thank you for your kind cooperation. We hope you will enjoy the show.

各位先生小姐，歡迎來到 Clairmont 戲院，今晚的表演將會有四幕以及一個中場休息。在表演過程中是不允許拍攝與拍照的。感謝你們的合作，希望你們能享受這個表演。

第三部　掌握資訊重點

有時英文字句都能理解，一下子聽很多卻找不到重點。一方面可能是因為情境的不熟悉造成，另一方面是聽到的資訊無法掌握，需要多練習。以下藉由情境延伸出 5W1H 的疑問句來練習找出文章或對話的重點資訊。大考一般較少詢問 how，而多以 5W 詢問資訊。以下練習資訊重點的掌握，仍以 5W1H 做範例解說：

Who 誰

當看到題目是要詢問 "who 誰" 的時候，名詞和代名詞最需要注意，但不只是人名，也包括人物職業和關係。在這篇範例中，詢問的是不是短文中的主角，而是說話者，所以要著重說話者跟主角之間的關係。

範例：

I've been asked by <u>coach Woodley</u> to say a few words on behalf of all his players. <u>Coach Woodley</u> didn't just <u>teach us</u> the game of basketball, he also <u>taught us</u> many important lessons about life. These are lessons we still use today and that we can pass on to our children and other young people.

我應 Woodley 教練的要求代表所有的球員們來講幾句話。Woodley 教練不只教我們打籃球，也教導我們許多重要的人生道理。這些道理我們至今仍然受用，還可以傳承給我們的孩子及其他年輕人。

Who is giving this speech?（誰在致詞？）
a）A basketball coach.（籃球教練）
b）The coach's son.（教練的兒子）
c）A basketball sportscaster.（籃球播報員）
d）<u>A basketball player.（籃球隊員）</u>

Coach Woodley（教練 Woodley）是主要描述的對象，說話者不停提到 teach us 教導我們，可見說話者與 coach Woodley 的關係是教練與球員。

When 何時

　　提到時間，最明顯的字包括數字以及時間相關的字，如 morning 早上、afternoon 下午、today 今天、tomorrow 明天、month 月、year 年等等，這些最基本的字一定要掌握到，但要注意的不只如此，有些難度高的題目會故意用明顯的時間用字來混淆。

範例：

W：When should I book our hotel room for our trip?
M：The sooner, the better. I've heard that it gets really busy that time of the year there.
W：I better get right on it!
女士：我什麼時候該為我們的旅行預訂飯店呢？
男士：愈快愈好。我聽說每年的那時候會是旺季。
女士：那麼我最好馬上進行。

When are they taking their trip?（他們何時要啟程旅行？）
a）As soon as possible（盡可能愈快愈好）
b) During the busy season（正當旺季的時候）
c) They haven't decided.（他們尚未決定。）
d) During off-season（適逢淡季的時候）

　　這段對話一開始就是詢問時間，之後也有關於時間的資訊，如：the sooner the better 越快越好，所以答案可能選 a）。但是也要小心題目雖然看似簡單，對話一開始提的是預訂旅館的時間，而題目問的是去旅行的時間，這兩者容易混淆。 所以 when 為疑問的題目雖然簡單，也要注意是否有陷阱。

Where 何地

　　問 where 地點的題目，除了要注意關於地點的名詞以外，最重要的就是要聽出情境的場合。整段對話或短文有可能都沒有提及地點，但透過對話或其他描述可以聯想到是在哪種情境，所以問地點其實就是在考驗對情境的熟悉度。

範例：

Your attention, please. The Ponte Verde Beach Lifeguard Service will be closing down now. We ask all <u>swimmers</u> to come out of the <u>water</u>. We also advise all <u>surfers</u> to come out of the <u>water</u> as well. The darker conditions make it difficult to see. Lifeguard service will resume at 9:00 tomorrow morning. Thank you and good night.

各位請注意，Ponte Verde 海灘的救生服務即將結束。請所有泳客都回到岸邊。同時也請衝浪的遊客上岸，因為較暗的天色會導致視線不清。救生服務將於明早九點恢復。謝謝大家，晚安。

Where does this announcement take place? 這段廣播的地點為何？
a）At a swimming pool（在游泳池）
b）In a hotel（在飯店）
<u>c）At a public beach（在公共海灘）</u>
d）By a harbor（在港口邊）

這篇廣播一開始就有說明是在 Beach 海灘，所以找到關鍵字就可以輕鬆答對。但有可能因為該海灘前的專有名詞始聽者錯過了 beach 這個字，那麼也可以從 swimmer 游泳者、surfer 衝浪者，或是重複提到的 water 水，而能聯想到是在海灘。另外，swimming pool 游泳池也不會因為天色變暗而需要關閉。遇到這種選項相近的情形，除了熟悉情境，最好也能預先閱讀試題。

What / Which 什麼 / 哪個

1．

What 疑問句是考題中最常出現的，因為使用 what 疑問句不只是問動作，也可以用來問人、問事件、甚至可以用來問時間地點等等。如：
What are the man and woman doing? 這男女在做什麼？（問動作）
What happened to your car? 你的車怎麼了？（問事件）
What did you say your name was? 你說你的名字是什麼？（問人名）
雖然很難找尋回答 what 疑問句的關鍵字，但這類型的問題，我們可以在聽的時後將焦點放在內容字上，即動詞和名詞。

範例：
W：How is that <u>book</u> you are <u>writing</u> coming along?
M：I've <u>gotten</u> most of it finished, but I'm stuck on how to <u>finish</u> it.
W：I can <u>read</u> what you <u>have</u> so far and <u>help</u> you with the rest.

女士：你正在寫的書進展如何？

男士：大部份已經完成，但是卡在不知道該如何結尾。

女士：讓我先讀目前已經完成的部份，然後幫你完成其餘的部份。

What is the man's problem?（這個男人有什麼困擾？）

a）He can't think of a good opening.（他想不出一個好開頭。）

b）He is too busy to write a book.（他太忙無法工作。）

c）He is having a hard time with the ending.（他對於結尾感到困難。）

根據名詞跟動詞：book 書、writing 寫、gotten 得到、finish 結束、read 閱讀、have 有、help 幫助、以及 rest 剩下的部份，就能掌握對話內容的大意。若能聽懂同屬於內容字的 finished 結束的、stuck 困住的，便能知道這位男仕的問題所在。其實了解內容字就能讓讀者很快地抓到該文章的重點。

2．

Which 也算是 what 的一種問法，Which statement is true?(哪一項陳述是正確的？）或下面範例問句 Which is the most important rule?（哪一個是最重要的規則）其實也等同於問 what is true? What is the most important? 同樣也是需要捉住內容字來掌握含義。但使用 which 來提問，通常都是要從三個或四個選項中挑選正確答案，所以一定要先看題目跟每個選項。

範例：

This is a reminder to all visitors of the zoo about which activities are acceptable and which activities are unacceptable while observing the various animal exhibits.

First and most important-do not feed the animals! The only exception to this rule is that feeding the elephants is permitted, but only with official feed sold by the zoo outside the elephant exhibit.

提醒參觀動物園的訪客，當參觀時，有些活動是可以被允許的，而有些則否。首先，也是最重要的是，千萬別餵食動物。餵食大象是唯一的例外，餵食大象是被允許的，但只能用在大象館外發售的園方飼料才可以。

Which is the most important rule?（什麼是最重要的規則？）

a）Not to take feathers home.（不要拿羽毛回家。）

b）Not to run in the zoo.（不要在園內奔跑。）

c) Not to feed the animals.（不要餵食動物。）

d) To buy food only at the zoo.（只能在園內購買食品。）

先看完各個選項，再聆聽就可以發現 feed 這個字是最常出現的，所以要注意 feed 餵食，而且題目中已經有提及 important，而短文中也有提到，所以接續其後的句子就是重點所在。

Why 為什麼

問 why 的題型主要針對文章或對話內容中的因果關係，不只是需要聽懂關鍵字，也必須了解前後因果。最簡單的情形是出現 "because 因為" 這個字，那麼該句就是決定性的關鍵句子。

M : I wonder whatever happened to my college friend George?

W : Isn't he the one who we called "The Bookman" because he never stopped studying?

M : Yeah, him. He must be somebody important by now.

男士： 我在想我的大學同學 George 現在不知道如何了？

女士： 他不就是以前那個不停念書，被我們稱作「書蟲」的人嗎？

男士： 是啊，就是他。他現在應該是個重要的大人物了。

Why did the man's friend have a nickname?

（為什麼這位男士的的朋友有個綽號？）

a) He almost never studied.（他幾乎不曾讀書。）

b) He was a hard-working student.（他是個用功的學生。）

c) He was an important person.（他是個大人物。）

d) He always read novels.（他總是讀小說。）

先看過題目後，知道問題的重點在 nickname 綽號的產生原因，所以我們可以先推測聽力中可能會出現 nickname 綽號、name 名字、call 稱呼等相關字眼，所以聽到 called，之後又加上聽到 because，那麼就可以確定之後那句就是答案了。

How 如何

問 how 如何的題形比較少出現，但運用 how 來問其他類型的資訊則很常見，例如問 how many （多少）、 how often（多常）等等，例如：How many of your students are going on to college? （你有多少學生去念大專？）How long have Frank and Melissa been going out? （Frank 和 Melissa 交往多久了？） 這些答案的關鍵字就是與數字或時間有關的用語。純粹問 how（如何）的類型在篇章中比較不容易找尋關鍵字，但如果在聽之前先看題目，就能夠掌握內容字（名詞和動詞為主），有助於了解整體含義並找到答案。

W：Mike is really up on things. He always seems to know what's going on.

M：He must read the newspaper every day or at least read some magazines.

W：Actually, he told me he goes to a website every night and every morning. It gives him all he needs.

女士：Mike 真的很熟悉各種事物。他似乎總是知道發生了什麼狀況。

男士：他一定是每天看報紙，不然至少看了一些雜誌。

男士：事實上，他告訴我他每天晚上和早上都會瀏覽網頁，提供他所需的所有資訊。

How does Mike keep up with current events? （Mike 是如何得知時事？）

a）He reads the news on the Internet. （他在網路上看新聞。）

b）He subscribes to the newspaper. （他訂閱報紙。）

c）He reads news magazines. （他閱讀新聞雜誌。）

d）He watches the morning and evening news.
　　（他看晨間和夜間的電視新聞。）

根據關鍵字 things 事物、know 知道、 read 閱讀（出現兩次）、 newspaper 報紙、 magazine 雜誌、 told 告訴、 website 網站、 gives 給予、 needs 需求，可知答案 a）和 c）最有可能，要再更仔細聽就會發現程度的不同，看網站上的新聞是每天早晚，而看雜誌則是 at least 至少，所以答案是 a）。

大考英文聽力題型範例

題型

　　依據測驗目標設計，評量考生了解詞彙、句子、對話、篇章的聽解能力。題型分為四種（如下表），全部為四選一的選擇題，共 40 題。

題型	說明	題數（配分比例）
看圖辨義	評量考生對常用詞彙（content words）及句型之聽解能力。	10（20%）
對答	評量考生能否聽懂一個敘述或問題，並做出適當回應的能力。	10（20%）
簡短對話	評量考生對日常生活對話的聽解能力。	10（30%）
短文聽解	評量考生對簡短陳述的聽解能力。	10（30%）

（一）看圖辨義

　　說明：含單題及題組。試題本上有數幅圖畫，每一圖畫有一個或二個相關的試題。每題請聽語音播出的試題及四個選項，根據圖意選出一個最適當的選項，並將答案畫記在答案卡之「選擇題答案區」，每題（組）播放一次。

單題

（讀）

A.

（聽）

Look at Picture A. What are the boys doing?

(A) They're singing.

(B) They're watching TV.

(C) They're playing basketball.

(D) They're reading the newspaper.　　　　　　　　　答案：C

題組

第 1、2 題為題組

（讀）B.

（聽）

For Questions 1 and 2, please look at Picture B.

Question 1. Where are these people?

(A) They're in a city park.

(B) They're in a classroom.

(C) They're in a restaurant.

(D) They're in a movie theater.　　　　　　　　　答案：B

Question 2. How many children are there in the picture?

(A) Two.

(B) Three.

(C) Four.

(D) Five.　　　　　　　　　答案：D

（二）對答

說明：請聽語音播出的一個問句或直述句後，依試題本所列的選項，選出一個最適當的回應選項，並將答案畫記在答案卡之「選擇題答案區」，每題播放一次。

（讀）

(A) You're right.

(B) I think so too.

(C) It's on the sofa.

(D) Mary will go with you.　　　　　　　　　　　　　　答案：C

（聽）

Where's the book I bought yesterday?

（三）簡短對話

說明：含單題與題組。請聽語音播出的一段對話和相關的問題，依試題本所列的選項，選出一個最適當的選項。並將答案畫記在答案卡之「選擇題答案區」，每題（組）播放一次。

單題

（讀）

(A) He loves Jane.

(B) He likes to help.

(C) He hurt his hand.

(D) He needs some help.　　　　　　　　　　　　　　答案：D

（聽）

Man: Jane, do you think you can give me a hand with this?

Woman: I'd love to help, but I've got to go over to my aunt's house in a
minute.

Question. Which is true about the man?

題組
第 3、4 題為題組

（讀）

3.
(A) Late at night.
(B) In the evening.
(C) Precisely at noon.
(D) In early morning.   答案：D

4.
(A) Eating the food.
(B) Going to church.
(C) Opening the gifts.
(D) Decorating the Christmas tree.   答案：A

（聽）

For Questions 3 and 4, you will listen to a short conversation.

Woman: So, John, tell me, what do you guys in Canada do on Christmas
Day? What do you eat? When do you open the gifts?

Man: Well, Anita, the routine in Canada for Christmas is quite simple. The
kids get very excited on the 25th because early in the morning, at
around seven o'clock, that's when we open the gifts.

Woman: Oh, really?

Man: That's right. But that's not the most exciting part of the day.

Woman: Oh, it's not? What is then?

Man: The food is.

Woman: The food?

Man: Yes, and it's the most exciting part of the day.

（四）短文聽解

> 說明：每兩題為一題組。請聽語音播出的一段訊息，從試題本中選出一個最適當的選項，並將答案畫記在答案卡之「選擇題答案區」，每題組播放一次。

第 5、6 題為題組

（讀）

5. What is Wonderland?
(A) A play.
(B) An expensive mall.
(C) A national museum.
(D) An amusement park.　　　　　　　　　　　　　　答案：D

6. What do the local residents think about Wonderland?
(A) It brings nothing but good business.
(B) It is one of the greatest achievements of mankind.
(C) It has caused problems for people living in the neighborhood.
(D) It is a good example of how recycling works for the community.
　　　　　　　　　　　　　　　　　　　　　　　　　　答案：C

（聽）

Questions 5 and 6 are based on the following report.

Woman: Wonderland is perhaps the most popular vacation spot for families. It attracts tourists and provides jobs for the local residents in its hotels and shopping malls.But now it is called "the tragic kingdom." The neighbors suffer from traffic jams that last for miles and it takes hours to park the car. Empty cans, bottles and garbage are everywhere. The whole place is becoming polluted. Most of all, prices of goods are skyrocketing. People pay more for living here.

看圖辨義

公共場所－休閒活動

學習重點

慢跑（jogging）是許多人喜愛的休閒活動，可以保持健康，鍛鍊體力；慢跑時通常穿著運動鞋（running shoes）、休閒服（casual wear），有些人還喜歡戴耳機（earphones）聽著音樂慢跑。

情境介紹及導引

David and Emily exercise regularly. They often jog on the weekends. Whenever they run, they wear shorts or warm-up suits and put on running shoes to protect their feet. Sometimes Emily wears earphones and listens to music while running. If you go to the park this weekend, you'll probably see them jogging together.

範 例

此圖片中，主題是人物的動作，此處你會聽到四句話，其中只有一句是最符合圖片內容的描述。

Look at the picture. What are they doing?

a) They are dancing.

b) They are eating.

c) They are jogging.

d) They are singing.

答案：c)

a. Information Focus

圖片中的人物穿著休閒服、運動鞋,並且有擺動手臂的姿勢,得知他們是在跑步。

b. Language Skills

重點字彙:jog(慢跑)、shorts(短褲)、warm-up suits(保暖衣物)。

句法:描述人物進行中的動作:人 + is / are + V-ing。

c. Tips for Listening

動詞加上 ing 的發音方式與原形動詞不太相同,如本題中的 dancing, eating, jogging, singing,請自行大聲朗誦三次,以熟悉其發音。

🎧 練習題  A-02

請聽以下看圖辨義題的描述,並從四個選項中,選出最適當的答案。

1 _____

2 _____

3 _____

1

◎解答

a）She's riding a horse.

（她在騎馬。）

◎聽力原文

Look at the picture. What is she doing?

a）She's riding a horse.

b）She's taking a walk.

c）She's cleaning a stable.

d）She's wearing a dress.

◎中譯

請看圖，她在做什麼？

a）她在騎馬。

b）她在走路。

c）她在打掃馬廄。

d）她在穿洋裝。

◎解析

圖中可看出一位女子正在騎馬，所以答案是a）。她不是在走路或打掃馬廄，也不是在穿洋裝，所以b）、c）、d）非正確答案。

2

◎解答

b）She's painting.（她在畫畫。）

◎聽力原文

Look at the picture. What is she doing?

a）She's cooking.

b）She's painting.

c）She's washing.

d）She's writing.

◎中譯

請看圖，她在做甚麼？

a）她在煮東西。

b）她在畫畫。

c）她在洗東西。

d）她在寫東西。

◎解析

圖中的情境是一位女子在畫圖，所以b）是最適合的答案。

3

◎解答

c）They're sitting on the floor.

（她們正坐在地板上。）

◎聽力原文

Look at the picture. What are they doing?

a）They're reading a sign.

b）They're paying for a computer.

c）Theyvre sitting on the floor.

d　They're standing on a stool.

◎中譯

請看圖，她們在做甚麼？

a）她們在閱讀標誌。

b）她們在付款買電腦。

c）她們正坐在地板上。

d）她們站在凳子上。

◎解析

圖中有兩個女孩坐在地上，一個在看書，一個在打電腦，所以正確的描述應是c）They're sitting on the floor.（她們正坐在地板上。）

看圖辨義

體能活動

🎧 **學習重點**

學校的體能活動包括各種球類（volleyball, baseball, tennis）、游泳（swimming）、划船（rowing），以打排球為例，排球場地是以網子（net）作為兩方的分界線，常見的排球動作有發球（serve）、傳球（pass）、殺球（smash）、攔網（block）等。

🎧 **情境介紹及導引**

In the PE class, Iris learns to play a variety of sports such as baseball, basketball, tennis, and volleyball. Iris enjoys the volleyball the best and learns to serve, pass, smash and block the ball. As you can see from the picture below, volleyball players must try to return the ball across the net.

範例

此圖片中，主題是人物的動作，此處你會聽到四句話，其中只有一句是最符合圖片內容的描述。

Look at the picture. What are they doing?

a) They are swimming in the pool.

b) The players are pulling the net.

c) They're playing volleyball.

d) The athletes are lifting weights.

答案：c)

說明

a. Information Focus

圖片中的場地有網子，其中的一位球員正舉起手準備殺球，可以推知他們在打排球
"They're playing volleyball." 。

b. Language Skills

重點字彙：pool（水池）、pull（拉）、athlete / player（運動員）、
lift weights（舉重）。

特定詞組：打各種球類：play ＋ baseball / basketball / tennis / volleyball

c. Tips for Listening

本則聽力重點是熟悉 V-ing 的念法，如 swimming, pulling, playing, lifting，
以及其他名詞，如 pool, net, volleyball, weights.

練習題　A-04

請聽以下看圖辨義題的描述，並從四個選項中，選出最適當的答案。

1 _____

2 _____

3 _____

2 詳解

1

◎解答

b) He is swimming.（他在游泳。）

◎聽力原文

Look at the picture. What is he doing?

a) He is taking a shower.

b) He is swimming.

c) He is cleaning the pool.

d) He is flying over water.

◎中譯

請看圖，他在做什麼？

a) 他在洗澡。

b) 他在游泳。

c) 他在清理泳池。

d) 他正飛過水面。

◎解析

圖片中的情境是男子在游泳池中游泳，所以答案 b) 是最適合的答案。

2

◎解答

b) The girl is hitting the ball.

（這位女孩在擊球。）

◎聽力原文

Look at the picture. What is she doing?

a) The girl is serving the ball.

b) The girl is hitting the ball.

c) The girl is playing at the net.

d) The girl is chasing the ball.

◎中譯

請看圖，她在做什麼？

a) 這位女孩在發球。

b) 這位女孩在擊球。

c) 這位女孩在上網擊球。

d) 這位女孩在追球。

◎解析

女孩雙眼盯著球，雙手握著球拍，明顯是正要擊球，所以答案應是 b)。

3

◎解答

c) They are rowing the boat.

（他們在划船。）

◎聽力原文

Look at the picture. What are they doing?

a) They are fishing.

b) They are getting off the boat.

c) They are rowing the boat.

d) They are boarding the bus.

◎中譯

請看圖，他們在做什麼？

a) 他們在捕魚。

b) 他們正要下船。

c) 他們在划船。

d) 他們正要上公車。

◎解析

圖中每個人都雙手握槳在水面上划船，所以答案 c) 最為適合。。

看圖辨義

3

校園藝文活動

學校的藝文活動主要是閱讀（reading）、繪畫（painting / drawing）、聆聽音樂（listening to music）、歌唱（singing）等。

情境介紹及導引

Education in literature and the arts is an important part of students' life. In Taiwan, students regularly go to the library to read and learn to appreciate good books. In art programs, students are taught to paint or draw pictures. In music classes, students listen to music or sing songs. In these classes, teachers give lectures to introduce famous writers, artists and musicians.

範例  A-05

此圖片中，主題是人物的動作，此處你會聽到四句話，其中只有一句是最符合圖片內容的描述。

_____

Look at the picture. What are they doing?

a) The students are drawing on the board.

b) The students are listening to music.

c) The teacher is looking at papers.

d) A student is giving a lecture.

答案：c)

a. Information Focus

圖片中站著的女士，年齡較長，看得出來是老師，她正看著文件，因此正確的描述
是 "The teacher is looking at papers."。

b. Language Skills

其他字彙：literature（文學）、appreciate（欣賞）、board（板子）、papers
（文件）、lecture（演講）。

特定詞組：reading a book（閱讀）、drawing a picture（畫圖）、listening
to music（聽音樂）、singing a song（唱歌）、giving a lecture（演
講）、looking at something（看著某事物）。

c. Tips for Listening

常用來表示位置或方向的字詞，如 drawing on the board, looking at papers
裡面的 on, at，雖然不是「重讀」所在，卻常出現，多加練習並記憶，可以幫助判
斷句子內容的正確性。

🎧 練習題　A-06

請聽以下看圖辨義題的描述，並從四個選項中，選出最適當的答案。

❶ _____

❷.1 _____

❷.2 _____

❸ _____

1

◎解答

c）The teacher is writing something.
　（這位老師在寫東西。）

◎聽力原文

Look at the picture. What are they doing?

a）They are looking at the calendar.
b）They're working on the computer.
c）The teacher is writing something.
d）The students are writing on the blackboard.

◎中譯

請看圖，她們在做什麼？

a）她們在看日曆。
b）她們在電腦前工作。
c）這位老師在寫東西。
d）學生們在黑板上書寫。

◎解析

圖中學生看著老師，老師握筆在書上書寫，所以 c）The teacher is writing something.（這位老師在寫東西。）最符合情境。

2.1

◎解答

a）The graduates are singing.
　（畢業生們在唱歌。）

◎聽力原文

Look at the Picture. What are they doing?

a）The graduates are singing.
b）The singers are clapping.
c）The students are leaving the room.
d）They are wearing bathrobes.

◎中譯

請看圖，他們在做什麼？

a）畢業生們在唱歌。
b）歌手們在鼓掌。
c）學生們正要離開室內。
d）他們在穿浴袍。

◎解析

從畢業生們的表情與姿勢判斷，選項 a）The graduates are singing.（畢業生們在唱歌。）最為合理。他們沒有拍手、離開室內，也沒有穿浴袍，故 b）、c）、d）為非。

2.2

◎解答

c）They are in an auditorium.
　（他們在大禮堂裡。）

◎聽力原文

Look at the picture. Where are they?

a）The students are standing outdoors.
b）They are sitting on the benches.
c）They are in an auditorium.
d）They are listening to a lecture.

◎中譯

請看圖，他們在哪裡？

a）學生們正站在室外。
b）他們坐在長凳上。
c）他們在大禮堂裡。
d）他們在聽演講。

◎解析

依圖中的燈光及背景判斷，這群畢業生最有可能在室內，因此選 c）They are in an auditorium.（他們在大禮堂裡。）。

3

◎解答

d）They are studying together.
（他們正在一起學習。）

◎聽力原文

Look at the picture. What are they doing?

a）The students are listening to a lecture.
b）They are sharing a calculator.
c）The professor has written all over the board.
d）They are studying together.

◎中譯

請看圖，他們在做什麼？

a）學生在聽演講。
b）他們共用一臺計算機。
c）教授已經寫滿整個黑板。
d）他們正在一起學習。

◎解析

圖中的孩子們一起坐著接受老師的指導，所以 d）They are studying together.（他們正在一起學習。）最符合情境。

居家活動

🎧 學習重點

一般的居家活動包括澆花（water plants）、晾衣服（air-dry clothes）、泡茶（make tea）、看報（read newspapers）等，以晾衣服為例，通常需要有曬衣繩（clothesline）、架子（rack），有時候還需要椅子或凳子（chair / stool）才能搆得著繩子，如以下圖片所示。

🎧 情境介紹及導引

Rachel regularly helps with household chores. She waters the plants and cleans the table every day. On the weekend, she helps her mother air-dry clothes. The task requires her to stand on a stool so she can pin the clothes on the clothesline. After the chores are done, Rachel and her mother usually make tea and read newspapers to relax.

 範例 A-07

此圖片中，主題是人物所在位置，此處你會聽到四句話，其中只有一句是最符合圖片內容的描述。

_____

Look at the picture. What is she doing?

a) She's drinking from a glass.

b) She's planting a tree.

c) She's clearing the table.

d) She's standing on a stool.　　答案：d)

說明

a. Information Focus

圖片中的女孩站在凳子上晾衣服，可以知道正確的描述是 "She's standing on a stool."。

b. Language Skills

重點字彙：household chores（家事）、planting a tree（種樹）、wiping / cleaning the table（擦桌子）。

c. Tips for Listening

此句的聽力重點在於句中動詞（drinking, planting, clearing, standing）的語意，其次是接續其後的名詞（glass, tree, table, stool）。

 練習題 A-08

請聽以下看圖辨義題的描述，並從四個選項中，選出最適當的答案。

1.1 _____

1.2 _____

2 _____

3 _____

4 詳解

1.1

◎解答

b) He is reading a newspaper.
（他在看報紙。）

◎聽力原文

Look at the picture. What is he doing?
a) He is cleaning the table.
b) He is reading a newspaper.
c) He is working at a desk.
d) He is eating his dinner.

◎中譯

請看圖。他在做什麼？
a) 他在清潔桌子。
b) 他在看報紙。
c) 他在桌前工作。
d) 他在吃晚餐。

◎解析

男士雙手拿著報紙閱讀，選項 b) 最為合適。圖中未見桌子和晚餐，故選項 a)、c)、d) 為非。

1.2

◎解答

b) He is in the living room.
（他在客廳裡。）

◎聽力原文

Look at the picture. Where is he?
a) He is in a library.
b) He is in the living room.
c) He is in a restaurant.
d) He is in a classroom.

◎中譯

請看圖。他在哪裡？
a) 他在圖書館裡。
b) 他在客廳裡。
c) 他在餐廳裡。
d) 他在教室裡。

◎解析

圖裡有窗簾、沙發，且這位男士穿著拖鞋，可推斷地點應為客廳；所以 b) 是最適合的答案。

2

◎解答

a) He is watering the plant.
（他在給植物澆水。）

◎聽力原文

Look at the picture. What is he doing?
a) He is watering the plant.
b) He is drinking the water.
c) He is taking a shower.
d) He is mopping the floor.

◎中譯

請看圖。他在做什麼？
a) 他在給植物澆水。
b) 他在喝水。
c) 他在淋浴。
d) 他在拖地。

◎解析

圖中男士拿著澆花器在澆水，所以應該選擇 a)。water 在此作動詞用，指「給⋯⋯澆水、灌溉」。

3

◎解答

d) One woman is serving drinks.

　（一位女士正端上飲料。）

◎聽力原文

Look at the picture. Which statement is true?

a) The books are on the table.

b) They are reading newspapers.

c) One woman is giving a lecture.

d) One woman is serving drinks.

◎中譯

請看圖。以下敘述何者為真？

a) 書本在桌上。

b) 她們在看報。

c) 一位女士在演講。

d) 一位女士正端上飲料。

◎解析

圖中兩位女士坐著，另一位女士正端上飲料，因此應選擇 d)。

5

商店購物

學習重點

在商店或賣場購物（buy, shop, purchase）時，常需要先瀏覽商品（browse）、挑選商品（pick out）、試穿（try on）或試吃（sample）、核對標價（check the price），決定購買再付款（pay for the items）。

情境介紹及導引

Vicky and Vera usually go to the department stores to buy new clothes. They browse through the items on the sales racks, pick out the pieces they like, and try them on in the fitting room. Being smart shoppers, they always check the prices to make sure the clothes are priced reasonably.

範例 A-09

此圖片中，主題是人物在做的動作，此處你會聽到四句話，其中只有一句是最符合圖片內容的描述。

Look at the picture. What are they doing?
a) They're checking the price.
b) They're paying for the shirt.
c) They're trying on their shirt.
d) They're hanging up their clothes.

答案：a)

a. Information Focus

圖片中的兩位女孩正在看衣服的標價牌，可以知道正確的描述是 "They're checking the price."。

b. Language Skills

其他字彙：item（貨品項目）、sales rack（貨架）、fitting room（試衣間）。

挑選商品：pick out ＋ 商品；試穿／試用：try on ＋ 衣服／其他商品

試吃／品嚐：sample ＋ 食物／飲料；付款：pay for ＋ 購買的商品

c. Tips for Listening

本則的重點是聽懂動詞（checking, paying, trying, hanging）的語意，以及接續其後的名詞（price, shirt, clothes）。

🎧 練習題 ◀A-10▶

請聽以下看圖辨義題的描述，並從四個選項中，選出最適當的答案。

① _____

2.1 _____

2.2 _____

③ _____

⁵ 詳解

1

◎解答

d) The woman is shopping for food.
（這位女士在採購食品。）

◎聽力原文

Look at the picture. Which statement is true?
a) The cashier is counting money.
b) The customer is sampling the food.
c) The woman is playing cards.
d) The woman is shopping for food.

◎中譯

請看圖。以下敘述何者為真？
a) 這位收銀員在算錢。
b) 這位顧客在試吃。
c) 這位女士在玩牌。
d) 這位女士在採購食品。

◎解析

圖片中的女士正拿起食品在選購，故答案選d) 最適合。

2.1

◎解答

a) She's shopping for food.
（她正在採購食品。）
◎聽力原文

Look at the picture. What is she doing?
a) She's shopping for food.

b) She's picking up clothes.
c) She's holding the boxes.
d) She's cooking the vegetables.

◎中譯

請看圖。她在做什麼？
a) 她在採購食品。
b) 她在收拾衣服。
c) 她抱著箱子。
d) 她在煮菜。

◎解析

圖中的女士正在挑選蔬果，故答案選a)。圖中沒有衣服和箱子，女士也沒有烹煮的動作，故b)、c)、d) 為非。

2.2

◎解答

c) There is a shopping cart in front of her.（她面前有一臺購物推車。）

◎聽力原文

Look at the picture. Which statement is true?
a) She's in a drugstore.
b) She's in a photo studio.
c) There is a shopping cart in front of her.
d) She's waiting in line.

◎中譯

請看圖。以下敘述何者為真？
a) 她在藥局內。
b) 她在照相館內。
c) 她面前有一臺購物推車。
d) 她正在排隊。

圖片中的女士正在超市選購蔬果，面前有購物車，故答案選 c ）最恰當。

3

◎解答

c) She's looking at a window
   display.（她在看櫥窗的陳設品。）

◎聽力原文

Look at the picture. What is she
doing?
a) She's applying makeup.
b) She's decorating the store.
c) She's looking at a window display.
d) She's trying on clothes.

◎中譯

請看圖。她在做什麼？
a ）她在化妝。
b ）她在裝飾店面。
c ）她在看櫥窗的陳設品。
d ）她在試穿衣服。

◎解析

圖中的女生站在商店櫥窗前往內觀看，故選
項 c ）最貼切。

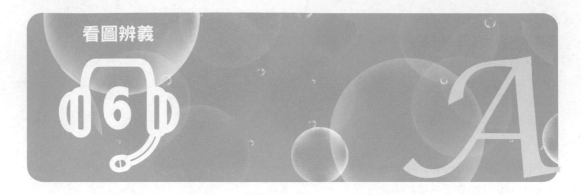

搭乘大眾運輸工具

 學習重點

搭乘（take / ride / board）大眾運輸工具（public transportation）是日常生活的一部份，包括公車（bus / coach）、火車（train）、捷運（rapid transit）、渡輪（ferry）等，這些工具提供人們便利的（convenient）、安全（safe）、又節能（energy saving）的服務。

 情境介紹及導引

Charles takes public transportation whenever he can. During the week he takes the bus to work, and on the weekends he makes day trips by train and rapid transit system. Taking public transportation is safe and convenient. Charles is happy that he can save money and help protect the environment by not driving a car.

範例 🎧 A-11

此圖片中，主題是人物的動作，此處你會聽到四句話，其中只有一句是最符合圖片內容的描述。

_____

Look at the picture. What are they doing?

a）The passengers are getting off the bus.

b）The passengers are waiting for the bus.

c）The passengers are waving to the bus.

d）The passengers are getting on the bus.

答案：d）

a. Information Focus

圖片人物的臉都是朝著公車車門，並有舉腳搭乘的動作，因此 "The passengers are getting on the bus." 是正確的描述。

b. Language Skills

重點字彙：passenger（乘客）、get on（「登」車）、get off（「下」車）、wait（等候）、wave（揮手）。

c. Tips for Listening

介系詞 on 及 off 在句子中都不是重讀（stress）所在，但是兩者的發音方式不同，仍然可以區別得出來。

🎧 練習題  ▶A-12

請聽以下看圖辨義題的描述，並從四個選項中，選出最適當的答案。

1 ＿＿＿＿＿＿

2.1 ＿＿＿＿＿＿

2.2 ＿＿＿＿＿＿

3 ＿＿＿＿＿＿

6 詳解

1

◎解答

d) They're getting on a bus.
（他們正要上公車。）

◎聽力原文

Look at the picture. What are they doing?
a) They're sitting at computers.
b) They're going down the stairs.
c) They're driving along the road.
d) They're getting on a bus.

◎中譯

請看圖。他們在做什麼？
a) 他們坐在電腦前。
b) 他們在下樓梯。
c) 他們正沿路開車。
d) 他們正要上公車。

◎解析

這群小朋友在一臺公車旁正要搭乘，所以答案選 d) 最適合。

2.1

◎解答

c) They are getting off the ferry.
（他們正在下船。）

◎聽力原文

Look at the picture. What are they doing?
a) They are boarding the bus.
b) They are riding the train.

c) They are getting off the ferry.
d) They are getting in the van.

◎中譯

請看圖。他們在做什麼？
a) 他們正要搭公車。
b) 他們正要搭乘火車。
c) 他們正在下船。
d) 他們正要坐上一臺廂型車。

◎解析

圖中的人們正經由連接的船板，從船艙走出來到岸上碼頭，故答案選 c) 最貼切。

2.2

◎解答

b) They are on a dock.
（他們在碼頭上。）

◎聽力原文

Look at the picture. Where are they?
a) They are in a hotel lobby.
b) They are on a dock.
c) They are in a restaurant.
d) They are in a hospital.

◎中譯

請看圖。他們在哪裡？
a) 他們在旅館大廳。
b) 他們在碼頭上。
c) 他們在餐廳裡。
d) 他們在一間醫院。

◎解析

圖中的人們已經從船艙離開到岸上的碼頭，故推測得知答案為 b)。

3

◎解答

b) The man is helping the passenger off the train.

（這位男士正協助乘客下火車。）

◎聽力原文

Look at the picture. Which statement is true?

a) The man is wearing a raincoat.

b) The man is helping the passenger off the train.

c) The people are boarding the train.

d) The people are buying umbrellas.

◎中譯

請看圖。以下敘述何者為真？

a) 這位男士身穿雨衣。

b) 這位男士正協助乘客下火車。

c) 人們正要上火車。

d) 人們正在買雨傘。

◎解析

圖中的男士正替下車的乘客撐傘，所以最符合圖片情境的敘述是 b) 選項。

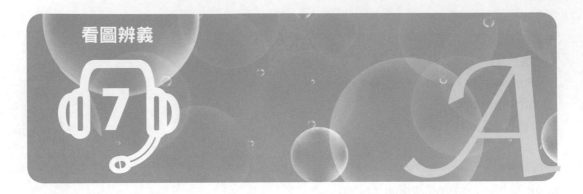

街道上人物的動作

🎧 學習重點

在街道上常會見到工作人員清掃街道（sweep the street），他們通常身著工作褲（work pants, overalls, coveralls），頭戴便帽（cap）或安全帽（helmet），使用的工具如掃帚（broom）、清潔刷（cleaning brush）、畚箕（dustpan）、垃圾桶（trash can）等。

🎧 情境介紹及導引

On the way to school or work, we often see people working on the street, with brooms, cleaning brushes, and dustpans under their arms. These workers empty trash cans and sweep the streets. The sweepers usually wear work pants or overalls. They also wear helmets to protect their heads.

 A-13

此圖片中，主題是人物的動作，此處你會聽到四句話，其中只有一句最符合圖片內容的描述。

Look at the picture. What is he doing?

a) The worker is parking his car.

b) The worker is sleeping in the street.

c) The worker is sweeping the street.

d) The worker is pushing the shopping cart.

答案：c)

a. Information Focus

圖片中的工作人員手拿長柄刷在清潔地面，因此 "The worker is sweeping the street." 是正確的描述。

b. Language Skills

重點字彙：park（停車）、push（推）、shopping cart（購物車）。

c. Tips for Listening

選項 b) 的 sleeping 與 sweeping 發音相似，混淆聽者判斷。

🎧 練習題  A-14

請聽以下看圖辨義題的描述，並從四個選項中，選出最適當的答案。

1.1 ＿＿＿＿＿＿

1.2 ＿＿＿＿＿＿

2 ＿＿＿＿＿＿

3 ＿＿＿＿＿＿

1.1

◎解答

d) They're working outside.
（他們在室外工作。）

◎聽力原文

Look at the picture. What are they doing?

a) They're waiting for a bus.
b) They're entering a building.
c) They're fixing a truck.
d) They're working outside.

◎中譯

請看圖。他們在做什麼？

a) 他們在等公車。
b) 他們正走進一棟大樓。
c) 他們正在修一臺卡車。
d) 他們在室外工作。

◎解析

圖中的人們正在進行維修工程，地點是室外，故最佳選項為 d)。

1.2

◎解答

c) They are wearing helmets.
（他們戴著安全帽。）

◎聽力原文

Look at the picture. Which statement is true?

a) They are carrying boxes in their hands.
b) They are wearing suits and ties.
c) They are wearing helmets.
d) There are four persons.

◎中譯

請看圖。以下敘述何者為真？

a) 他們手中正拿著盒子。
b) 他們穿西裝打領帶。
c) 他們戴著安全帽。
d) 有四個人。

◎解析

圖中可見三人正在工作，手上分別拿著工具，兩個人頭上都戴著安全帽，故 c) 的描述較符合。

2

◎解答

a) They're crossing the street.
（他們正在過馬路。）

◎聽力原文

Look at the picture. What are they doing?

a) They're crossing the street.
b) They're shopping in a mall.
c) They're packing their suitcases.
d) They're putting on their jackets.

◎中譯

請看圖。他們在做什麼？

a) 他們正在過馬路。
b) 他們在購物中心買東西。
c) 他們在打包行李。
d) 他們正在穿外套。

52　　看圖辨義

◎解析

圖中的行人正在穿越斑馬線，故答案選 a)。
圖中未見 mall（購物商場）、 suitcase（行
李箱），也沒有穿外套的動作，故 b)、 c)、
d)為非。

3

◎解答

c) She's using a pay phone.
　（她正在使用公共電話。）

◎聽力原文

Look at the picture. What is she
doing?
a) She's talking in the hall.
b) She's standing on the rail.
c) She's using a pay phone.
d) She's carrying a backpack.

◎中譯

請看圖。她在做什麼？
a) 她正在大廳說話。
b) 她正站在軌道上。
c) 她正在使用公共電話。
d) 她正背著背包。

◎解析

圖中的女士正站在戶外打公用電話（pay
phone），故答案 c)最適合。

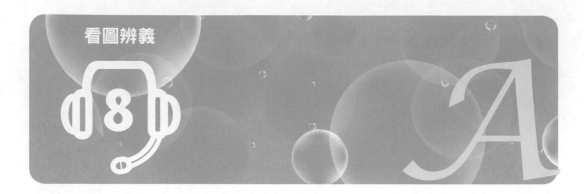

看圖辨義

8

餐廳進食

🎧 **學習重點**

日常生活中常有外食（eat out）機會，選擇用餐地點是很重要的，例如有些咖啡館（café）提供戶外用餐（outdoor dining），營造不同的用餐氣氛（create a different dining atmosphere）。

🎧 **情境介紹及導引**

Gary went to Italy this summer. When he visited an old castle, he saw people eating at an outdoor café. With sunshine and fresh air, the café has a relaxing atmosphere. From the tables, the diners have a view of a nearby grassy area where young people lie on the grass and sunbathe.

範例  A-15

此圖片中，主題是人物的動作，此處你會聽到四句話，其中只有一句最符合圖片內容的描述。

_____

Look at the picture. What are they doing?

a) They're eating at an outdoor café.

b) They're lying on the grass.

c) They're dining inside a castle.

d) They're having a sunbath.　答案：a)

a. Information Focus

圖片中的背景是一棟城堡式建築物，圖中的人們都在戶外用餐，因此 "They're eating at an outdoor café." 是正確的描述。

b. Language Skills

重點字彙：outdoor（戶外的）、dine（用餐）、lie（躺、臥）、castle（城堡）、sunbath（日光浴）、relaxing（令人輕鬆愉快的）。

c. Tips for Listening

動詞後面若接續代表地點的字詞（at / in / on ＋ 地方），通常是與進行該動作有關的地點：

如 eating / dining ＋ at a restaurant / at an outdoor café / inside a castle，或 lying ＋ on the floor / on the grass

🎧 練習題 A-16

請聽以下看圖辨義題的描述，並從四個選項中，選出最適當的答案。

1.1 _____

1.2 _____

2 _____

3 _____

詳解

1.1

◎解答

d) He's looking at the menu.

（他正在看菜單。）

◎聽力原文

Look at the picture. What is he doing?

a) He's signing the papers.

b) He's looking in the phone book.

c) He's calculating the bill.

d) He's looking at the menu.

◎中譯

請看圖。他在做什麼？

a) 他正在簽文件。

b) 他正在查看電話簿。

c) 他正在計算帳單。

d) 他正在看菜單。

◎解析

圖中的男士坐在擺有水和餐具的桌子前，所以推測他在「看菜單」，答案選 d)。

1.2

◎解答

d) He is in a restaurant.

（他在一間餐廳裡。）

◎聽力原文

Look at the picture. Where is he?

a) He is on a bus.

b) He is in a park.

c) He is in a telephone booth.

d) He is in a restaurant.

◎中譯

請看圖。他在哪裡？

a) 他在公車上。

b) 他在公園內。

c) 他在電話亭裡。

d) 他在一間餐廳裡。

◎解析

由圖片中桌上擺放的餐具推斷，男士應該是在餐廳內，故答案選 d)。

2

◎解答

a) He is drinking tea.

（他正在喝茶。）

◎聽力原文

Look at the picture. What is he doing?

a) He is drinking tea.

b) He is making coffee.

c) He is having lunch.

d) He is making a pie.

◎中譯

請看圖。他在做什麼？

a) 他正在喝茶。

b) 他正在泡咖啡。

c) 他正在吃午餐。

d) 他正在做派。

◎解析

圖中的男士手持杯子喝飲料，所以選項 a) 較合理。

3

◎解答

b）He's serving the wine.

　　（他在斟酒。）

◎聽力原文

Look at the picture. What is he doing?

a）He's cleaning the table.

b）He's serving the wine.

c）He's washing the glasses.

d）He's watering the lawn.

◎中譯

請看圖。他在做什麼？

a）他在清桌子。

b）他在斟酒。

c）他在洗玻璃杯。

d）他在替草坪澆水。

◎解析

圖片中的男士穿著正式，一手拿酒瓶倒酒，
一手端著放有杯子的盤子，所以選項 b ）為
正確描述。

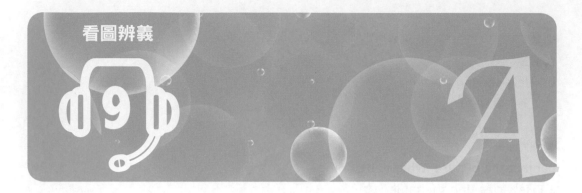

大眾娛樂活動

音樂會（concert）是許多人喜愛的娛樂活動（entertainment），例如欣賞交響樂團表演（symphony），觀眾（audience）常會感到如癡如醉（fascinated），樂曲結束時都會鼓掌歡呼（clapping and cheering）。

 情境介紹及導引

Ivan is a lover of classical music and goes to the concerts regularly for entertainment. This evening as he listens to a symphony in the concert hall, he notices that the audience, like him, is fascinated with the beauty of the music. They clap and cheer as the performance ends.

範例 A-17

此圖片中，主題是人物的動作，此處你會聽到四句話，其中只有一句最符合圖片內容的描述。

_____

Look at the picture. Which statement is true?

a) The play is about to start.

b) The musicians are on break.

c) The concert has already begun.

d) The audience are clapping and cheering.

答案：c)

說明

a. Information Focus

圖片中央的男士正在指揮樂團演奏，旁邊的觀眾在聆聽，表示音樂會已經開始了，"The concert has already begun." 是正確選項。

b. Language Skills

重點字彙：play / performance（表演）、musician（音樂家，樂師）、
　　　　　 on break（休息）。

c. Tips for Listening

本則聽力重點是 "is about to start"（即將開始）及 " has already begun"（已經開始）的分別，請注意發音及句法的差異處。

 練習題 A-18

請聽以下看圖辨義題的描述，並從四個選項中，選出最適當的答案。

1.1 _____

1.2 _____

2 _____

3 _____

9 詳解

1.1

◎解答

a) They are watching a performance.
（他們在看表演。）

◎聽力原文

Look at the picture. What are they doing?

a) They are watching a performance.
b) They are drinking at a bar.
c) They are camping in a forest.
d) They are listening to a lecture.

◎中譯

請看圖，他們在做什麼？

a) 他們在看表演。
b) 他們在酒吧喝飲料。
c) 他們在森林裡露營。
d) 他們在聽演說。

◎解析

圖中前方兩人拿著電吉他在彈唱，後方站著一群人觀看表演，因此選項 a) 最符合情境。

1.2

◎解答

a) The musicians are playing at the beach.（樂手們在海邊演奏。）

◎聽力原文

Look at the picture. Which statement is true?

a) The musicians are playing at the beach.

b) The concert is sold out.
c) The guitar players are in a performance hall.
d) The audience is clapping.

◎中譯

請看圖，以下描述何者為真？

a) 樂手們在海邊演奏。
b) 音樂會的票已經全部售出。
c) 吉他手在表演廳裡。
d) 聽眾在鼓掌。

◎解析

圖片中沒有售票的情境、表演不是在室內舉行，也沒有人在鼓掌，因此 b)、c) 和 d) 皆非，只有 a) 是正確描述。

2

◎解答

c) There is a firework display.
（正在放煙火。）

◎聽力原文

Look at the picture. Which statement is true?

a) A rocket is being launched.
b) The stars are shining brightly.
c) There is a firework display.
d) The building is on fire.

◎中譯

請看圖，以下描述何者為真？

a) 火箭正要發射。
b) 星星正閃耀著光輝。
c) 正在放煙火。
d) 大樓著火了。

圖片中的夜空佈滿美麗的煙火，因此答案選
c）。名詞 display 在此指「展示；表演」的
意思。

3

◎解答

a）She's dancing in the woods.
（她在林間跳舞。）

◎聽力原文

Look at the picture. What is she
doing?
a）She's dancing in the woods.
b）She's picking the coconuts.
c）She's planting the fruit.
d）She's playing the drums.

◎中譯

請看圖，她在做什麼？
a）她在林間跳舞。
b）她在摘椰子。
c）她在種水果。
d）她在打鼓。

◎解析

圖中可見熱帶森林（woods），還有一位穿
著草裙的女孩在舞蹈，因此 a）的描述最貼
切。

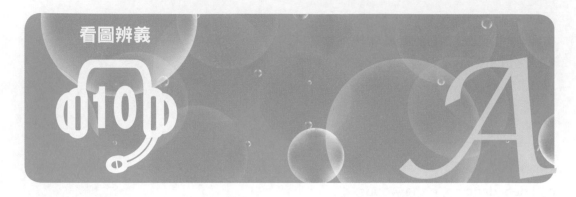

看圖辨義

⑩10

美髮理容

 學習重點

一般人為了改變髮型（hairdo／hairstyle）會去美髮沙龍（hair salon）請設計師（stylist）服務，美髮的項目通常包括洗髮（shampoo）、剪髮（cut）、上捲子（curl）、染髮（color／dye）、燙髮（perm）等。

 情境介紹及導引

Many people visit hair salons regularly. Hair salons provide a variety of services from cuts and styling, to color and perms. A basic visit usually involves a shampoo and haircut. Some customers may request services such as an easy trim or styling with rollers or a curling iron.

範例 A-19

此圖片中，主題是人物的動作，此處你會聽到四句話，其中只有一句最符合圖片內容的描述。

_____

Look at the picture. What is the woman doing?

a) The woman is curling her hair.

b) The woman is shampooing her hair.

c) The woman is having her hair cut.

d) The woman is coloring her hair.

答案：c)

 說明

a. Information Focus

圖中的設計師正拿著剪刀幫客人剪髮，因此 "The woman is having her hair cut." 是正確的描述。

b. Language Skills

請別人做髮型：人 + have/ has/ get(s) + his/ her hair + cut / colored / permed。

c. Tips for Listening

本則聽力重點是要熟悉跟髮型設計有關的一般動詞，如 shampoo, curl, cut, color, dye, perm 等。

練習題　A-20

請聽以下看圖辨義題的描述，並從四個選項中，選出最適當的答案。

1 _____

2 _____

3.1 _____

3.2 _____

詳解

1

◎解答

c) One girl is putting up the other
girl's hair.
（一個女孩正為另一個女孩綁頭髮。）

◎聽力原文

Look at the picture. What are they
doing?
a) Both girls put their hair in curlers.
b) They are studying in the library.
c) One girl is putting up the other
girl's hair.
d) They are looking at magazines.

◎中譯

請看圖。她們在做什麼？
a) 兩個女孩都在上髮捲。
b) 她們正在圖書館念書。
c) 一個女孩正為另一個女孩綁頭髮。
d) 她們在看雜誌。

◎解析

put up 是指「綁起；掛起」的動作。圖中
站立的女孩正在為另一個女孩綁頭髮，故答
案選 c) 最合適。

2

◎解答

b) He's getting his hair cut.
（他在剪髮。）

◎聽力原文

Look at the picture. What is he doing?
a) He's getting his teeth cleaned.
b) He's getting his hair cut.
c) He's getting his hair dyed.
d) He's getting his head measured.

◎中譯

請看圖。他正在做什麼？
a) 他在清潔牙齒。
b) 他在剪髮。
c) 他在染髮。
d) 他在量頭圍。

◎解析

圖中男士正坐著讓人剪頭髮，故答案選 b)。
hair 和 head 發音相近，要小心聽辨。

3.1

◎解答

c) They are doing hair at a beauty
shop.（她們在美容院弄頭髮。）

◎聽力原文

Look at the picture. What are they
doing?
a) They are swimming.
b) They are taking a bath.
c) They are doing hair at a beauty
shop.
d) They are measuring for a tablecloth.

◎中譯

請看圖。她們在做什麼？
a) 她們在游泳。
b) 她們在泡澡。
c) 她們在美容院弄頭髮。
d) 她們在測量桌布尺寸。

◎解析

圖中可見兩位女士，其中一位正在為另一位
沖頭髮，故答案選 c）最恰當。

3.2

◎解答

c）This is a hair salon.

（這裡是髮廊。）

◎聽力原文

Look at the picture. Where is this
place?

a）This is a shower room.

b）This is a dental clinic.

c）This is a hair salon.

d）This is a drugstore.

◎中譯

請看圖。這是什麼地點？

a）這裡是淋浴間。

b）這裡是牙醫診所。

c）這裡是髮廊。

d）這裡是藥局。

◎解析

題目是問地點，由圖中沖洗頭髮的動作推
測，地點是在髮廊內。

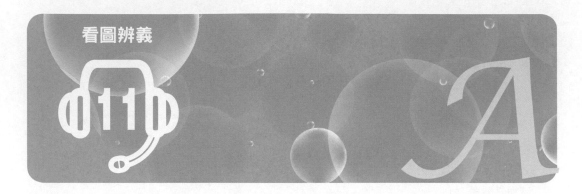

地點：商店及賣場

日常生活中常會去商店或賣場等處，例如在海鮮市場（sea food market），會看到許多賣海鮮的小販（vendor）， 站在陳列貨品的攤子（stand）旁邊，每種海鮮都有價格標籤（price tag），幫助顧客選取自己想賣的貨品。

 情境介紹及導引

Being an island surrounded by a rich environment of marine life, Taiwan is known for its fresh seafood. In several port cities, tourists can visit fish markets to buy from a vast inventory of marine products and sample some of the local seafood dishes at nearby restaurants.

範例　A-21

此圖片中，主題是圖片中的地點，此處你會聽到四句話，其中只有一句是最符合圖片內容的描述。

_____

Look at the picture. Where is this place?
a) This is a market.
b) This is a fishing pond.
c) This is a dock.
d) This is a playground.

答案：a)

a. Information Focus

圖中的男士身穿工作圍裙，站在擺滿海鮮的攤子旁，得知圖片地點是市場。

b. Language Skills

重點字彙：marine（海洋的）、fishing pond（魚池）、dock（碼頭）、
playground（遊樂場）。

c. Tips for Listening

此處問題是 "Where is this place?"，因此選項中的「地點名詞」，包括 market,
fishing pond, dock, playground 就是聽力重點所在，請熟悉這些字彙的發音。

🎧 練習題　A-22

請聽以下看圖辨義題的描述，並從四個選項中，選出最適當的答案。

❶ ＿＿＿＿＿＿＿

2.1 ＿＿＿＿＿＿＿

2.2 ＿＿＿＿＿＿＿

❸ ＿＿＿＿＿＿＿

詳解

1

◎解答

b) He's looking at the cameras.
（他在看相機。）

◎聽力原文

Look at the picture. What is he doing?
a) He's washing the cars.
b) He's looking at the cameras.
c) He's buying some clothes.
d) He's talking to a salesman.

◎中譯

請看圖。他在做什麼？
a) 他在洗車子。
b) 他在看相機。
c) 他在選購衣服。
d) 他正在和售貨員講話。

◎解析

圖片上一名男士正站在相機展示架前方觀看，故答案選 b) 最合適。

2.1

◎解答

a) This is a price list board.
（這是價目表。）

◎聽力原文

Look at the picture. What is it?
a) This is a price list board.
b) This is a flight schedule board.
c) This is a chopping board.
d) This is a chess board.

◎中譯

請看圖。這是什麼？
a) 這是價目表。
b) 這是航班時間表。
c) 這是砧板。
d) 這是棋盤。

◎解析

圖中掛板上可見 Coffee & Tea（咖啡和茶）的標題，下方列出飲料名和價格，所以推測答案應該選 a)。

2.2

◎解答

c) The shop serves different drinks.
（這間店提供不同的飲料。）

◎聽力原文

Look at the picture. Which statement is true?
a) The prices are higher than $15.00.
b) The store sells cups and glasses.
c) The shop serves different drinks.
d) All flights are delayed or canceled.

◎中譯

請看圖。下列敘述何者為真？
a) 價格都高於 15 美元。
b) 此店販售茶杯和玻璃杯。
c) 此店提供不同的飲料。
d) 所有的班機都延誤或取消了。

◎解析

由圖片中所列各式茶或咖啡飲料的名稱，可以推知答案為 c)。

3

◎解答

b）She's at a bakery.

（她在一家麵包店裡。）

◎聽力原文

Look at the picture. Where is she?

a）She's at a factory.

b）She's at a bakery.

c）She's at a dormitory.

d）She's at a fashion store.

◎中譯

請看圖。她在哪裡？

a）她在一間工廠裡。

b）她在一家麵包店裡。

c）她在宿舍裡。

d）她在一間時裝店內。

◎解析

題目問的是地點，由圖中的麵包架及陳列的
麵包可得知答案為 b）。

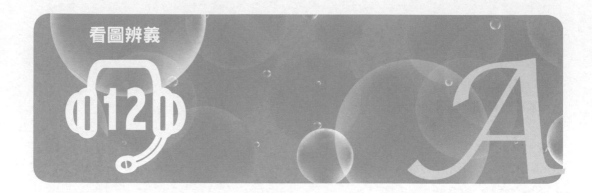

看圖辨義

12

地點：大眾運輸

學習重點

當搭乘大眾運輸工具時，坐在車廂（train carriage）中的乘客（passenger），有的戴著耳機（earphones）聽音樂，有的在看報紙（reading newspapers），有的在交談（having a conversation），有的則是閉目養神（sitting with eyes closed）。

情境介紹及導引

On trains and buses, it is common to see passengers reading newspapers or, with their eyes closed, taking a rest. Many people also listen to music through earphones or have a conversation with people sitting next to them. To be safe, remember to hold on to the handrail if you do not have a seat.

範例　A-23

此圖片中，主題是圖片中人物的動作，此處你會聽到四句話，其中只有一句最符合圖片內容的描述。

_____

Look at the picture. Which statement is true?

a) They are having a conversation.

b) The men are reading newspapers.

c) They are holding on to the handrail.

d) The passengers are sitting next to one another.

答案：d)

說明

a. Information Focus

圖片中的人物在車廂中並排而坐,因此 "The passengers are sitting next to one another." 是正確的描述。

b. Language Skills

重點字彙:hold on to(緊握)、handrail(扶手)、next to(緊鄰著)。

c. Tips for Listening

請記住特定詞組的發音,有助於聽懂句子的意思,如 reading newspapers(看報)、having a conversation(交談)、hold on to the handrail(緊握扶手);圖片中都是現在進行式的動作,注意聽 be + V-ing 裡的動詞發音,如 having, reading, holding, sitting。

練習題　A-24

請聽以下看圖辨義題的描述,並從四個選項中,選出最適當的答案。

1 ＿＿＿＿＿＿＿

2 ＿＿＿＿＿＿＿

3 ＿＿＿＿＿＿＿

12 詳解

1

◎解答

b) This is an airport.
（這是機場。）

◎聽力原文

Look at the picture. Where is this place?
a) This is a school.
b) This is an airport.
c) This is a post office.
d) This is a supermarket.

◎中譯

請看圖。這是什麼地方？
a) 這是學校。
b) 這是機場。
c) 這是郵局。
d) 這是超級市場。

◎解析

題目問的是地點（where），由圖中一架飛機停在跑道上，可推測地點是機場，所以選b)。

2

◎解答

c) The people are at the train station.
（人們在車站裡。）

◎聽力原文

Look at the picture. Where are the people?
a) The people are at a restaurant.
b) The people are at a party.
c) The people are at the train station.
d) The people are walking in the rain.

◎中譯

請看圖。人們在什麼地方？
a) 人們在餐廳裡。
b) 人們在舞會上。
c) 人們在車站裡。
d) 人們在雨中漫步。

◎解析

由圖片中的列車、指示牌以及來往的乘客，可知地點應該是車站內，故選 c)。

3

◎解答

d) He is in the aisle seat.
（他坐在靠走道的位置。）

◎聽力原文

Look at the picture. What is he doing?
a) He is spilling the drink.
b) He is sitting next to a woman.
c) He is sitting in the window seat.
d) He is in the aisle seat.

◎中譯

請看圖。他正在做什麼？
a) 他把飲料灑出來。
b) 他坐在一位女士的旁邊。
c) 他坐在靠窗的位子。
d) 他坐在靠走道的位子。

◎解析

由圖片顯示，這位男士坐在有雙排座位的車廂內，身旁靠窗的座位是空著的，所以答案選 d) 最合適。aisle 指「走道」，其中 s 不發音。

看圖辨義

13

地點：娛樂場所

學習重點

日常生活中常有機會參觀博物館（museum）、畫廊（gallery），或造訪名勝古蹟（historical sites），以畫廊為例，每隔一段時間都會有不同的展覽主題（exhibition themes），吸引有興趣的民眾參訪（visit）。

情境介紹及導引

Many people enjoy cultural activities such as visiting historical sites or churches famous for their architecture. Viewing works of art at a museum or gallery is another way of appreciating culture. Because most museums have a large collection, they rotate the works by organizing exhibitions on various themes.

此圖片中，主題是圖片中的地點，此處你會聽到四句話，其中只有一句是最符合圖片內容的描述。

Look at the picture. Where is this place?
a) This is a gallery.
b) This is a photo booth.
c) This is a movie theater.
d) This is a church.

答案：a)

🎧 說明

a. Information Focus

圖片顯示出掛滿畫作的展覽室，得知地點是一間畫廊。

b. Language Skills

重點字彙：photo booth（投幣式自動拍照亭）、movie theater（電影院）、
church（教堂）、architecture（建築物）、rotate（輪替）。

c. Tips for Listening

圖片的問題是 where 引導的疑問句，聽力的重點是地點名稱（gallery, photo
booth, movie theater, church）。

🎧 練習題 A-26

請聽以下看圖辨義題的描述，並從四個選項中，選出最適當的答案。

1.1 _____

1.2 _____

2 _____

3 _____

13 詳解

1.1

◎解答

a) The tourists are gathered at the square.（遊客們在廣場聚集。）

◎聽力原文

Look at the picture. Where are the tourists?

a) The tourists are gathered at the square.

b) The tourists are getting on the bus.

c) The tourists are in front of the skyscrapers.

d) The tourists are lining up.

◎中譯

請看圖。這些遊客在哪裡？

a) 遊客們在廣場聚集。

b) 遊客們要上巴士。

c) 遊客們站在摩天大樓前。

d) 遊客們在排隊。

◎解析

圖中可見一群遊客站在教堂前的廣場上，所以 a) 是合理描述。gather 為動詞「聚集，集合」。

1.2

◎解答

b) Some people are using cameras.（有些人在照相。）

◎聽力原文

Look at the picture. Which statement is true?

a) The buildings are for sale.

b) Some people are using cameras.

c) They are wearing audio tour headsets.

d) They are choosing souvenirs.

◎中譯

請看圖。下列敘述何者為真？

a) 這些樓房在出售。

b) 有些人在照相。

c) 他們戴著語音導覽耳機。

d) 他們在挑選紀念品。

◎解析

圖中可見右下角一名遊客正拿著相機拍照，故答案選 b) 最合理。圖中沒有待售的房子、導覽耳機或紀念品，故選項 a)、 c)、d) 為非。

2

◎解答

b) This is a museum.（這是博物館。）

◎聽力原文

Look at the picture. Where is this place?

a) This is a library.

b) This is a museum.

c) This is a schoolyard.

d) This is a kindergarten.

◎中譯

請看圖。這是什麼地方？

a) 這是圖書館。

b）這是博物館。

c）這是校園。

d）這是幼稚園。

◎解析

本題問的是地點（where），圖片中的人們站在一座雕像前，有位女士在向大家解說，可推知是在博物館內。

3

◎解答

b）There are people on the stairs.

（人們在階梯上。）

◎聽力原文

Look at the picture. Which statement is true?

a）There are people on the sidewalk.

b）There are people on the stairs.

c）There are street vendors.

d）There are factory workers.

◎中譯

請看圖。下列敘述何者為真？

a）人們在人行道上。

b）人們在階梯上。

c）有街頭小販。

d）有工廠工人。

◎解析

從圖中有人上下階梯的狀況判斷，選項 b）最合適。on the stairs 指的是位置「在階梯上」。

地點：自然風景

 學習重點

假日時常有機會出遊（have an outing），遠離塵囂（away from traffic or crowds），造訪鄉村（visit the countryside），鄉村的景物以農田（farm）為代表，人口較為稀少（less populated），也不常看到川流不息的交通（traffic）或人潮（crowds）。

 情境介紹及導引

Many people enjoy driving through the countryside. They find the rural scenes very relaxing. Because these areas are less populated, driving through the farmland allows you to get away from traffic or crowds. Next time when you visit the countryside, look out for the farms that lie between rolling hills.

範 例 A-27

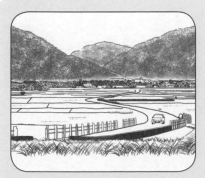

此圖片中，主題是圖片中的地點，此處你會聽到四句話，其中只有一句是最符合圖片內容的描述。

_____

Look at the picture. Where is this place?

a) This is an airport.

b) This is a harbor.

c) This is a city.

d) This is a farm.　　　　　　答案：d)

a. Information Focus

圖片中的主要景物是農田，因此 "This is a farm." 是正確的選項。

b. Language Skills

重點字彙：airport（機場）、harbor（港口）、city（城市）、rural（農村的）、
rolling hills（起伏的山巒）。

c. Tips for Listening

本文聽力的重點是地點名稱（airport、harbor、city、 farm），除了熟悉這些字
彙的發音，也須了解這些地點應有的景色或建築物。

🎧 練習題　A-28

請聽以下看圖辨義題的描述，並從四個選項中，選出最適當的答案。

1 ＿＿＿＿＿＿＿＿

2.1 ＿＿＿＿＿＿＿＿

2.2 ＿＿＿＿＿＿＿＿

3 ＿＿＿＿＿＿＿＿

14 詳解

1

◎解答

c) There is a waterfall.
（有一座瀑布。）

◎聽力原文

Look at the picture. Which statement is true?

a) There are several boats on the river.
b) The lake is calm.
c) There is a waterfall.
d) There are waves on the ocean.

◎中譯

請看圖。下列敘述何者為真？
a) 河中有幾艘船。
b) 湖面很平靜。
c) 有一座瀑布。
d) 海上有浪濤。

◎解析

圖中左方可見瀑布流入湖中，引起湖面陣陣漣漪，所以答案 c) 最適合。

2.1

◎解答

d) They are at the beach.
（他們在海灘上。）

◎聽力原文

Look at the picture. Where are these people?

a) They are in the swimming pool.
b) They are in the playground.
c) They are in the desert.
d) They are at the beach.

◎中譯

請看圖。這群人在什麼地方？
a) 他們在游泳池裡。
b) 他們在遊樂場。
c) 他們在沙漠裡。
d) 他們在海灘上。

◎解析

本題是問地點，從圖片中的遮陽傘和小朋友在沙灘上堆沙堡的動作，可知答案選 d) 最恰當。

2.2

◎解答

b) The woman is wearing a hat.
（這位女士戴著一頂帽子。）

◎聽力原文

Look at the picture. Which statement is true?

a) The woman is wearing an evening gown.
b) The woman is wearing a hat.
c) The children are crying.
d) They are eating dinner.

◎中譯

請看圖。下列敘述何者為真？
a) 這位女士穿著晚禮服。
b) 這位女士戴著一頂帽子。
c) 孩子們在哭。
d) 他們在吃晚餐。

◎解析

從圖中女士穿戴遮陽帽的打扮可知， 選項
b）是合適的敘述。女士並未穿著晚禮服
（evening gown）、孩子們也沒有哭泣或
吃晚餐，故其它選項為非。

3

◎解答

a) The waterfall is pouring down.
　（瀑布正傾瀉而下。）

◎聽力原文

Look at the picture. Which statement
is true?
a) The waterfall is pouring down.
b) It's raining heavily.
c) It is a puddle.
d) People are swimming in the river.

◎中譯

請看圖。下列敘述何者為真？
a）瀑布正傾瀉而下。
b）正下著傾盆大雨。
c）這是個水坑。
d）人們在河裡游泳。

◎解析

pour down 指「（河水）傾流而下；（雨）
傾盆而下」，由圖片可知答案 a）是正確描
述。

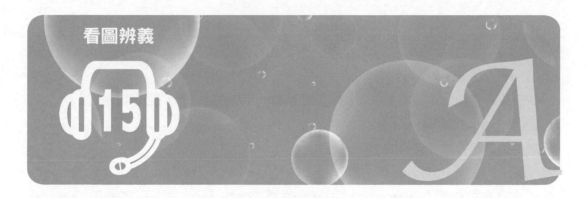

物品的位置

 學習重點

在日常生活中常有機會對他人描述物品的位置,例如介紹居家的擺設(room furnishings),包括桌椅(table and chair)、檯燈(electric lamp)、圖畫(picture)、盆栽(potted plants)、電器(electrical appliances)等。

 情境介紹及導引

Jean loves to show her friend around her apartment. In a corner of the living room, there's a table by the wall. On the table sit the phone, a potted plant, and a lamp. Jean also has an antique clock hanging on the wall.

範例 🎧 A-29

此圖片中,主題是圖片中的地點,此處你會聽到四句話,其中只有一句是最符合圖片內容的描述。

Look at the picture. Which statement is true?
a) A poster is above the telephone.
b) An electric lamp is under the picture.
c) There is a plant between the phone and the lamp.
d) There is a phone mounted on the wall.

答案:c)

說明

a. Information Focus

依照圖片所顯示，只有選項 c）有盆植物在電話和檯燈之間，是正確的描述。

b. Language Skills

常用來表示方向及位置的字詞：

i. 在……之上：above, on, on top of；在……之下：beneath, below, under

ii. 在……的前面：in front of；在兩者之間：between；在……的後面：behind

iii. 在……旁邊、靠近：by, beside, near；遠離：away from

c. Tips for Listening

本則聽力的重點是物品名稱，如 telephone, electric lamp, plant, wall；以及表示方向及位置的字詞，如 above, under, between, mounted on。

練習題 A-30

請聽以下看圖辨義題的描述，並從四個選項中，選出最適當的答案。

1.1 _____

1.2 _____

2 _____

3 _____

15 詳解

1.1

◎解答

c) There's a picture above the sofa.
（沙發上方有一幅畫。）

◎聽力原文

Look at the picture. Which statement
is true?
a) There's a television set in the
corner.
b) The bookcases are behind the
sofa.
c) There's a picture above the sofa.
d) The flower vase is on the table.

◎中譯

請看圖。以下敘述何者為真？
a) 角落有一臺電視機。
b) 書架位於沙發後方。
c) 沙發上方有一幅畫。
d) 桌上有花瓶。

◎解析

圖中沒有電視（television set）也沒有書
架（bookcase），花瓶（flower vase）
並非擺在桌上，故只有 c) 選項符合。

1.2

◎解答

c) This is a living room.
（這是客廳。）

◎聽力原文

Look at the picture. Which statement
is true?
a) The room is full of people.
b) This is a bedroom.
c) This is a living room.
d) This a florist shop.

◎中譯

請看圖。以下敘述何者為真？
a) 房間擠滿了人。
b) 這是臥房。
c) 這是客廳。
d) 這是一間花店。

◎解析

圖中沒有任何人（people）也非臥房
（bedroom），由其陳設可以推斷是客廳
（living room）。

2

◎解答

d) There are books on the shelves.
（書本在書架上。）

◎聽力原文

Look at the picture. Which statement
is true?
a) There is a staircase by the window.
b) There are toys on the chair.
c) There is a lamp on the table.
d) There are books on the shelves.

◎中譯

請看圖。以下敘述何者為真？
a) 窗戶旁邊是樓梯間。
b) 椅子上有玩具。
c) 桌上有一盞檯燈。
d) 書本在書架上。

圖中未見 staircase （樓梯）、toy （玩具）
或 lamp （檯燈），只有選項 d）是正確描
述。shelves 是 shelf「（書櫃等）架子」
的名詞複數。

3 ─────────────────────

◎解答

a）The forks lie to one side of the
　　plate.（叉子擺在盤子的一側。）

◎聽力原文

Look at the picture. Which statement
is true?

a）The forks lie to one side of the
　　plate.

b）The knives are set to the right of
　　the spoon.

c）A napkin lies unfolded on top of
　　the plate.

d）The knife and fork are side by
　　side.

◎中譯

請看圖。以下敘述何者為真？

a）叉子擺在盤子的一側。

b）刀子放在湯匙的右邊。

c）餐巾攤開在盤子上。

d）刀子和叉子並排擺放。

◎解析

lie「位於……」是描述位置時常用的動詞，
to one side of ＋（某物）則指「位於（某
物）的一側」，根據盤子周圍的餐具擺設觀
察，a）是合理描述。

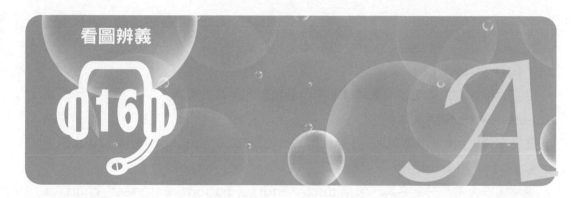

看圖辨義

人物的身分

 學習重點

我們在不同的工作場所（workplace），會遇到各種身分（identity）的人物，例如在醫院，會接觸到醫生（doctor）或護士（nurse）；在賣場結帳時，會與收銀員（cashier）互動；即使走在街道上，也有機會看到街頭藝人（street artist）的表演。

 情境介紹及導引

Sophia finds her job as a nurse rewarding because she gets to see patients recover. After work, Sophia usually buys groceries from a supermarket where her sister works as a cashier. Then Sophia goes home to eat dinner with her husband, who is a software engineer.

範例 A-31

此圖片中，主題是人物的身分，此處你會聽到四句話，其中只有一句是最符合圖片內容的描述。

_____

Look at the picture. Who are they?

a) They are a doctor and a nurse.

b) They are a nurse and a patient.

c) They are an engineer and a child.

d) They are a technician and student.

答案：b)

說明

a. Information Focus

從圖片中人物的衣著及場景環境，可以看出他們是護士與病人。

b. Language Skills

重點字彙：patient（病人）、engineer（工程師）、technician（技術人員）。

c. Tips for Listening

注意代表人物身分的名詞，包括 doctor, nurse, patient, engineer, child, technician, student；以及這些人物會出現的場景環境以及他們常穿的衣著。

練習題　A-32

請聽以下看圖辨義題的描述，並從四個選項中，選出最適當的答案。

1.1 _____

1.2 _____

2 _____

3 _____

16 詳解

1.1

◎解答

c) She's a cashier.
（她是收銀員。）

◎聽力原文

Look at the picture. Who is she?
a) She's a registered nurse.
b) She's a waitress.
c) She's a cashier.
d) She's a banker.

◎中譯

請看圖。她的身分是？
a) 她是合格護士。
b) 她是服務生。
c) 她是收銀員。
d) 她是銀行家。

◎解析

由圖片中的收銀機（cash register），及男士付錢、女士收錢的動作推測，女士是位收銀員（cashier）。

1.2

◎解答

c) They are at the checkout counter.
（他們在收銀臺。）

◎聽力原文

Look at the picture. Where are they?
a) They are in a bank.
b) They are in a park.
c) They are at the checkout counter.
d) They are at the front desk.

◎中譯

請看圖。他們在哪裡？
a) 他們在銀行裡。
b) 他們在公園內。
c) 他們在收銀臺。
d) 他們在接待櫃臺。

◎解析

本題是問地點，由圖片可推知地點應在商店內的收銀臺，故答案選 c) 最適合。checkout 指「付款；結帳」。

2

◎解答

d) He's a street cleaner.
（他是街道清潔工。）

◎聽力原文

Look at the picture. Which statement is true?
a) He's working at the cleaners.
b) He's going for a walk.
c) He's emptying the trash can.
d) He's a street cleaner.

◎中譯

請看圖。以下描述何者為真？
a) 他在乾洗店工作。
b) 他要去散步。
c) 他正清空垃圾桶。
d) 他是街道清潔工。

◎解析

由圖中男士手持掃把和畚箕及他的衣著推測，男士應是一名清潔工，故選 d)。選項 a) 的 cleaners 是指「乾洗店（常用複數）」。

❸

◎解答

b) They are street artists.

（她們是街頭藝術家。）

◎聽力原文

Look at the picture. Which statement
is true?

a) They're playing the same
    instruments.

b) They are street artists.

c) A big crowd is listening to music.

d) The violinist is wearing a dress.

◎中譯

請看圖。以下描述何者為真？

a) 她們演奏相同的樂器。

b) 她們是街頭藝術家。

c) 一大群人在聽音樂。

d) 小提琴演奏者穿著裙裝。

◎解析

由圖片可見，兩個人正演奏不同樂器且穿著
褲裝，也沒有一大群人圍繞，所以答案 b)
最貼切。street artist 指「街頭藝人」。

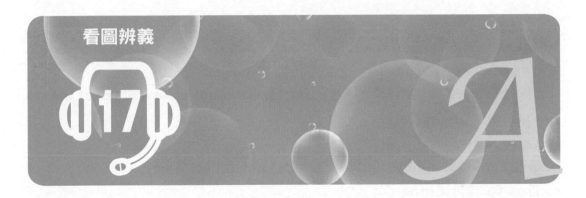

看圖辨義

事物的狀態

🎧 學習重點

在都會區維持順暢的交通動線（maintain smooth traffic flow），需要大家遵守交通規則（traffic regulations），包括車輛停放規定（parking regulations），即使像體積較小的摩托車（motorcycle），也要整齊地停靠在路邊（park at the roadside）。

🔊 情境介紹及導引

When we drive, it is important to follow traffic rules to help maintain smooth traffic flow. This includes following parking regulations so that cars and motorcycles are neatly lined up along the street by the roadside. Vehicles that do not park properly are likely to be towed by the police.

範例　A-33

此圖片中，主題是圖片中車子的狀態，此處你會聽到四句話，其中只有一句最符合圖片內容的描述。

Look at the picture. Which statement is true?

a) The motorcycle crashed into a bus.

b) The motorcycle is parked by the roadside.

c) The motorcycle is being towed by a policeman.

d) Motorcycles are lined up along the street.

答案：b)

a. Information Focus

圖片中只有一輛摩托車停靠在路邊，因此 "The motorcycle is parked at the roadside." 是正確的描述。

b. Language Skills

重點字彙：crash（撞壞）、tow（拖吊）、line up（排成一列）。

c. Tips for Listening

聽取描述車輛動作的動詞（如 crash, park, tow, line up）；表示方向性、動作者或地點的字詞（into a bus, by a policeman, at the roadside, along the street）。

🎧 練習題　A-34

請聽以下看圖辨義題的描述，並從四個選項中，選出最適當的答案。

1 ＿＿＿＿＿＿

2 ＿＿＿＿＿＿

3 ＿＿＿＿＿＿

詳解

1

◎解答

a) There are flags near the buildings.
（建築物附近有幾面旗子。）

◎聽力原文

Look at the picture. Which statement is true?
a) There are flags near the buildings.
b) There are many people on the street.
c) Some cars are parked along the street.
d) One of the buildings has already collapsed.

◎中譯

請看圖。下列描述何者為真？
a) 建築物附近有幾面旗子。
b) 街上有很多人。
c) 幾部車輛沿著街道停放。
d) 其中有棟房子已經倒塌。

◎解析

如圖片所示，街上有旗子（flags）和建築物（buildings），並無人與車輛，而且建築物完好，只有答案 a) 的描述最合理。

2

◎解答

d) There are a lock and a chain.
（有一組鎖和鎖鏈。）

◎聽力原文

Look at the picture. Which statement is true?

a) The door is unlocked.
b) There's a key in the lock.
c) There's a rock on the gate.
d) There is a lock and a chain.

◎中譯

請看圖。下列描述何者為真？
a) 門沒有上鎖。　　b) 門鎖上有把鑰匙。
c) 門上有顆石頭。　d) 有一組鎖和鎖鍊。

◎解析

由圖片可以判斷，門是上鎖的，但上面沒有鑰匙，只有鎖頭和鍊條，故答案選 d)。

3

◎解答

d) There is a cable-supported bridge across the river.
（有座鋼索吊橋橫跨河面。）

◎聽力原文

Look at the picture. Which statement is true?
a) There are boats sailing on the river.
b) There is an accident on the road.
c) There is heavy traffic on the bridge.
d) There is a cable-supported bridge across the river.

◎中譯

請看圖。下列描述何者為真？
a) 船隻航行於河面上。
b) 路上有一起意外事故。
c) 橋上交通繁忙。
d) 有座鋼索吊橋橫跨河面。

◎解析

河面沒有船、橋上無意外事故（accident），也沒有交通繁忙（heavy traffic），只有鋼索吊橋橫跨河面，故選 d)。cable 是指「纜繩；繩索」。

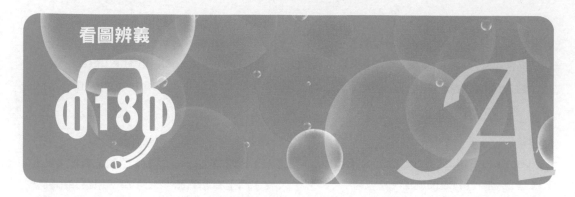

看圖辨義

18

衣著

🎧 學習重點

人們的衣著（clothing）會隨著不同的身分（identity）、場合（occasion）、天氣狀況（weather condition）而改變。例如學生在學校穿著制服（uniform）；男士在正式場合會穿西裝打領帶（a suit and tie）；夏季從事戶外活動最好戴著帽子（hat/cap）。

🎧 情境介紹及導引

Students in Taiwan, from grades one to twelve, wear uniforms to school. Many believe that students who wear uniforms perform better academically because they spend less time planning and choosing their daily clothing. Students usually have two sets of uniforms: one for attending classes and another for sports.

 範例 A-35

此圖片中，主題是圖片中人物的衣著，此處你會聽到四句話，其中只有一句最符合圖片內容的描述。

_____

Look at the picture. Which statement is true?

a) They are both wearing hats.

b) They are both dressed in jeans.

c) They are of the same height.

d) They have uniforms on.　　　答案：d)

說明

a. Information Focus

圖片顯示一對男女學生穿著制服，因此 " They have uniforms on." 是正確描述。

b. Language Skills

表示「穿著」的動詞：S + wear + 衣著；S + be dressed in + 衣著；
S + have + 衣著 + on

c. Tips for Listening

本段聽力重點是各種衣著的名詞，如 uniform, jeans, hat；以及表示穿著的動詞，
如 wearing, dressed, have...on。

練習題 A-36

請聽以下看圖辨義題的描述，並從四個選項中，選出最適當的答案。

1 _____

2.1 _____

2.2 _____

3 _____

18
詳解

1

◎解答
a）He's wearing a suit and tie.
（他穿西裝打領帶。）

◎聽力原文
Look at the picture. Which statement is true?
a）He's wearing a suit and tie.
b）He's wearing a hat.
c）He's carrying a suitcase.
d）He's dressed in a dark robe.

◎中譯
請看圖。下列敘述何者為真？
a）他穿西裝打領帶。
b）他戴著一頂帽子。
c）他拎著一只皮箱。
d）他穿著深色長袍。

◎解析
由圖片可知，男士穿著正式的淺色西裝（suit），沒有提皮箱（suitcase）也沒戴帽子（hat），所以答案選 a）。

2.1

◎解答
c）The boys are wearing caps.
（男孩們戴著球帽。）

◎聽力原文
Look at the picture. Which statement is true?

a）They're putting on their shorts.
b）One boy is taking off his sunglasses.
c）The boys are wearing caps.
d）The boys are playing chess.

◎中譯
請看圖。下列敘述何者為真？
a）他們正換上短褲。
b）其中一個男孩正摘下太陽眼鏡。
c）男孩們戴著球帽。
d）男孩們在下棋。

◎解析
圖中兩個男孩都穿運動服戴球帽（cap），所以 c）是正確描述。圖中男孩沒有戴太陽眼鏡（sunglasses）、也沒有在下棋（play chess），而且只有一名男孩穿著短褲（shorts）故選項 a）、b）、d）為非。

2.2

◎解答
b）They are having outdoor activities.
（他們在戶外運動。）

◎聽力原文
Look at the picture. Which statement is true?
a）They are in a restaurant.
b）They are having outdoor activities.
c）They are sitting on a bench.
d）They are lying on the grass.

◎中譯
請看圖。下列敘述何者為真？
a）他們在餐廳內。
b）他們在戶外運動。
c）他們坐在長椅上。

d）他們躺在草地上。

◎解析

本題是詢問地點或動作相關的描述，圖片可見地點在戶外，從男孩們的穿著和動作可推測 b）是正確描述。 outdoor 是形容詞「戶外的」。

3

◎解答

a）The man's hat is on backwards.
（男士的帽子是朝後戴的。）

◎聽力原文

Look at the picture. Which statement is true?
a）The man's hat is on backwards.
b）The man has on a long-sleeved shirt.
c）The man is wearing sunglasses.
d）The T-shirt has one vertical line.

◎中譯

請看圖。下列敘述何者為真？
a）男士的帽子是朝後戴的。
b）男士穿著長袖上衣。
c）男士戴著太陽眼鏡。
d）這件 T 恤上有一條直線。

◎解析

圖中的男士穿著短袖上衣，沒有戴太陽眼鏡，故只有 a）選項的描述正確。backwards「向後；倒回」是形容方向的副詞。

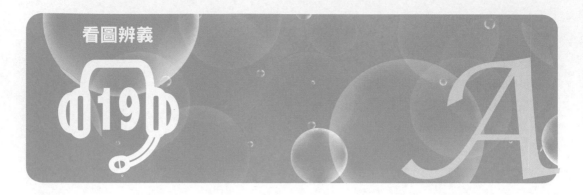

看圖辨義

19

動物

 學習重點

人們的休閒活動（leisure activity）有很多種，比較特殊的是觀賞動物的競賽活動，例如賽狗（dog race），在歐美部份國家會選取適合賽跑的品種（breed），像是灰狗（greyhound）、惠比特犬（whippet）、哈士奇（husky）等，比較著名的賽狗活動是美加地區的拉雪橇競賽（sled dog racing）。

 情境介紹及導引

The sport of dog racing is a popular leisure activity in some parts of the world. Like horse racing, people bet on the greyhound races, but the amateur form of the sport, where no financial interest involves, also exists.

範例 A-37

此圖片中，主題是圖片中狗的動作，此處你會聽到四句話，其中只有一句是最符合圖片內容的描述。

_____

Look at the picture. Which statement is true?

a) The dogs are resting.

b) The dogs are racing.

c) The dogs are riding the sled.

d) The dogs are fighting.　　　　答案：b)

🎧 說明

a. **Information Focus**

圖片顯示一群狗在賽跑，因此 "The dogs are racing." 是正確描述。

b. **Language Skills**

重點字彙：rest（休息）、race（賽跑）、sled（雪橇）、fight（打架）。

c. **Tips for Listening**

本段聽力重點是幾個 V-ing（現在分詞）的念法，包括 resting, racing, riding, fighting；其中 resting 與 racing 發音相似，混淆聽者的判斷。

🎧 **練習題**  A-38

請聽以下看圖辨義題的描述，並從四個選項中，選出最適當的答案。

1 _____

2 _____

3.1 _____

3.2 _____

1

◎解答

c) The ducks are on the ground.
（鴨子在陸地上。）

◎聽力原文

Look at the picture. Which statement is true?
a) There are birds in the tree.
b) There are dogs by the pond.
c) The ducks are on the ground.
d) They are swimming in the lake.

◎中譯

請看圖。以下敘述何者為真？
a) 樹上有鳥兒。
b) 池邊有狗兒。
c) 鴨子在陸地上。
d) 牠們在湖中游泳。

◎解析

由圖片可知，鴨子在陸地上行走，不是在樹上（in the tree）也不是在湖中游泳（swimming in the lake），故答案選 c ）最合適。

2

◎解答

c) The cattle are eating grass.
（牛正在吃草。）

◎聽力原文

Look at the picture. Which statement is true?

a) The cattle are being milked.
b) The cattle are being led out.
c) The cattle are eating grass.
d) The cattle are racing.

◎中譯

請看圖。下列敘述何者為真？
a) 牛正被擠奶。
b) 牛被放出來。
c) 牛正在吃草。
d) 牛在賽跑。

◎解析

由圖片可見，乳牛被關在柵欄內伸出頭吃草，故答案選 c ）。其他動詞 milk（擠奶）、lead out（放出來）、race（賽跑）皆不符合圖中動作。

3.1

◎解答

b) The boy is wearing boots.
（男孩穿著靴子。）

◎聽力原文

Look at the picture. Which statement is true?
a) The dog is running after the boy.
b) The boy is wearing boots.
c) The dog is licking the boy's face.
d) The boy is waving to the dog.

◎中譯

請看圖。下列敘述何者為真？
a) 狗兒追著男孩跑。
b) 男孩穿著靴子。
c) 狗兒在舔男孩的臉。
d) 男孩向狗兒揮手。

◎解析

由圖片可見，小男孩穿著靴子（boots）踩在水中，因此 b）選項最恰當。圖中的狗兒沒有追逐男孩（run after the boy）、舔男孩的臉（lick the boy's face），男孩也沒有向狗兒揮手（wave to the dog），故選項 a）、c）、d）為非。

3.2

◎解答

a）They are in the river.

（他們在河裡。）

◎聽力原文

Look at the picture. Where is this place?

a）They are in the river.

b）They are on the seashore.

c）They are in a library.

d）They are in a museum.

◎中譯

請看圖。這是什麼地方？

a）他們在河裡。

b）他們在海岸邊。

c）他們在圖書館。

d）他們在博物館。

◎解析

本題主要問的是地點（where），由圖片中的水流和河岸可推知，男孩跟狗兒是站在河裡，所以選 a）。

 看圖辨義

人的表情及狀態

 學習重點

不同的環境會帶給人們不同的心境（mood），而隨之產生各種臉部的表情（expression），例如當我們坐在公園的長椅上，聆聽蟲鳴鳥囀（chirp），享受微風拂面（a breeze caresses the face），這時心情自然平和快樂。

 情境介紹及導引

Sitting on a park bench is a good way to relax. One can feel the gentle breeze, hear the birds singing, and enjoy the fresh air. It doesn't have to be a big fancy park. Grass on the ground, a bench under a tree, and the sun shining down from the sky are all it takes.

範例　A-39

此圖片中，主題是女士的表情及狀態，此處你會聽到四句話，其中只有一句是最符合圖片內容的描述。

―――――――――

Look at the picture. Which statement is true?

a) She's relaxing on the bench.

b) She's standing beside a streetlamp.

c) She's working hard in the office.

d) She's writing a letter on the computer.

答案：a)

說明

a. Information Focus

圖片中的女士坐在公園的長椅上閉目養神，嘴角微笑，得知 "She's relaxing on the bench." 是正確的選項。

b. Language Skills

重點字彙：relax（放鬆）、bench（長椅）、streetlamp（街燈）。

c. Tips for Listening

本段聽力的重點在與狀態有關的動詞，如 relax, stand, work, write，以及跟地點有關的字詞，如 on the bench, beside a streetlamp, in the office, on the computer。

練習題 A-40

請聽以下看圖辨義題的描述，並從四個選項中，選出最適當的答案。

1 _____

2 _____

3 _____

1

◎解答

b）She is in a park.（她在公園裡。）

◎聽力原文

Look at the picture. Where is she?

a）She is in the living room.

b）She is in a park.

c）She is on the beach.

d）She is in a library.

◎中譯

請看圖。這位女士在什麼地方？

a）她在客廳。

b）她在公園裡。

c）她在海灘。

d）她在圖書館。

◎解析

題目重點是詢問地點（where），圖片中的女士坐在樹下長椅上，可推測應是在公園內，故選 b）。

2

◎解答

d）The children are happy.
（孩子們很快樂。）

◎聽力原文

Look at the picture. Which statement is true?

a）The children are bored.

b）The children are sick.

c）The children are sad.

d）The children are happy.

◎中譯

請看圖。下列敘述何者為真？

a）孩子們感到無聊。

b）孩子們生病了。

c）孩子們很難過。

d）孩子們很快樂。

◎解析

圖中的孩子們互相搭肩且笑容滿面，可知應選表開心的形容詞 d）。其他選項中的 bored（感到無聊）、sick（生病的）、sad（難過的）皆不符合。

3

◎解答

a）The woman is pregnant.
（這位女士懷孕了。）

◎聽力原文

Look at the picture. Which statement is true?

a）The woman is pregnant.

b）The woman is embarrassed.

c）The woman is depressed.

d）The woman is breast-feeding.

◎中譯

請看圖。下列敘述何者為真？

a）這位女士懷孕了。

b）這位女士感到不好意思。

c）這位女士很沮喪。

d）這位女士正在餵母乳。

◎解析

從圖中女士挺著大肚子以及背景的醫院可知，答案應選 a）最恰當。

對答

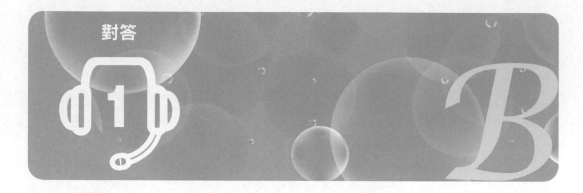

圖書館情境

 學習重點

對學生而言，圖書館的主要功能不外乎借閱書籍（check out books）和複習課業（review schoolwork），例如兩位學生為了即將到來的暑假，上圖書館選擇要閱讀的書籍，而引發了以下的對答。

 情境介紹及導引

Tim and Lisa are in the library discussing their reading list for the upcoming summer vacation. Tim is interested in science fiction while Lisa wants to read more vampire novels. Tim picks up a classic novel by a famous American writer.

 範 例 🎧 B-01

在以下的對答中，你會聽到一個人問問題，接著再讀取四個選項，其中只有一個是正確的回應。

Haven't you read that book?

_____

a) No, it's not ready.（不，還沒好。）

b) Four dollars and fifty cents（四塊錢五十分）

c) Yes, but I am reading it again.（是的，但我要再讀一次。）

d) Yes, I like science fiction novels.（是的，我喜歡科幻小說。）

答案：c)

說明

a. Information Focus

以上對答中女士提問的目的是「是否有看過那本書」，正確的回應方式是告訴對方有看過那本書，並想再讀一遍 " Yes, but I am reading it again."。

b. Language Skills

其他字彙：upcoming（即將來臨的）、science fiction（科幻小說）、vampire（吸血鬼）、novel（小說）、classic（古典的）。

句法：Have 開頭的問句：Have ／ Has ＋ S ＋ V–ed；問句的重點在 V–ed 所表示的動作是否「完成」。

c. Tips for Listening

本題屬於 yes ／ no question，通常以 yes ／ no 來回應問題。

選項 a）與問題無關，其中 ready 與問題中的 read 發音相似，混淆聽者判斷；

選項 b）是回應有關價格多少的問題（如 How much is the book?）；

選項 d）是回應類似 " Do you like that book? " 的問題。

練習題 (B-02)

請聽以下對答題，選出適當的回應。

1 _____

a) Who's the author?   b) Thanks, I just got it.

c) It was found a few years ago.   d) Yes, it is my favorite book.

2 _____

a) But I was planning to wear them tonight.

b) I'll try to return them by tomorrow.

c) Get them to me as soon as you find them.

d) I asked for a raise.

3 _____

a) I read it to my daughter when she was young.

b) I prefer novels to nonfiction.

c) It was written many years ago.

d) The author is John Steinbeck.

詳解

1

◎解答

a) Who's the author?（作者是誰？）

◎聽力原文

Can you help me find this book?

◎中譯

你能幫我找這本書嗎？

a) 作者是誰？

b) 謝謝，我拿到了。

c) 這幾年前就被找到了。

d) 沒錯，這是我最喜歡的書。

◎解析

從題目中得知說話者想找一本書，只有 a) 回問有關這本書的資訊，故 a) 是最適合的答案。

2

◎解答

c) Get them to me as soon as you find them.（一找到就立刻給我。）

◎聽力原文

When do you need those books you asked for?

◎中譯

你什麼時候要拿到你詢問的這些書？

a) 但我打算今晚就穿。

b) 我會盡量在明天就歸還。

c) 一找到就立刻給我。

d) 我要求加薪。

◎解析

因為題目是詢問什麼時候可以拿到書，所以回答應與時間有關，a) 、b) 、c) 的回答都與取書無關，只有 c) 的答案最符合題意。

3

◎解答

d) The author is John Steinbeck.
（作者是 John Steinbeck。）

◎聽力原文

Who wrote that book you're reading?

◎中譯

你正在讀的那本書是誰寫的？

a) 我在女兒年紀還小的時候讀給她聽。

b) 我喜歡小說勝過散文。

c) 這本書是很多年前寫的。

d) 作者是 John Steinbeck。

◎解析

題目詢問書的作者是誰，因此只有 d) 的回答最為切題。

學校課業

 學習重點

與學校課業相關的主題，包括課程選修、考試、撰寫報告、獎學金等，以申請獎學金
（apply for a scholarship）為例，有些人可能怕自己資格不夠好，而有以下的對話。

 情境介紹及導引

Jeff is about to begin his studies in a private school. He is concerned that his family may not be able to afford the tuition. Jeff is thinking of working part-time to help pay for the expense. He seeks the teacher's advice and is told to consider a scholarship application.

範例 🎧 B-03

在以下的對答中，你會聽到一個人問問題，接著再讀取四個選項，其中只有一個
是正確的回應。

Why don't you apply for a scholarship next year?

_____

a) I don't think I can afford it.（我不認為我負擔得起。）

b) I don't think I'd qualify for one.（我不認為我夠資格。）

c) I think they recruited enough athletes.
（我認為他們已招募足夠的運動員。）

d) I should invite more scholars to our campus.
（我應該邀請更多學者來我們學校。）

答案：b)

說明

a. Information Focus

提問的目的是「為何不申請獎學金」，正確的回應是說明具體的理由：" I don't think I'd qualify for one. "（我不認為我夠資格。）。

b. Language Skills

其他字彙：apply for（申請）、scholarship（獎學金）、afford（負擔得起）、qualify（合格）、recruit（聘用）、scholar（學者）、tuition（學費）。

合格或享有某條件：人 ＋ qualify for ＋ 優惠條件 / 身分資格

c. Tips for Listening

選項 c) 的 "...recruited enough athletes." 是回應類似 "Why don't you apply for a job in the sports team?" 的問題，跟 scholarship 無關，混淆聽者判斷。

 練習題　B-04

請聽以下對答題，選出適當的回應。

1 _____

a) That's probably a wise decision.

b) It's a classy operation.

c) We didn't have enough time.

d) We will go to a classical music concert.

2 _____

a) I had the time of my life.

b) There was very little time left when I answered the last question.

c) Time will tell if my answers are correct.

d) I bought it before the date expired.

3 _____

a) I paid more attention to material objects.

b) I went to the school library last Monday.

c) The finding supported my original theory.

d) I did a lot of research at the university library.

1

◎解答

a）That's probably a wise decision.
（這或許是個明智的決定。）

◎聽力原文

Should we take classes to learn how to use it?

◎中譯

我們是否應該上課學習如何使用它？

a）這或許是個明智的決定。

b）這是一次漂亮的運作。

c）我們之前沒有足夠的時間。

d）我們將參加一場古典音樂會。

◎解析

說話者詢問對方意見，答案中只有 That's probably a wise decision. 給予肯定的回覆，所以應選 a）。選項 b）的 classy 容易和 classes 混淆，要小心聽辨。

2

◎解答

b）There was very little time left when I answered the last question.（當我答完最後一題時所剩時間也不多了。）

◎聽力原文

Did you answer all the questions before time expired?

◎中譯

你有在時限內回答完所有問題嗎？

a）我有過美好時光。

b）當我回答完最後一個問題時所剩時間也不多了。

c）時間會證明我的答案是否正確。

d）我在過期之前買了它。

◎解析

本題是在詢問「限時回答問題」的情境，所以只有 a）最適合。選項 d）的 date expired（過期日）易與問句中的 time expired（時間到）混淆，要小心分辨。

3

◎解答

d）I did a lot of research at the university library.
（我在大學圖書館做了很多研究。）

◎聽力原文

Where did you find the research material to support your finding?

◎中譯

你從那裡找到研究資料來支持你的研究結果？

a）我特別留意資料物件。

b）我上週一去了學校圖書館。

c）這項發現支持了我原本的理論。

d）我在大學圖書館做了很多研究。

◎解析

說話者詢問研究資料的來源，答案 d）回答在研究上下了很多工夫，因此 d）最符合題意。

師生互動

 學習重點

師生之間的對答通常是針對學生的課業（schoolwork）、在校行為（behavior at school）、同儕相處（get along with others）或其他特殊狀況有關，例如老師要找一位學生私下談話時，會詢問對方 "May I have a word with you?"。

 情境介紹及導引

Nancy's home room teacher, Ms. Lin, is experienced, dedicated and caring. She pays attention to students' performance and behavior at school. Whenever someone does not do her homework, gets a poor test result, or has problems getting along with others, she can expect Ms. Lin to have a word with her.

 範例 B-05

在以下的對答中，你會聽到一個人問問題，接著再讀取四個選項，其中只有一個是正確的回應。

May I have a word with you?

＿＿＿＿＿＿＿＿＿＿

a）I play crossword every day.（我每天都玩填字遊戲。）

b）What is it about?（是關於什麼事？）

c）Thank you for your time.（謝謝你費事了。）

d）OK, let's solve math word problems.

（好啊，讓我們來解決數學的敘述題）

答案：b）

 說明

a. Information Focus

提問的目的是「想要進一步說話」，正確的回應是問對方要談什麼事情：" What is it about? "。

b. Language Skills

其他字彙：homeroom teacher（導師）、get along with（與……和睦相處）、 have a word with sb.（跟某人說句話）、crossword（填字遊戲）。

感謝某人某事：thank ＋ 人 ＋ for ＋ 事物 / V-ing

c. Tips for Listening

選項 a）及 d）的 crossword, math word 與問題的 word 用字相同，但與題意無關，是用來混淆聽者的判斷。

練習題　B-06

請聽以下對答題，選出適當的回應。

1 _____

a) OK. What time should I call you?

b) Yes. The warning signals are flashing.

c) No, you are not stupid.

d) I didn't mean to do it!

2 _____

a) I think you have the right.

b) That's probably a good idea.

c) I don't think they are right.

d) You should turn to the right again.

3 _____

a) I don't mind if no one else does.

b) No thanks, I've already eaten my lunch.

c) Did you make that lunch yourself?

d) We eat lunch from 12:30 to 1:30 every day.

1

◎解答

d) I didn't mean to do it!
（我不是故意要這麼做的！）

◎聽力原文

Would you warn me the next time you're going to do something stupid?

◎中譯

你下次要做傻事時可以先警告我一聲嗎？

a) 沒問題。我應該幾點打給你？

b) 沒錯。警示號誌正在閃爍。

c) 不，你並不笨。

d) 我不是故意要這麼做的！

◎解析

對於問句的責備，選項 d) I didn't mean to do it!（我不是故意要這麼做的！）的解釋是合理選項。

2

◎解答

b) That's probably a good idea.
（這可能是個好主意。）

◎聽力原文

Do you want me to write this again?

◎中譯

你要我把這個重寫一次嗎？

a) 我認為你有這個權利。

b) 這可能是個好主意。

c) 我不認為他們是對的。

d) 你應該再一次右轉。

◎解析

問句中的 write（書寫）和選項 a)、c)、d) 中的 right（權利、右邊）發音相同，小心不要混淆。本題詢問對方的意願，根據題意應選 b) That's probably a good idea.（這可能是個好主意。）

3

◎解答

a) I don't mind if no one else does.
（如果其他人都不介意，我也不介意。）

◎聽力原文

Could I eat my lunch in here?

◎中譯

我能在這兒吃午餐嗎？

a) 如果其他人都不介意，我也不介意。

b) 不了，謝謝，我已經吃過午餐。

c) 那份午餐是你自己做的嗎？

d) 我們每天 12:30 到 1:30 吃午餐。

◎解析

題目是禮貌性請求對方允許，只有選項 a) I don't mind if no one else does.（如果其他人都不介意，我也不介意。）的回應與問題相關。

對答

幫忙做家事

 學習重點

在居家的情境中常會有幫忙家事的時候，像是掃地（sweep the floor）、倒垃圾（take out the garbage / trash）、整理房間（clean the room）、顧爐火（keep an eye on the stove）、幫忙寄信（mail a letter）等。

 情境介紹及導引

Sam is his mother's best helper. Whenever she is busy, she can always count on Sam to lend an extra hand. At home, Sam sweeps the floor, takes out the trash, and cleans the rooms. Today, Sam's mother has to go to the grocery store to buy soy sauce and some eggs while food is cooking on the stove.

範例 B-07

在以下的對答中，你會聽到一個人問問題，接著再讀取四個選項，其中只有一個是正確的回應。

Would you come keep an eye on the stove for me?

_____

a）Yes, I put a pot on the stove.（是的，我把鍋子放在火爐上。）

b）I'll be right there.（我馬上就來。）

c）I see what you mean.（我懂你的意思。）

d）Where would you like me to put it?（你要我把它放在哪兒？） 答案：b）

說明

a. Information Focus

提問目的是「幫忙來顧爐火」，正確的回應是答應對方：" I'll be right there. "（我馬上就來。）；如果不能幫忙也要說明理由：" I'm busy right now. "。

b. Language Skills

其他字彙：lend an extra hand（幫忙）、keep an eye on（注意）、
　　　　　stove（爐子）。

客氣請對方幫忙的說法：Would you ＋ V ...，V 是指要對方幫忙的事情。

c. Tips for Listening

選項 a）的 stove 及 c）的 "...would you..." 是重複題目裡相同的字，但與題意無關。

練習題 B-08

請聽以下對答題，選出適當的回應。

1 _____

a）You will have many chances to learn software programs.

b）I wish I had a copy of it, too.

c）I think it was a new record.

d）I did. But I ran out of tape halfway through.

2 _____

a）It's your turn.

b）I turned the machine on.

c）Yes. It's garbage day.

d）I bought a new garbage can yesterday.

3 _____

a）OK, I will write an email to you right away.

b）Actually, I'm going to the dentist.

c）Can it wait until I get back from the post office?

d）Yeah, I'm going to check out some books.

1

◎解答
d）I did. But I ran out of tape halfway through.
（我有，不過錄到一半帶子就用完了。）

◎聽力原文
How come you didn't record that TV program for me?

◎中譯
你怎麼沒有幫我錄電視節目？
a）你會有很多機會學習軟體程式。
b）我希望我也有個備份。
c）我想這是一項新紀錄。
d）我有，不過錄到一半帶子就用完了。

◎解析
題目是在問為何沒有錄節目，只有答案 d）回答原因。選項 a）的 program（程式）和選項 c）的 record（記錄）意在混淆聽者，要小心聽辨。

2

◎解答
a）It's your turn.
（輪到你了。）

◎聽力原文
Whose turn is it to take out the garbage today?

◎中譯
今天輪到誰把垃圾拿出去？

a）輪到你了。
b）我已經發動機器了。
c）沒錯，今天是倒垃圾日。
d）我昨天買了一個新垃圾桶。

◎解析
題目中的 whose turn is it 是問「輪到誰……?」，所以應該選擇 a），說明是輪到某人。

3

◎解答
b）Actually, I'm going to the dentist.
（其實我是要去看牙醫。）

◎聽力原文
If you're going to the post office, would you mail this letter for me?

◎中譯
你要去郵局的話，能幫我寄這封信嗎？
a）好的，我會馬上寫封電子郵件給你。
b）其實我是要去看牙醫。
c）能等我從郵局回來再說嗎？
d）是啊，我正要借閱一些書。

◎解析
題目詢問是否去郵局路上順便幫忙寄信，只有選項 b）說明目的地並非郵局。選項 a）的 email 和選項 c）的 post office 皆與問題無關。

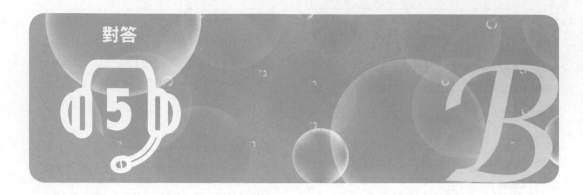

家具購置或更換

在居家的情境中,有時會遇到需要購置(buy, purchase)或更換(replace)家具的時候,例如選購新的沙發(sofa)時,常要考慮沙發的樣式(style)及顏色(color)是否搭配現有的室內裝潢(match the decor of the room)。

 情境介紹及導引

Walt is moving into a new apartment and is looking for new furniture. He needs to replace the sofa, but it is difficult to find one that matches the tropical resort theme he is trying to create. Today he goes to a furniture store with a friend, hoping to find a sofa that matches the decor of his living room.

範例 B-09

在以下的對答中,你會聽到一個人問問題,接著再讀取四個選項,其中只有一個是正確的回應。

Does this sofa match the decor of my room?

_____

a) The other tie is nicer.(另外一條領帶更好。)

b) The one over there is better.(那邊的那張「沙發」比較好。)

c) You might want to bring a sweater, too.(你可能也要帶件毛衣。)

d) You can light several candles with just one match.
（你可以只用一根火柴點亮幾支蠟燭。）

答案:b)

🎧 說明

a. Information Focus

提問的目的是「這張沙發是否搭配裝潢」，可能的回應方式有：

同意：Yes, it goes well with your wall.（是的，它很搭配你的牆壁。）

不同意：The one over there is better.（那邊的那張「沙發」比較好。）

b. Language Skills

重點字彙：match（搭配）、decor（室內裝潢）、tropical resort theme（熱帶休閒主題）。

c. Tips for Listening

選項 a ）是指衣服的搭配與題意無關；選項 d ）裡的 match 是指火柴，與題目的 match（搭配）字義不同，混淆聽者判斷。

🎧 練習題 B-10

請聽以下對答題，選出適當的回應。

1 _____

a) Yes, and they're good for jogging long distances.

b) Yes, but the sound isn't as clear as these old ones.

c) Yes, but they don't taste as good as these pears.

d) Yes, she is a very impressive public speaker.

2 _____

a) There should be another one in my bag.

b) I put the book back on the shelf yesterday.

c) Sorry, we don't have those books either.

d) I was thinking the same thing, too.

3 _____

a) The light switch is over there.

b) It's a 30-watt bulb.

c) Wait. I think I have a spare.

d) It's very easy to replace a light bulb.

5 詳解

1

◎解答

b）Yes, but the sound isn't as clear as these old ones.

（是啊，但是它的聲音不如舊的那套音響那麼清晰。）

◎聽力原文

Did you buy a new pair of speakers?

◎中譯

你新買了一套音響嗎？

a）是啊，它們很適合長跑使用。

b）是啊，但是它的聲音不如舊的那套音響那麼清晰。

c）是啊，但是它們嚐起來不像這些梨子那麼美味。

d）是啊，她是一位令人印象極深刻的演講者。

◎解析

關鍵是問是否買了新的音響（speaker），只有選項 b）回應新音響的音質。選項 c）的 pear（梨子）和 pair 發音相同，容易混淆；選項 d）的 speaker 指的是「講者」。

2

◎解答

d）I was thinking the same thing, too.

（我也在想同樣的事情。）

◎聽力原文

I think we're going to need some more bookshelves.

◎中譯

我想我們會需要多幾個書架。

a）在我包包裡應該有另一個。

b）昨天我把書放回書架上了。

c）抱歉，我們也沒有那些書。

d）我也在想同樣的事情。

◎解析

需要增加的是 bookshelves（書架），所以 d）選項的回答最適合。

3

◎解答

c）Wait. I think I have a spare.

（等等，我想我有一個多的。）

◎聽力原文

Where can I purchase a replacement light bulb?

◎中譯

我在哪裡可以買到電燈泡來替換呢？

a）電燈開關在那邊。

b）這是 30 瓦的燈泡。

c）等等，我想我有一個多的。

d）換燈泡是件很容易的事。

◎解析

題目是問哪裡可以買到電燈泡來替換，只有 c）選項合理回應這個問題。replacement 在此指「替換品」，意思與 spare「備用品」相似。

對答

設備使用與維護

學習重點

校園常見的設備（facilities）如電梯（elevator）、電腦（computer）、販賣機（vending machine）、影印機（copier），因為使用頻繁，難免發生故障（breakdown）的情形，這時就需要進行維修（maintenance）。

情境介紹及導引

Donna arrives at school this morning and finds a small crowd of students waiting in front of the elevator. Due to regular maintenance, only one elevator is working. It is inconvenient, but Donna understands that equipments and facilities such as computers, copiers, vending machines, and elevators should be regularly checked to prevent breakdowns.

範例 B-11

在以下的對答中，你會聽到一個人問問題，接著再讀取四個選項，其中只有一個是正確的回應。

Why is only one elevator working today?

_____

a) It's working quite well if you ask me.

（如果你問我，我覺得它運轉得很好。）

b) Because I took the express elevator.（因為我搭了直達電梯。）

c) The train runs smoothly on the elevated rail.

（火車在高架軌道上行駛順利。）

d) I think they're doing some maintenance work.

（我想他們正在做維修工作。）

答案：d)

 說明

a. Information Focus

提問的目的是「為何只有一臺電梯在動」，正確的回應是告知原因 " I think they're doing some maintenance work. "。

b. Language Skills

重點字彙：express elevator（直達電梯）、smoothly（順暢地）、elevated rail（高架軌道）。

c. Tips for Listening

選項 a）的 working 及選項 b）的 elevator，是重覆題目中的字彙，選項 c）的 elevated 與 elevator 發音近似，皆與題意無關。

練習題　B-12

請聽以下對答題，選出適當的回應。

1 _____

a) Thanks for fixing it.

b) No, John broke it.

c) Yes, I bought a new computer yesterday.

d) Are you sure? You'd better double-check.

2 _____

a) Yes, use this one over here instead.

b) No, you don't.

c) Not all the time.

d) I created a new user account on my computer.

3 _____

a) I'll ask you later.

b) Would you get me a soda, too?

c) It was working fine a minute ago.

d) I just applied for a vendor's license.

6 詳解

1

◎解答

d）Are you sure? You'd better double-check.

（你確定嗎？你最好再檢查一遍。）

◎聽力原文

The computer seems to have broken.

◎中譯

電腦似乎壞了。

a）謝謝你修好它。

b）不，是約翰弄壞的。

c）是的，我昨天買了一臺新電腦。

d）你確定嗎？你最好再檢查一遍。

◎解析

說話者認為電腦似乎故障，所以請求再檢查一次（double-check）是合理回應，因此選 d）。

2

◎解答

a）Yes, use this one over here instead.

（有的，請改用這邊這臺電腦。）

◎聽力原文

Is anyone using this computer?

◎中譯

有人正在使用這臺電腦嗎？

a）有的，請改用這邊這臺電腦。

b）不，你不必。

c）不總是如此。

d）我在我的電腦上新設了一個使用者帳號。

◎解析

題目是問有沒有人正在用這台電腦，a）的回答 yes 表示有人正在使用，所以請他改用另一臺。b）、c）、d）的回應與問題無關。

3

◎解答

c）It was working fine a minute ago.

（它一分鐘前還好好的。）

◎聽力原文

Is this vending machine broken?

◎中譯

這臺販賣機壞掉了嗎？

a）我待會會問你。

b）請你也給我一杯汽水好嗎？

c）它一分鐘前還好好的。

d）我剛申請了販售執照。

◎解析

問題詢問的是販賣機的運作狀況，所以答案選 c）最能符合情境。

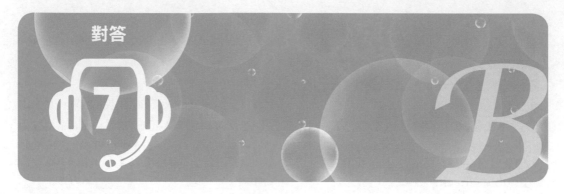

家庭娛樂活動

學習重點

常見的家庭娛樂活動包括收看電視節目（TV program）、電玩遊戲（video game）、家庭旅遊（family travel）等。以家庭旅遊為例，從選擇旅遊地點（choose a travel destination）、旅遊規畫（travel plan）、到預約（make the reservations）交通工具及飯店，都得事前先安排（arrange in advance），才會有快樂的家庭假期。

情境介紹及導引

The Lee family is planning a family trip. Before they make plans, the family has to agree on a travel destination. After the plan is decided, the family will contact the travel agent to make all necessary arrangements, which include booking flights and making hotel reservations.

範 例 🎧 B-13

在以下的對答中，你會聽到一個人問問題，接著再讀取四個選項，其中只有一個是正確的回應。

M：Who is responsible for making the travel reservations?

_____

a）The travel agent can make all the arrangements.
（旅行社會做好所有的安排。）

b）The reservations are made prior to the time of travel.
（旅遊前先做預約。）

c）The hotel rooms were very comfortable.（飯店房間非常舒適。）

d）The seats are all reserved in this restaurant.（餐廳的座位都被預約了。）

答案：a）

a. Information Focus

提問的目的是「誰做預約」，正確的回應是具體告知負責預約的人 "The travel agent can make all the arrangements."。

b. Language Skills

重點字彙：travel agent（旅行社專員）、arrangements（準備事項）、prior to（在……之前）、comfortable（舒適的）、book flights（訂機票）。

c. Tips for Listening

以疑問詞 who 開頭的問句，關鍵在問人；選項 b）的 reservations 是重複題目的用字，選項 d）的 reserved 則是發音類似，都跟「人」無關。

 練習題　B-14

請聽以下對答題，選出適當的回應。

1 _____

a) Let's go out for dinner tonight.

b) My favorite show is on at 7:00.

c) Go ahead and change the channel.

d) The remote control is on the table.

2 _____

a) Sure. They always do.

b) That would be a very nice gift.

c) I have seen that movie before.

d) What do you want to see?

3 _____

a) We are going to eat dinner.

b) My vacation begins in two days.

c) We still haven't made plans.

d) We went to Kenting last summer.

7 詳解

1

◎解答

b）My favorite show is on at 7:00.
（我最喜歡的節目是七點播出。）

◎聽力原文

Is there anything good on TV tonight?

◎中譯

今晚有什麼好看的電視節目呢？
a）我們今天晚上出去吃飯吧。
b）我最喜歡的節目是七點播出。
c）去換個頻道吧。
d）遙控器在桌上。

◎解析

說話者是詢問電視上有什麼好看的節目，所以 b）的回答最適當。

2

◎解答

d）What do you want to see?
（你想看什麼片呢？）

◎聽力原文

Shall we rent a video tonight?

◎中譯

今晚租個影片來看吧？
a）好啊。他們總是這麼做。
b）那會是個很棒的禮物。
c）那部電影我之前看過了。
d）你想看什麼片呢？

◎解析

說話者是提議去租影片來看，只有選項 d）針對提議給予肯定的回應。

3

◎解答

c）We still haven't made plans.
（我們還沒做計畫呢！）

◎聽力原文

Where are you going on your vacation?

◎中譯

你打算去哪裡度假呢？
a）我們打算去吃晚餐。
b）我的假期兩天後開始。
c）我們還沒做計畫呢！
d）去年夏天我們去了墾丁。

◎解析

說話者是詢問度假的地點，所以 c）是合理回答。選項 d）回答的是過去發生的動作，不符合題意。

社交禮儀

 學習重點

對於初次見面的人,如果想與對方保持聯絡(keep in touch with somebody),就需要禮貌的詢問對方的姓名、電話、或電郵(name, phone number, e-mail address)。

 情境介紹及導引

Harrison is a car salesperson. One day a man comes to the showroom and looks at the latest model. The man is interested in the car but would like to look around more. Harrison thinks it's a good idea to get the name and contact number of this potential customer.

範 例 🎧 B-15

在以下的對答中,你會聽到一個人問問題,接著再讀取四個選項,其中只有一個是正確的回應。

May I have your name and phone number?

_____

a) Hold on. Please make yourself at home.(等一等,請不用客氣。)

b) Excuse me?(抱歉,請再說一次。)

c) I don't know. He didn't say.(我不知道,他沒說。)

d) Please print your name in the blank.

（請在空格中以正楷寫出你的名字。）

答案:b)

a. Information Focus

提問的目的是「詢問聯絡方式」，可能的回應如下：

告知對方聯絡方式：My name is Conny Wilson, and my mobile number is
0910123456.

不知道對方的問題：Excuse me?

b. Language Skills

"May I..." 為首的問句是客氣的詢問對方自己是否能夠做某件事情。

Excuse me? 通常是用在沒有聽清楚談話內容時，客氣地要求對方再重複一次。

c. Tips for Listening

選項 a）的 hold on（等一等）似乎與題目的 phone 有點關係，但卻與題意無關。

 練習題　B-16

請聽以下對答題，選出適當的回應。

1 _____

a）Why do you ask? Did you change it again?

b）How can I address this?

c）Please send it to my new e-mail address.

d）I send e-mail every day.

2 _____

a）I am not familiar with the instructor.

b）I don't think so.

c）We felt sorry about that.

d）I read the introduction.

3 _____

a）It's very nice to meet you.

b）I haven't told you my name yet.

c）Tell me some old-fashioned names.

d）How should I know?

詳解

1

◎解答

a) Why do you ask? Did you change it again?

（為什麼這麼問？你又換了新的郵件地址嗎？）

◎聽力原文

Do you have my e-mail address?

◎中譯

你有我的電子郵件地址嗎？

a) 為什麼這麼問？你又換了新的郵件地址嗎？

b) 我要怎麼寫地址？

c) 請寄到我新的電子郵件信箱。

d) 我每天寄電子郵件。

◎解析

說話者是確認對方是否有他的電子郵件地址，所以 a) 為合理回答。

2

◎解答

b) I don't think so.

（我不這麼認為。）

◎聽力原文

I'm sorry, but have we been introduced?

◎中譯

抱歉，我們已經互相介紹過了嗎？

a) 我和指導老師不太熟。

b) 我不這麼認為。

c) 我們為那件事感到抱歉。

d) 我已經讀了引言。

◎解析

問題在詢問雙方是否已經互相「介紹」認識過，所以最適合的答案是 b)。introduce（介紹）和選項 a) 的 instructor（指導者）發音相近，勿混淆。

3

◎解答

b) I haven't told you my name yet.

（我還沒告訴你的名字呢。）

◎聽力原文

What did you say your name was?

◎中譯

請問您說您的名字是？

a) 很高興認識你。

b) 我還沒告訴你我的名字呢。

c) 告訴我一些很老套的名字吧。

d) 我怎麼知道？

◎解析

問題是想要再次詢問對方的姓名，所以選項 b) 較合理。

表達關心、致意

🎧 **學習重點**

在一般社交情境下，常有機會對別人表示關心或是禮貌性地致意，例如看見對方臉色不佳時，會問道 "You don't look so well." 或 "What happened to you?"，對方通常會回應具體的理由，如頭痛（headache）、胃痛（stomachache）或喉嚨痛（sore throat）。

🎧 **情境介紹及導引**

Jon didn't feel well the entire weekend. He had a mild headache and sore throat. On Monday morning, his stomach was not feeling right, either, but he had to visit a customer. Jon decided that he would take the rest of the day off after the meeting.

範例

在以下的對答中，你會聽到一個人問問題，接著再讀取四個選項，其中只有一個是正確的回應。

You don't look so well. Are you sick or something?

a）I gave it a good look, but I didn't see any errors.
（我仔細的看過，但沒看出問題。）
b）I remember now. It was Mary who took the day off sick.
（我現在想起來了，Mary 那天請病假。）
c）I think I can do this pretty well.（我認為我可以做得很好。）
d）It's just a mild headache.（只是有點頭痛。）

答案：d）

說明

a. Information Focus

提問的目的是「問候對方是否身體不適」，正確的回應是告知身體不適的情況：

"It's just a mild headache."

b. Language Skills

重點字彙：error（錯誤）、take the day off（請假）、mild（輕微的）。

c. Tips for Listening

選項 a）的 look、選項 b）的 sick、及選項 c）的 well 都是重覆問題裡的字彙，混淆聽者的判斷。

 練習題 B-18

請聽以下對答題，選出適當的回應。

1 _____

a) Absolutely.

b) Scientifically.

c) Instantly.

d) Primarily.

2 _____

a) I'm sorry I'm late.

b) Well, I've been there before.

c) How very nice it was of you!

d) Fine, thanks.

3 _____

a) I ran into a telephone pole.

b) It happened two days ago.

c) I'm running out of money.

d) I bought it from a car dealer.

9 詳解

1

◎解答

a）Absolutely.

（好得很。）

◎聽力原文

Are you feeling all right?

◎中譯

你還好嗎？

a）好得很。

b）合乎科學地。

c）即時地。

d）首要地。

◎解析

副詞 absolutely（當然；沒錯）常用於肯定的回應，語氣較 yes 更為強烈。b）、c）、d）皆答非所問。

2

◎解答

d）Fine, thanks.

（我很好，謝謝。）

◎聽力原文

How have you been lately?

◎中譯

你最近好嗎？

a）抱歉，我來晚了。

b）嗯，我曾經去過那裡。

c）你人真好！

d）我很好，謝謝。

◎解析

how 詢問的是「（狀況、狀態）如何」，選項 d）是貼切且禮貌的回應。選項 a）的 late（晚到的）和題目的 lately（最近）容易混淆，要小心聽辨。

3

◎解答

a）I ran into a telephone pole.

（我撞到電線桿。）

◎聽力原文

What happened to your car?

◎中譯

你的車發生了什麼事？

a）我撞到電線桿。

b）兩天前發生的。

c）我的錢用完了。

d）我從車商那兒買的。

◎解析

What happened...? 是詢問「事情發生的狀況」，因此選項 a）說明駕車撞到電線桿的回應最適當。

對答 10 B

八卦閒聊

學習重點

朋友碰面常會閒聊（gossip），話題通常會圍繞在引發好奇的事情或人物上，例如談論一位新進人員（newcomer）的外貌如何，而有如下的對話。

情境介紹及導引

Mina's company just hired a new marketing vice president, and everyone is dying to find out more about this newcomer. Since Mina is the receptionist and has briefly seen the new VP when she came for the job interview, everyone is asking Mina to describe what this new top executive looks like.

範例 B-19

在以下的對答中，你會聽到一個人問問題，接著再讀取四個選項，其中只有一個是正確的回應。

Can you describe what the newcomer looks like?

_____

a) It looks like she's going to move to another apartment.
（看起來她將搬到別的公寓。）

b) I can describe what she is looking at.（我能形容她在看什麼。）

c) It's hard to, since her appearance is always changing.
（很難耶，她的外貌一直在變。）

d) The welcome party will be held next Monday.
（迎新會將在下週一舉行。）

答案：c)

a. Information Focus

提問的目的是「新人長什麼樣子」，正確的回應是告知對方你對該人物外貌的描述或看法：" It's hard to, since her appearance is always changing. "。

b. Language Skills

重點字彙：describe（形容，描述）、look like（看起來如何）、look at（注意看）、apartment（公寓）、appearance（外貌）、welcome party（迎新會）。

c. Tips for Listening

選項 a) 的 looks like 和選項 b) 的 describe 只是重複試題的單字，與題意無關，混淆聽者判斷。

 練習題

請聽以下對答題，選出適當的回應。

1 ＿＿＿＿＿＿＿＿

a) No, were you late for class?

b) Yeah, some college professors were very strict.

c) Oh no! Did you get hurt?

d) No, how did it go?

2 ＿＿＿＿＿＿＿＿

a) Who's that guy she's with?

b) The café is very famous in this area.

c) When do you think she'll be back?

d) I have known her for nearly all my life.

3 ＿＿＿＿＿＿＿＿

a) When will they be back?

b) I'm afraid I can't right now.

c) Oh, that's old news.

d) They already went out to lunch.

詳解

1

◎解答

d) No, how did it go?
（沒有，是怎樣啊？）

◎聽力原文

Did I tell you I ran into one of my old college professors the other day?

◎中譯

我有沒有告訴你某天我在路上巧遇以前的大學教授？

a) 沒有，你上課遲到了嗎？
b) 是啊，有些大學教授是非常嚴格的。
c) 喔，不會吧！你受傷了嗎？
d) 沒有，是怎樣阿？

◎解析

run into sb 在此指「巧遇（某人）」。此題是 yes/no 的問題，故選項 d) 回答 no 之後接著詢問碰面的狀況，是合理回應。

2

◎解答

a) Who's that guy she's with?
（和她在一起的那個男的是誰？）

◎聽力原文

Hey, isn't that Margaret sitting at that café over there?

◎中譯

嘿，坐在那間咖啡廳裡的不就是瑪格莉特嗎？

a) 和她在一起的那個男的是誰？
b) 那間咖啡廳在這一帶非常有名。
c) 你覺得她何時會回來？
d) 我已經認識她將近一輩子了。

◎解析

問題是想確認在咖啡廳的女子是否是認識的人，所以選項 a) 提出相關的問題是合理回應。

3

◎解答

c) Oh, that's old news.
（喔，那是舊聞了！）

◎聽力原文

How long have Frank and Melissa been going out?

◎中譯

法蘭克和梅莉莎已經交往多久了？

a) 他們何時會回來？
b) 我現在恐怕沒辦法。
c) 喔，那是舊聞了！
d) 他們已經出去吃午餐了。

◎解析

how long 問的是兩人交往的時間長短，只有選項 c) 表示已經有好一段時間。此處的 go out 指的是「交往」，並非「外出」。

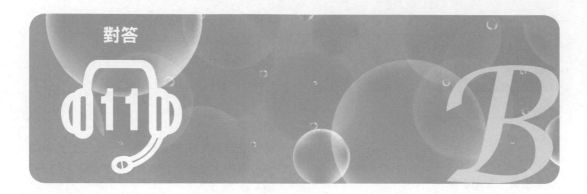

穿著選擇

🎧 學習重點

當遇到要去正式場合，包括約會（date）、婚宴（banquet）、接待會（reception），都會對穿著選擇（clothing selection）特別慎重，甚至連配件（accessories），如領帶（tie）、圍巾（scarf）、首飾（jewelry）都得搭配得宜（match well）。

🎧 情境介紹及導引

What to wear depends on the occasion. People dress formally to go to banquets and receptions. The men will put on a tie and the ladies wear a scarf or accessories. When you go on a date, first find out where you're going so you can dress appropriately and with taste.

  B-21

在以下的對答中，你會聽到一個人問問題，接著再讀取四個選項，其中只有一個是正確的回應。

What are you wearing for your big date?

_____

a) He has good taste in clothes.（他對服裝的品味很好。）

b) Yes, I have a dental appointment.（是的，我要去看牙齒。）

c) I think I might be able to borrow something from my friend.
（我想可以從朋友那兒借些衣服來。）

d) I always do my laundry by myself.（我一直都自己洗衣服。）　　答案：c)

說明

a. Information Focus

提問的目的是「約會穿什麼」，正確的回應是告知對方想穿的服飾或是交代服裝的來源："I think I might be able to borrow something from my friend."。

b. Language Skills

重點字彙：big date（重要的約會）、taste（品味）、dental appointment（牙科的約診）、laundry（清洗的衣物）、appropriately（適當地）。

c. Tips for Listening

問題的聽力重點是疑問詞 what 及動詞 wear；選項 a）的 clothes 及選項 d）的 laundry，都與「衣物」有關，但與題意無關，選項 b）的 appointment 也解釋為約會，但指的是牙醫的約診。

 練習題 B-22

請聽以下對答題，選出適當的回應。

1 _____

a) I think you should wear the black ones instead.

b) They know when they see a good match for you.

c) They are in the closet.

d) I have many pairs of shoes.

2 _____

a) The banquet is held on Sunday.

b) Don't you like it?

c) I put on a blue dress last time.

d) I like it when you dress up like that.

3 _____

a) Bring a nice gift.

b) Whatever is comfortable.

c) The receptionist should dress professionally.

d) It's at the Red Carpet Hotel downtown.

詳解

1

◎解答

a）I think you should wear the black ones instead.

（我倒覺得你應該穿那雙黑色的。）

◎聽力原文

Do these shoes match my suit?

◎中譯

這鞋子和我的套裝搭配嗎？

a）我倒覺得你應該穿那雙黑色的。

b）當他們看到適合你的就會知道了。

c）他們在衣櫥裡。

d）我有很多雙鞋子。

◎解析

對話問的是鞋子和衣服是否搭配，所以 a）提出其他搭配建議是合理回應。選項 b）的 match 是名詞「匹配者」，和題目中的動詞 match「搭配」詞性及字義皆不同。

2

◎解答

b）Don't you like it?（你不喜歡嗎？）

◎聽力原文

Is that the dress you're going to wear to the banquet?

◎中譯

那就是你打算穿去赴宴的洋裝嗎？

a）宴會將於週日舉辦。

b）你不喜歡嗎？

c）我上次是穿藍色洋裝。

d）我喜歡妳像那樣盛裝打扮的時候。

◎解析

題目是要確認對方是否穿著那件洋裝赴宴，所以選項 b）回問對方喜好是合理回應。選項 d）的 dress up 指「盛裝打扮」，與題目中的 dress「洋裝」意思不同。

3

◎解答

b）Whatever is comfortable.

（穿起來自在的都可以。）

◎聽力原文

What should I wear at the reception dinner tonight?

◎中譯

我該穿什麼服裝出席今晚的宴會？

a）帶份不錯的禮物吧。

b）穿起來自在的都可以。

c）接待人員應該穿得有模有樣。

d）位在市中心的紅毯飯店。

◎解析

問題是詢問服裝建議，故答案選 b）為合理回應。名詞 reception 在此指「宴會，接待會」，和選項 c）的 receptionist「接待人員」無關。

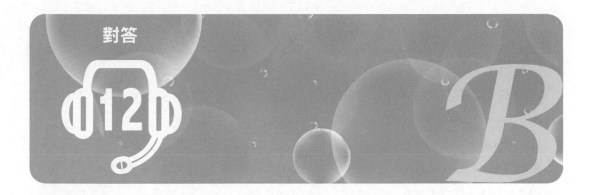

對答

聚會邀約

 學習重點

在一般社交情境下，常有機會邀約（invite）別人一起聚餐（dine together）、參加聚會（get-together）、或是較正式的宴會（如 Christmas party），對方的回應通常是樂意接受（happily accept），或是婉拒（politely decline）。

 情境介紹及導引

When you receive an invitation to an event such as a get-together, dinner, or party, it's a good idea to happily accept. If you have to decline, do it politely. Thank the inviter and give them a reason that will not hurt their feelings.

範例 B-23

在以下的對答中，你會聽到一個人問問題，接著再讀取四個選項，其中只有一個是正確的回應。

Would you like to join us for dinner?

_____

a) I'm sorry. I'll be at your place any minute now.
（抱歉，我馬上就會到你那。）
b) The steak here is supposed to be wonderful.
（這裡的牛排應該是很讚的。）
c) It's better to join a club in high school.（高中時最好參加個社團。）
d) Thanks, but I've got more work to do.
（多謝，但我已有許多工作要忙。）

答案：d)

a. Information Focus

提問的目的是「邀約對方一起晚餐」，正確的回應是婉拒並說明原因 "Thanks, but I've got more work to do."。

b. Language Skills

重點字彙：join（加入）、be supposed to（應該）、club（社團）。

c. Tips for Listening

Would you like to ＋ V 是客氣的詢問對方是否要做某件事情，常會出現在社交邀約等情境的對話中；婉拒他人的邀請，可以先說 thanks，接著用轉折語氣的 but，並說明不去的理由。

練習題 B-24

請聽以下對答題，選出適當的回應。

1 _____

a) I was busy.

b) I hope he has fun.

c) The game was exciting last night.

d) I would rather go to a movie.

2 _____

a) Christmas is a time for celebration.

b) Probably, but I won't know until the day before the party.

c) Yes, I went to the Christmas party.

d) This is my favorite Christmas gift.

3 _____

a) I'm sending out the invitations next week.

b) Not as many as last year.

c) I hope I get an invitation, too.

d) The party will be held on Sunday.

12 詳解

1

◎解答

d）I would rather go to a movie.

（我寧可去看電影。）

◎聽力原文

What do you say we go to a ball game on Friday?

◎中譯

你覺得我們週五去看球賽如何？

a）我很忙。

b）希望他玩得愉快。

c）昨晚的比賽非常刺激。

d）我寧可去看電影。

◎解析

What do you say「你覺得呢？」、「怎麼樣？」的問句常用來徵詢對方意見，因此，選項 d）回答「我寧可去看電影」是合理的回應。

2

◎解答

b）Probably, but I won't know until the day before the party.

（也許吧，但我要到舞會前一天才能確定。）

◎聽力原文

Will you be going to the Christmas party?

◎中譯

你會參加聖誕舞會嗎？

a）聖誕節是個慶祝的好時機。

b）也許吧，但我要到舞會前一天才能確定。

c）是啊，我參加過聖誕節舞會了。

d）這是我最喜歡的聖誕禮物。

◎解析

對話問對方是否會去參加聖誕舞會，以 b）的回答最合理。

3

◎解答

b）Not as many as last year.

（不會像去年那麼多。）

◎聽力原文

How many people are you planning to invite to the party?

◎中譯

你打算邀請多少人來舞會呢？

a）我下週會寄出邀請函。

b）不會像去年那麼多。

c）我希望我也會獲得邀請。

d）舞會將在週口舉行。

◎解析

How many people 是問「人數」，只有選項 b）not as many as...「不像……那樣多」和數量有關。題中雖提到 invite「邀請」的動作，但並非問題的重點。

尋求協助

 學習重點

人們常有機會尋求他人的幫助（ask others for help），例如詢問時間（Do you have the time?）、提取物品（Could you hold this for me?）、或是幫忙找零（Could I get change for this bill?）。

 情境介紹及導引

When traveling in the United States, we usually carry large bills such as fifty- and twenty-dollar bills. If we need 20 one-dollar bills or coins to use for the bus or the vending machine, we can go to the bank and ask the teller for change for a twenty.

範例 ◖B-25◗

在以下的對答中，你會聽到一個人問問題，接著再讀取四個選項，其中只有一個是正確的回應。

Could I get change for this bill?

_____

a）No. I don't think Bill has changed much.
（不，我不認為 Bill 改變很多。）

b）I'm sorry, but I don't have any small coins.
（抱歉，我沒有任何零錢。）

c）I paid that bill last week.（我上週付了那份帳單。）

d）I wish I could change your mind.（我希望能夠改變你的心意。）

答案：b）

說明

a. Information Focus
提問的目的是「拜託對方找零」，可能的回應如下：

肯定：Here you are.（給你。）

否定：I'm sorry, but I don't have any small coins.（抱歉，我沒有任何零錢。）

b. Language Skills
尋求他人協助的客套用語：Could you ＋ V？

c. Tips for Listening
選項 a）的 Bill 是指人名，選項 c）的 bill 是指帳單，與題目的 bill（鈔票）代表不同的意義；題目的 change 是名詞（零錢），選項 d）的 change 是動詞（改變）。

練習題　B-26

請聽以下對答題，選出適當的回應。

1 ＿＿＿＿＿＿＿

a）Be my guest, please.

b）No one is stopping you.

c）I will hold a meeting later.

d）No problem.

2 ＿＿＿＿＿＿＿

a）No. I feel fine.

b）That always gives me a headache, too.

c）Yes, I will go and see a doctor.

d）Look in the top drawer.

3 ＿＿＿＿＿＿＿

a）It's four past five.

b）How many do you need?

c）No, thank you.

d）Time passes so swiftly.

1

◎解答

d）No problem.

（沒問題。）

◎聽力原文

Could you hold this for me?

◎中譯

可以請你幫我拿著這個嗎？

a）請隨意，不用客氣。

b）沒有人會阻止你。

c）我待會要召開會議。

d）沒問題。

◎解析

問句是請人協助拿著東西，所以答案選 d） 最合理。選項 c）的 hold 是「召開（會議）； 舉辦（派對）」之意，與題目中的 hold「拿， 舉」意思不同。

2

◎解答

d）Look in the top drawer.

（找看看最上層的抽屜。）

◎聽力原文

Do you have anything for a headache?

◎中譯

你有治療頭痛的東西嗎？

a）不，我很好。

b）那也總是令我頭痛。

c）是的，我會去看醫生。

d）找看看最上層的抽屜。

◎解析

Do you have 是詢問對方「有沒有……?」， 只有選項 d）點出頭痛藥存放的地點， drawer 指「抽屜」。

3

◎解答

a）It's four past five.

（五點四分。）

◎聽力原文

Excuse me. Do you have the time?

◎中譯

抱歉。你知道現在幾點嗎？

a）五點四分。

b）你需要多少個？

c）不，謝了。

d）時光飛逝啊。

◎解析

the time 是指「現在的時刻」，本題是詢 問現在的時間，所以答案選 a）最恰當。

對答

14

提供協助

 學習重點

在日常生活中我們常有機會對他人伸出援手（give a helping hand），例如讓別人搭便車（give someone a ride / lift），幫別人接電話（answer someone else's phone），或是為人指路（give directions）。

 情境介紹及導引

It's in our nature to help those in need. Even when we're busy, we still try to give a helping hand whenever we can. To help others, we can give our friends a ride, answer our colleagues' phone, or give directions to people from out of town.

範例 B-27

在以下的對答中，你會聽到一個人問問題，接著再讀取四個選項，其中只有一個是正確的回應。

Does anyone need a ride?

_____

a) I used to ride a bike every day.（我之前每天都騎腳踏車。）

b) I'm going to buy a car this weekend.（我這個週末要去買輛車。）

c) I really like fast rides.（我真的很喜歡坐快速的遊樂設施。）

d) How nice of you to ask!（你這樣邀請實在太好了！）

答案：d)

說明

a. Information Focus

提問的目的是「是否有人要搭便車」，可能的回應如下：

肯定：How nice of you to ask!（你這樣邀請實在太好了！）

婉謝：Thanks, but I'll walk.（謝了，我走路回去。）

b. Language Skills

重點字彙：ride（搭乘）、fast rides（指遊樂園裡的設施）、colleague（同事）。

c. Tips for Listening

選項 a）的 ride a bike 與題目的 ride 詞性與用法不同（前者是動詞，後者是名詞）；

"How nice of you" 是客氣並且帶著愉悅的心情來回應別人的幫忙。

練習題 B-28

請聽以下對答題，選出適當的回應。

1 _____

a）Thanks, but I'll call you.

b）Thanks, but Cole doesn't have a car.

c）Thanks, but I don't have a driver's license.

d）Thanks, but I'll walk.

2 _____

a）I'm sorry, but I'm completely decided.

b）You can get change for that bill over there.

c）I'm sorry, but I didn't catch your name.

d）I'm on my way home.

3 _____

a）I don't know who it was that called.

b）Don't forget to take any messages.

c）Hurry up. He's waiting on the line.

d）The answer to this question is still unknown.

14 詳解

1

◎解答

d）Thanks, but I'll walk.
（謝了，我用走的。）

◎聽力原文

Shall I call you a taxi?

◎中譯

需要幫你叫計程車嗎？
a）謝了，我會再打給你。
b）謝了，但 Cole 沒有車。
c）謝了，但我沒有駕照。
d）謝了，我用走的。

◎解析

Shall I 的問句是禮貌性的詢問對方「是否需要幫忙叫車」，只有選項 d）是合理回應。call a taxi 指「打電話叫車」。

2

◎解答

a）I'm sorry, but I'm completely
decided.
（很抱歉，我已經下定決心了。）

◎聽力原文

Is there any way I can change your
mind?

◎中譯

有沒有任何辦法可以讓你改變心意？
a）很抱歉，我已經下定決心了。
b）你可以到那邊換零錢。

c）抱歉，我沒有聽到您的大名。
d）我在回家的路上。

◎解析

題目 Is there any way...? 是問「有沒有任何辦法……?」，而 change your mind 是「改變心意」，只有 a）的回答最合理。選項 b）的 change「零錢」和選項 d）的 way「路上」和題目關鍵字發音相同，要小心聽辨。

3

◎解答

b）Don't forget to take any messages.
（別忘了記下所有留言訊息。）

◎聽力原文

Shall I answer your phone while
you're gone?

◎中譯

你不在的時候需要我幫你接電話嗎？
a）我不知道那通電話是誰打來的。
b）別忘了記下所有留言訊息。
c）快點，他在電話上等著。
d）此問題的答案仍然未知。

◎解析

題目中的 answer your phone 是「接聽電話」，因此回答 take messages 「記下留言訊息」是合理回應。

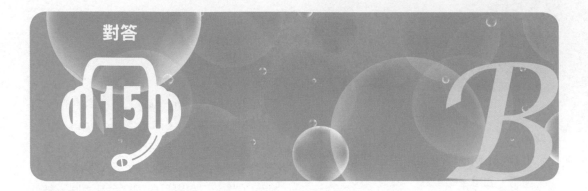

餐廳結帳

 學習重點

在餐廳結帳時（pay a bill），常會碰到是否要留下小費（leave a tip）的問題，有些餐廳是帳單內含（included in the bill），有些則是除了帳單外，另須支付額外的費用（additional payment）。

 情境介紹及導引

We usually pay a service charge with a meal. In countries like Japan or Taiwan, service charge is already included in the bill, generally around 10%. In the United States, customers usually leave a tip between 15 and 20% to the waiters, sometimes more if they do an excellent job.

範例 🎧 B-29

在以下的對答中，你會聽到一個人問問題，接著再讀取四個選項，其中只有一個是正確的回應。

Should we leave a tip?

_____

a) This is just the tip of the iceberg.（這只是冰山一角。）

b) We accept cash only.（我們只收現金。）

c) A service charge has already been included in the bill.
（服務費已經包含在帳單內了。）

d) We don't have to leave until tomorrow.（我們明天才離開。） 答案：c

a. Information Focus

提問的目的是「是否該留點小費」，可能的回應方式如下：

支付：A 15% tip should be fine.（付 15% 的小費就好了。）

不用支付：A service charge has already been included in the bill.
（服務費已經包含在帳單內了。）

b. Language Skills

重點字彙：service charge（服務費）、leave（留置）、tip（小費）、iceberg（冰
山）。

c. Tips for Listening

選項 a）的 tip 是指事物的頂端，與題目的 tip（小費）同字不同義；選項 b）是指
支付的工具（cash or credit cards）與題意無關；選項 d）的 leave 解釋為「離
開」，與題目的 leave（留置）同字不同義。

🎧 練習題　🔊B-30

請聽以下對答題，選出適當的回應。

1 ＿＿＿＿＿＿＿

a) It is already included in the price.

b) The price includes breakfast and dinner.

c) Please tell me some cooking tips.

d) Both cash and credit cards are accepted.

2 ＿＿＿＿＿＿＿

a) Yes, I'll pay the bill tomorrow.

b) Bill is in charge of the next project.

c) They will not pass the bill until the next session.

d) I'll send it immediately.

3 ＿＿＿＿＿＿＿

a) I don't think so. My order was more expensive.

b) I don't have problems with split ends.

c) OK. It'll be my treat.

d) I don't have 50 dollars.

1

◎解答

a）It is already included in the price.
　（已包含在價格內了。）

◎聽力原文

Has the tip already been included in the bill?

◎中譯

帳單上的價錢已含小費了嗎？
a）已包含在價格內了。
b）這個價錢包含早餐和晚餐。
c）請傳授我一些烹飪技巧。
d）可接受現金和刷卡。

◎解析

題目的關鍵動詞是 include「包含」，bill 則指「帳單」，所以選項 a）回答「已包含在價格內」是合理回應。

2

◎解答

d）I'll send it immediately.
　（我會立刻寄出。）

◎聽力原文

Would you send me the bill?

◎中譯

可否請你寄帳單給我？
a）是的，明天我會去付清。
b）Bill 負責下一個專案。
c）他們到下個會期才會批准法案。
d）我會立刻寄出。

◎解析

本題的關鍵字為 bill「帳單」，題目是要求對方寄帳單給他，所以選項 d）為合理回應。選項 b）的 Bill 是人名、選項 c）的 bill 則指「法案」，皆不符題意。

3

◎解答

a）I don't think so. My order was more expensive.
　（我不這麼想，我點的東西比較貴。）

◎聽力原文

Why don't we split the bill fifty-fifty?

◎中譯

這帳單我們就各付一半吧？
a）我不這麼想，我點的東西比較貴。
b）我沒有髮尾分岔的問題。
c）好吧，這餐我請客。
d）我沒有五十元。

◎解析

題中的 split the bill 指「對分帳單；各付各的」，所以答案選 a）是合理回應。選項 b）的 split 為形容詞「分岔的」。

服飾選購

學習重點

一般人在選購衣服時，都會對價格（price）、材質（material）、尺寸（size），加以考量，有時還需要試穿，才知道是否合身。

情境介紹及導引

Mark needs to get a new jacket. At the department store, he finds one with good material for a reasonable price, but is not sure what size to get. The salesperson suggests that he tries on a medium, but Mark thinks a large is better because he does not want a tight fit.

  B-31

範例

在以下的對答中，你會聽到一個人問問題，接著再讀取四個選項，其中只有一個是正確的回應。

Do you fit a meduim?

_____

a) No, medium rare, please.（不，三分熟就好。）

b) Yes, I will.（是的，我願意。）

c) Well, a large would be better.（嗯，大號的比較好。）

d) You look very fit.（你看起很健康。）

答案：c）

a. Information Focus

提問的目的是「中號是否合身」，可能的回應：

肯定："Yes, it fits me well."

否定："Well, a large would be better."。

b. Language Skills

重點字彙：fit（合身）、medium（「尺寸」中號）、medium rare（「牛排熟度」
三分熟）。

c. Tips for Listening

選項 a）的 medium rare 是指牛排的熟度，與衣服尺寸無關；選項 d）的 fit 代表
身體健康，與題意無關。

 練習題　B-32

請聽以下對答題，選出適當的回應。

1 ＿＿＿＿＿＿＿

a) Where can I find them?

b) Any size is fine.

c) No. That's not my style.

d) I'll look into it.

2 ＿＿＿＿＿＿＿

a) Your new desk is big.

b) I have a new desk in my office.

c) A good desk makes a big difference.

d) I would try that new furniture store.

3 ＿＿＿＿＿＿＿

a) It's going to be a vest.

b) It's a blend of silk and cotton.

c) I eat a high-fiber diet.

d) I think a light shade of blue might be nice.

16 詳解

1

◎解答

c）No. That's not my style.
（不，那不是我的風格。）

◎聽力原文

Is this the hat you were looking for?

◎中譯

這是你在找的帽子嗎？
a）我在哪裡可以找到它們？
b）任何尺寸都好。
c）不，那不是我的風格。
d）我會調查看看。

◎解析

題目是確認對方「是否在找這類型的帽子」，無關位置或尺寸，只有選項 c）是合理回應。選項 d）的 look into「調查」和題目的 looking 發音相近，要小心聽辨。

2

◎解答

d）I would try that new furniture store.
（我會去那家新家具行看看。）

◎聽力原文

Where is a good place to buy a new desk?

◎中譯

要買新桌子該去哪裡好呢？
a）你的新桌子很大。
b）我辦公室有張新桌子。

c）好桌子真的差很多。
d）我會去那家新傢俱行看看。

◎解析

題目中的 where 是問哪裡可選購新桌子，只有選項 d）提到地點。furniture store 指「傢俱行」。

3

◎解答

b）It's a blend of silk and cotton.
（它是由絲和棉混紡而成。）

◎聽力原文

What kind of fabric is that made out of?

◎中譯

那是什麼質料做成的？
a）會織成一件背心。
b）它是由絲和棉混紡而成。
c）我吃高纖食品。
d）我想淡藍色會很不錯。

◎解析

題目關鍵字為 fabric（布料），因此選項 b）回答 silk（絲）和 cotton（棉）等材質是合理回應。選項 c）的 fiber（纖維）和 fabric 發音相近，要小心聽辨。

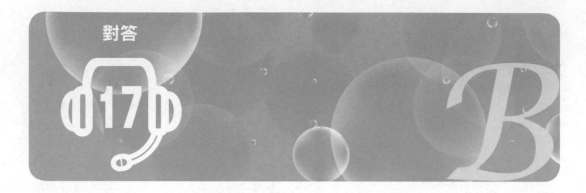

詢問方向

🎧 **學習重點**

搬進新社區或出外旅行時，遇到路況不熟、找不到方向的時候，就需要問路（ask for directions），如找不到入口或出口（entrance / exit）、公車或地鐵路線（bus / subway line）、或是特定的標的物，如書店（a bookstore）。

🎧 **情境介紹及導引**

Cora recently moved to a new neighborhood. On the weekend, she decided to take a walk and become acquainted with the shops. Cora is a book lover, so finding a good bookstore is at the top of her list. She stops a passerby and asks for directions.

範例   B-33

> 在以下的對答中，你會聽到一個人問問題，接著再讀取四個選項，其中只有一個是正確的回應。
>
> Do you know of any good bookstores in the area?
>
> _____
>
> a) No, there aren't that many, are there?（不，沒有那麼多，不是嗎？）
> b) No, unfortunately I'm not from here, either.
>   （很不巧，我也不是這裡的人。）
> c) I know some good books to read.（我知道一些好書可讀。）
> d) No, I don't know the title of the book.（不，我不知道書名。）
>
> 答案：b)

說明

a. Information Focus

提問的目的是「哪裡有書店」，可能的回應：

肯定：There is one on the street corner.（街角那兒有一間。）

否定：No, unfortunately I'm not from here, either.

（很不巧，我也不是這裡的人。）

b. Language Skills

重點字彙：area（地區）、unfortunately（不幸地，不巧地）、acquaint（熟悉）。

c. Tips for Listening

選項 a）的 many 與題目的 any 發音相近；選項 c）及 d）的 book 是重複題目裡的字彙，並未回答書店的位置。

練習題 B-34

請聽以下對答題，選出適當的回應。

1 _____

a）Sure, it's over to the right.

b）I already have an exit strategy.

c）I'm not ready to leave yet.

d）You can get in through there.

2 _____

a）The airport is very close to downtown.

b）I'll pick you up when you arrive at the airport.

c）With this traffic, you should take the train.

d）These buses are never on time.

3 _____

a）I would take the number seven.

b）I would take the subway if I were you.

c）The hotel is very near the subway station.

d）The subway is faster than the bus.

a）機場非常靠近市中心。

b）當你抵達機場時我會去接你。

c）以目前交通狀況來看，你應該搭火車。

d）這些巴士從沒準時過。

1

◎解答

a）Sure, it's over to the right.

（沒問題，就在右手邊。）

◎聽力原文

Excuse me, could you direct me to the exit, please?

◎中譯

不好意思，可以請你指引我出口的方向嗎？

a）沒問題，就在右手邊。

b）我已經想到退場的策略了。

c）我尚未準備離開。

d）你可以從那邊進去。

◎解析

題中的動詞 direct 是「指示方向」，exit 則指「出口」，所以回答應該跟方向或方位有關，因此選 a）最合理。選項 b）的 exit 是指「退場策略」，與題意無關。

2

◎解答

c）With this traffic, you should take the train.

（以目前交通狀況來看，你應該搭火車。）

◎聽力原文

What's the quickest way to the airport?

◎中譯

哪一個是到機場最快的方式？

◎解析

題目是問到機場「最快的方式」（the quickest way），所以選項 c）根據交通狀況建議 take the train（搭火車）是合理回應。

3

◎解答

a）I would take the number seven.

（我會搭七號線。）

◎聽力原文

Which subway line should I take to go downtown?

◎中譯

到市中心要搭哪一條地鐵線？

a）我會搭七號線。

b）如果我是你，我會選擇搭地鐵。

c）飯店很靠近地鐵站。

d）地鐵會比公車快。

◎解析

題目是問 Which subway line「哪條地鐵線」，選項 a）回答 the number seven「七號線」 最恰當。選項 b）和 d）是回應 "Should I take the subway or the bus?" 這類的問題。

郵件處理

 學習重點

郵寄包裹（package delivery）時，需要考慮的事項包括收件人的地點（location of recipient）、運送方式（mode of transportation）、運送工具（means），如果想要快點送到指定地點，很多人會選擇用貨機（air freighter）運送的快捷郵件（express mail）。

 情境介紹及導引

Roger is sending his graduate school application to a school in Boston. To send the package through express mail, Roger goes to a convenience store, fills out a form, and inserts the documents in the courier's envelope. Roger needs to make sure the package arrives before the deadline.

範 例 B-35

在以下的對答中，你會聽到一個人問問題，接著再讀取四個選項，其中只有一個是正確的回應。

How quickly can I get this package to Boston?

_____

a）About 60 miles an hour（時速大約 60 英里）
b）By noon tomorrow（明天中午以前）
c）A chartered airplane（一架包機）
d）By express mail（用快捷郵件）

答案：b）

a. Information Focus

提問的目的是「郵件多快到達目的地」，所以是問跟「時間」有關的資訊，正確的
回應是告知具體的時間，如 "By noon tomorrow"。

b. Language Skills

重點字彙：package（包裹），by ＋ 時間（在……以前）、charter（包租）、
courier（快遞信差）。

c. Tips for Listening

本句聽力重點是 how quickly（多快）及 get this package to（讓包裹到……），
選項 a）About 60 miles an hour 是指「速度」，似乎可以回應 how quickly，
但是跟提問的目的不符，選項 c）是指運送工具，選項 d）是指運送方式。

 練習題 B-36

請聽以下對答題，選出適當的回應。

1 _____

a）Just these letters, please.

b）Please send me some water.

c）First class, please.

d）Please don't end it.

2 _____

a）Yes. It's delivered at the same time every day.

b）I've already sent an e-mail to the client.

c）I delivered a package this morning.

d）It's supposed to be here by 10:00 a.m.

3 _____

a）I called them yesterday.

b）They said sometime today.

c）He arrived safe and sound.

d）I told them I would buy it soon.

1

◎解答

c) First class, please.
（平信，謝謝。）

◎聽力原文

How would you like to send this?

◎中譯

你希望以什麼方式寄送？
a) 只有這些信件，麻煩了。
b) 請遞些水給我。
c) 平信，謝謝。
d) 請勿結束它。

◎解析

題目的 how 是問「方式」，此類問題通常是詢問郵件包裹的寄送方式，因此只有選項 c) 最合理。選項 b) 的 send 是指「送上；遞上」，與題意不符；選項 d) 的 end 則和 send 發音相近，勿混淆。

2

◎解答

d) It's supposed to be here by 10:00 a.m.
（它應該上午十點前就要送到這裡了。）

◎聽力原文

Is the mail delivered in the morning or afternoon?

◎中譯

信件是上午或下午送到？
a) 是的，每天都在同樣的時間送達。
b) 我已經寄電子郵件給客戶了。
c) 我今早已寄出一件包裹。
d) 它應該上午十點前就要送到這裡了。

◎解析

問題是確認郵件送達的時間，因此選項 d) 回答應該送達的時間是合理回應。be supposed to + V「應該」是預期的語氣，常指「應該要發生卻沒發生」。

3

◎解答

b) They said sometime today.
（他們說今天的某個時候會到。）

◎聽力原文

When is the delivery supposed to arrive?

◎中譯

運送物品應該何時會送達呢？
a) 我昨天已經打給他們了。
b) 他們說今天的某個時候會到。
c) 他平安抵達了。
d) 我告訴他們我很快就會去買。

◎解析

題目 when 是問何時會送達，所以回答應與時間有關； sometime 可指稱「（過去或未來的）某個時候」，所以是合理回應。

致謝及致歉

 學習重點

在接受別人的幫助或是招待（reception）後，必須向對方表示謝意（express gratitude）；反之，如果犯了錯，造成他人的不便及損失，則應該向對方道歉（apologize to 某人 for 某事）。

 情境介紹及導引

Showing sincere appreciation is the best way to repay an act of kindness. There is no need to feel that we have to pay the person back right away. It is okay to wait until an opportunity comes up for us to return the favor in a natural way.

範例 B-37

在以下的對答中，你會聽到一個人問問題，接著再讀取四個選項，其中只有一個是正確的回應。

What can I ever do to repay your kindness?

_____

a）There's no easier way to do it.（做這件事沒有捷徑。）

b）You can pay the bill later.（你可以待會兒再付帳。）

c）Don't worry about it, really.（不用放在心上，真的。）

d）I can't tell you, either.（我也沒法告訴你。）

答案：c）

說明

a. Information Focus
提問的目的是「如何報答對方的善意」，正確的回應是 " Don't worry about it, really. "。

b. Language Skills
重點字彙：repay（報答）、kindness（善意）、worry（憂心）、favor（恩惠）。

c. Tips for Listening
本段聽力是以 What 為首的疑問句，雖然是問對方「要做什麼事」，但重點是動詞 repay your kindness，正確的回答是不用對方做任何事情；選項 b）的 pay 與 repay 發音相似，用來混淆聽者判斷；選項 a）及 d）皆與題意無關。

 練習題 B-38

請聽以下對答題，選出適當的回應。

1 _____

a) I don't think you should.

b) I should go there sometime.

c) I will make you a job offer.

d) I don't think it's necessary.

2 _____

a) How do you do?

b) I'm fine, how about you?

c) The pleasure was all mine.

d) I'm looking forward to it, too!

3 _____

a) You're very welcome.

b) The roses, please.

c) In the garden.

d) How much did you pay?

19 詳解

1

◎解答

d）I don't think it's necessary.
（我不覺得有這個必要。）

◎聽力原文

Don't you think you should offer an apology?

◎中譯

你難道不該道個歉嗎？
a）我不認為你該這麼做。
b）我該找個時間去那裡。
c）我會給你工作機會。
d）我不覺得有這個必要。

◎解析

題目的 Don't you think you should...? 是委婉詢問對方是否應該道個歉，因此選項 d）的回答最合理。選項 c）中的 job offer 是名詞「工作機會」，和題目中的動詞 offer 意思不同。

2

◎解答

c）The pleasure was all mine.
（那是我的榮幸。）

◎聽力原文

I had a great time. Thank you!

◎中譯

我玩得很愉快，謝謝你！
a）你好嗎？
b）我很好，你呢？
c）那是我的榮幸。
d）我對此也很期待。

◎解析

題目對話的目的在致謝，表示玩得很盡興，而選項 c）回答 The pleasure was all mine.「榮幸之至」是合理的回應。

3

◎解答

a）You're very welcome.
（實在不必客氣。）

◎聽力原文

Thank you for the beautiful flowers.

◎中譯

謝謝你送這麼漂亮的花。
a）實在不必客氣。
b）請給我玫瑰花。
c）在花園裡。
d）你付了多少錢？

◎解析

對話是感謝對方送花，所以回答「不客氣」是合理回應，故答案選 a）。題目中的 flowers 非特指 rose（玫瑰）或 garden（花園），也與價錢無關。

旅遊見聞

學習重點

旅遊有助增廣見聞（to broaden horizons of learning），結識不同文化的人們（to meet people from different cultures）；帶著愉快和好奇的心情旅遊，即使在旅程中遇到天候不佳的狀況，也能自得其樂（be content with oneself）。

情境介紹及導引

Traveling is not only fun but also broadens the mind. We get to meet people from different cultures and see how they live. In Italy, the birthplace of the European Renaissance, one learns to appreciate paintings and sculptures created by great artists. Travelers are always fascinated by Italy's cultural achievements.

在以下的對答中，你會聽到一個人問問題，接著再讀取四個選項，其中只有一個是正確的回應。

How was your trip to Italy?

———————————————

a）My family first came to Italy in 1904.
（我的家族在 1904 年來到義大利。）

b）It will be a good trip.（那將會是美好的旅程。）

c）There is an Italian restaurant on the corner of the street.
（街角上有間義大利餐廳。）

d）It rained a lot, but I had fun.（雨下得很大，不過我覺得蠻好玩的。）

答案：d）

a. Information Focus

提問的目的是「旅程如何」，正確的回應是" It rained a lot, but I had fun. "。

b. Language Skills

重點字彙：trip（旅行）、family（指家族）、corner（角落）。

c. Tips for Listening

句法" How ＋ is / are / was / were ＋ 事物 "是詢問對方「某件事情如何」，因此聽力重點是接續在 how 後面的「事物」，此處是指 trip to Italy，問句動詞是用過去式 was，表示答話者已去過義大利，選項 b)" It will be a good trip. "時間點是未來，沒有正確回應問題的重點「此次旅程的感受如何？」。

請聽以下對答題，選出適當的回應。

1 _____

a) I enjoyed the carnival the most.

b) I bought a map from an airport gift shop.

c) The city is very crowded.

d) I thought they were very hospitable.

2 _____

a) Yes. I'll be there for a while.

b) Once, when I was in college.

c) Yes, two times a day.

d) If I could save up enough money.

3 _____

a) We plan to visit some friends in Seattle before we fly home.

b) I'll never go there again because the weather is awful.

c) We visited the most famous museum in the country.

d) Usually we go to Hawaii, but this time we went skiing.

20 詳解

1

◎解答

d）I thought they were very hospitable.
（我覺得他們很熱情好客。）

◎聽力原文

How did you find the people in Brazil?

◎中譯

你覺得巴西人怎麼樣？
a）我最喜歡嘉年華會。
b）我在機場的禮品店買了張地圖。
c）城市非常擁擠。
d）我覺得他們很熱情好客。

◎解析

題目 How did you find...? 是問「對巴西人的印象」，所以 d）的回應最貼切。hospitable 通常形容人的特質「好客的」。

2

◎解答

b）Once, when I was in college.
（我在念大學的時候去過一次。）

◎聽力原文

Have you ever been to South America?

◎中譯

你有去過南美洲嗎？
a）是的，我將會去那裡一陣子。
b）我在念大學的時候去過一次。
c）是的，一天兩次。
d）如果我能存夠錢的話。

◎解析

Have you ever...? 是詢問過去的經驗，所以選項 b）說明大學時去過一次為合理答案。

3

◎解答

a）We plan to visit some friends in Seattle before we fly home.
（我們計畫搭機返家前先到西雅圖拜訪朋友。）

◎聽力原文

What is the last place you'll visit on your vacation?

◎中譯

你假期的最後一站會去拜訪哪個地方？
a）我們計畫搭機返家前先到西雅圖拜訪朋友。
b）天氣實在糟糕透頂，我再也不去那裡了。
c）我們去參觀了全國最有名的博物館。
d）通常我們會去夏威夷，但這次改去滑雪。

◎解析

題目問的是旅程中的最後一站，帶有未來式的語氣，只有 a）回答「計畫去拜訪朋友」為合理回應。選項 b）回答天氣因素與題意無關，選項 c）、d）皆是過去時態也不符題意。

簡短對話

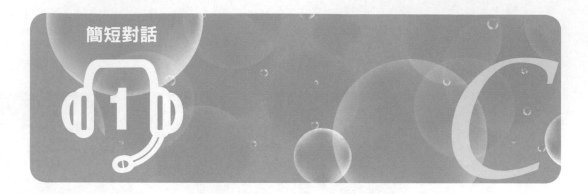

簡短對話

1

家居修繕問題

 學習重點

在家中常會遇到一些設備發生問題，例如水管漏水（leaking）、電視沒有畫面（no picture）、或是冷氣故障（out of order），這時就需要找人修繕了。

 情境介紹及導引

It's time for lunch, and Ben walks to the bathroom to wash his hands. He finds the bathroom flooded. With water overflowing, it looks like one of the pipes is leaking. Ben goes to the kitchen to tell his wife, Cindy, about the situation. They must fix the flooded bathroom right away.

範例 🎧 C-01

在簡短對話裡，你會聽到兩個人（通常是一男一女）的交談，接著再依據談話內容，找出他們需要找誰來幫忙。

M：We'd better call for help. I think one of our pipes is leaking.

W：What happened?

M：I'm not sure, but there's water all over the bathroom floor.

Who will they probably call for help?（他們可能會打電話找誰幫忙？）

_____

a）A tour guide.（導遊。）

b）A plumber.（水管技工。）

c）An automobile mechanic.（汽車技師。）

d）A teacher.（老師。）

答案：b）

說明

a. Information Focus

問題的重點是「找誰來修繕？」，從對話中的關鍵字彙 pipe, leaking, water，得知可能是水管漏水的問題，應該要找修水管的技工（plumber）。

b. Language Skills

其他字彙：pipe（輸送管）、bathroom（浴室）、flood（淹水）、overflow（溢出）、situation（情況）。

c. Tips for Listening

兩人之間的對話常會有所謂的「起頭語」，例如本段對話的 " We'd better call for help. "，表示有狀況發生，需要幫忙，後面接續的文字，應該是描述所發生的問題。

練習題　C-02

請聽以下的對話題，並回答相關的問題。

1 ＿＿＿＿＿＿

a) Find the man's contact lens.

b) Get in touch with the man.

c) Make the repairs take longer.

d) Accept the man's television.

2 ＿＿＿＿＿＿

a) It was unplugged.

b) The batteries needed to be replaced.

c) The remote control was broken.

d) The TV was too far away.

3 ＿＿＿＿＿＿

a) He thinks it's strange.

b) He thinks it's something to laugh about.

c) He thinks the woman is playing a joke.

d) He thinks he should have done it.

1

◎解答

b) Get in touch with the man.

（聯絡這位男士。）

◎聽力原文

M：Have you finished fixing my TV?

W：No, but when I finish, I'll contact you.

M：How much longer should it be?

What will the woman probably do after fixing the television?

◎中譯

男士：我的電視修好了嗎？

女士：還沒有，不過一修好我就會聯絡您。

男士：大概還要多久？

這位女士在修完電視後可能會怎麼做？

a) 去找這位男士的隱形眼鏡。

b) 聯絡這位男士。

c) 花更長的時間修理。

d) 接受這位男士的電視。

◎解析

在文中提到：when I finish, I'll contact you... 因此正確答案為 b)。選項 a) 的 contact lens「隱形眼鏡」用意在混淆聽者，而男士沒有要求拖延時間，也沒有要送女士電視機，故 a)、c)、d) 為非。

2

◎解答

b) The batteries needed to be replaced.

（這些電池需要更新。）

◎聽力原文

W：I think the remote control is broken. I keep pressing the power button, but nothing happens.

M：These batteries are old. Try these new ones.

W：That's much better.

Why couldn't the woman turn on the TV?

◎中譯

女士：我覺得遙控器壞了。我一直按電源開關，但都沒有反應。

男士：這些電池是舊的。試試看這些新的。

女士：現在好多了。

這位女士為什麼打不開電視？

a) 電視沒有插電。

b) 這些電池需要更新。

c) 遙控器壞掉了。

d) 電視擺太遠了。

◎解析

對話中可知，當換過電池後，女士立刻覺得情況改善，顯然問題就是出在電池上。因此 b) 是正確答案。

3

◎解答

a) He thinks it's strange.

（他對這個狀況感到奇怪。）

◎聽力原文

M：That's funny...did you pay the telephone bill this month?

W：Yes, just today. Why?

M：I think our line's been cut; there's no dial tone.

How does the man feel about this situation?

◎中譯

男士：奇怪 ...... 這個月電話費你付了嗎？

女士：有啊，今天付的。怎麼了？

男士：我想電話線被切掉了，我聽不到任何
　　　撥號音。

這位男士對這個情況感到如何？

a）他對這個狀況感到奇怪。

b）他覺得很好笑。

c）他覺得這位女士在開玩笑。

d）他覺得自己應該去繳電話費。

◎解析

文中 ''That's funny...'' 並非真的感到有趣，
而是指「奇怪的；不正常的」，所以 a）是
正確的答案。

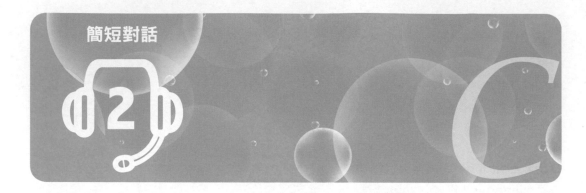

簡短對話

遊學、旅行

 學習重點

遊學是很多年輕學子嚮往的生活經驗，除了學習他國語言，還可以做志工（volunteer）幫助他人，例如到巴西（Brazil）遊學，得先學習葡萄牙文（Portuguese），才能更深入了解當地民情及社會。

 情境介紹及導引

Kevin is telling Lisa about a friend who is learning Portuguese, the official language of Brazil. Kevin's friend loves to travel and is dedicated to helping other people in need. Going to South America is a good way for Kevin's friend to combine her passions for travel and doing voluntary work.

範例 C-03

在簡短對話裡，你會聽到兩個人（通常是一男一女）的交談，接著再依據談話內容，找出男士的朋友學習葡語的原因。

M: My friend is learning Portuguese so she can go to Brazil and volunteer there.

W: That's great! She must be really dedicated to helping other people.

M: Yeah, and it's also a good way for her to follow her other passion, which is traveling.

Why is the man's friend learning Portuguese?

（這位男士的朋友為何要學葡語？）

a) She wants to travel and aid people in need.
（她想要旅遊並幫助窮困的人。）

b) She wants to be a linguist.（她想要成為語言學家。）

c) She wants to help people in her native country.
（她想要在家鄉幫助他人。）

d) She wants to teach Portuguese.（她想要教葡語。）   答案：a)

📢 說明

a. Information Focus

問題的重點是「學習葡語的原因」，從對話中的關鍵字彙 Brazil, volunteer, helping other people, passion, traveling， 得知她喜歡旅遊並且樂於幫助當地人士。

b. Language Skills

其他字彙：dedicated（奉獻的）、passion（熱情）、linguist（語言學家）。

奉獻 / 致力於某事物：人 + is / are + dedicated to + V-ing / 事物

c. Tips for Listening

請注意 Brazil 及 volunteer 的重音都在後面的音節。

 練習題　C-04

請聽以下的對話題，並回答相關的問題。

1 _____

a) Paris is far away.   b) They have to raise much more money.

c) He wants the trip to go far.   d) He doesn't want to go to Paris.

2 _____

a) She has gotten really dark.   b) She has become a very good swimmer.

c) She lives by the ocean.   d) She has recovered from an illness.

3 _____

a) Make a guess.   b) Go camping.

c) Make a fire.   d) Learn about nature.

1

◎解答

b) They have to raise much more
money.（他們必須籌更多的錢。）

◎聽力原文

M : Do you think we'll be able to raise enough money for the trip this year?

W : I hope so. I've always wanted to go to Pairs.

M : Well, we've still got a long way to go.

What does the man mean?

◎中譯

男士：你覺得我們能為今年的旅行籌到足夠的錢嗎？

女士：我希望如此。我一直都想去巴黎。

男士：嗯，我們還有漫漫長路要走。

這位男士所指的意思是？
a) 巴黎很遠。
b) 他們必須籌更多的錢。
c) 他希望去遠行。
d) 他並不想去巴黎。

◎解析

a long way to go 指「（距離目標）還差得遠」，男子的意思是需要繼續努力以籌到更多資金，所以選項 b) They have to raise much more money.（他們必須籌更多的錢。）是最適合的答案。

2

◎解答

a) She has gotten really dark.
（她真的變黑了。）

◎聽力原文

M : Wow! You're really tanned!

W : I spent a lot of time at the beach when I visited my family.

M : Oh, no wonder!

What can you conclude about the woman?

◎中譯

男士：哇！你曬的真黑！

女士：我去看家人時，在海灘上消磨了許多時間。

男士：哦，難怪！

關於這位女士，你能得出什麼結論？
a) 她真的變黑了。
b) 她已成為一位很出色的泳者。
c) 她住在海邊。
d) 她已經從疾病中痊癒。

◎解析

第一句提到：You're really tanned，可以得知女士曬黑了，因此正確答案為 a) She has gotten really dark.（她真的變黑了。）

3

c) Make a fire.（升火。）

◎聽力原文

W：Where did you learn how to make a campfire like that?

M：I went to summer camp every year as a child.

W：So, I guess you know a lot about nature then.

What did the man just do?

◎中譯

女士：你在哪裡學會升營火？

男士：我小時候每年都去夏令營。

女士：那麼，我想你知道很多大自然的事囉。

這位男士剛剛做了什麼？

a) 進行猜測。

b) 去露營。

c) 升火。

d) 學習有關大自然的事情。

◎解析

第一句即提到：make a campfire like that，可知男士剛升起營火，所以答案中只有 c) Make a fire.（升火。）為正確答案。

簡短對話

3

選擇禮物

 學習重點

選購禮物常會遇到的問題包括：買什麼（clothes / painting）、價格（expensive / inexpensive）、何處選購（online / at a real store）等問題，例如一位女士要上網選購禮物給她的姊妹，而與朋友有如下對話。

 情境介紹及導引

Peggy's sister is celebrating her birthday soon, and Peggy hopes to find the perfect gift from an online store. Many beautiful clothes are available online, but Peggy wants to order something different this year. A painting by her sister's favorite artist, if it is not too expensive, may be a good choice.

 範例 C-05

在簡短對話裡，你會聽到兩個人（通常是一男一女）的交談，接著再依據談話內容，找出女士為何要使用電腦。

M：Are you playing with your computer?

W：Actually, I'm using it to order a present for my sister. Her birthday is next week.

M：Really? What are you going to get her?

W： It is something for her house.

M：Maybe it's some designer clothes?

W：No, it's not clothes and it's not made by a designer, it's made by an artist.

M : OK, I've got it.

W : That's right! I'm giving my sister a painting by her favorite artist.

Why is the woman using the computer?（這位女士為何要使用電腦？）

_____

a) She wants to watch a movie.（她想要看一部電影。）

b) She wants to play computer games.（她想玩電腦遊戲。）

c) She wants to buy a gift online.（她想上網購買禮物。）

d) She is writing an email to her sister.（她正寫信給她的姊妹。）　答案：c)

🎧 說明

a. Information Focus

問題的重點是「為何要用電腦」，從對話中的關鍵句" I'm using it to order a present for my sister. "得知她是上網購買禮物。

b. Language Skills

重要字彙：available（買得到的）、order（訂購）、designer（設計師）、artist（藝術家）、painting（繪畫）、favorite（特別喜愛的）、online（網路上）。

c. Tips for Listening

內容較長的對話通常從前幾句的關鍵字彙就可以判斷出對話的主題，例如以上對話的 computer, order, present, birthday，這些字彙都不艱深，只要熟悉發音就能輕鬆掌握對話內容。

 練習題　C-06

請聽以下的對話題，並回答相關的問題。

1.1 _____ 請聽對話 **1**，回答以下 2 題。

a) The woman's shopping experience.

b) Gift ideas for New Year.

c) The woman's niece.

d) A jewelry store.

 **1.2** _____

a) A home entertainment system.

b) Jewelry.

c) Clothes.

d) Make-up.

 **2** _____

a) Tom.

b) The man.

c) John.

d) The woman.

 3 _____

a) The woman bought him a nice gift.

b) He received many presents.

c) He looks forward to his birthday.

d) He is expecting a baby boy.

1

◎聽力原文

M：Have you finished your New Year's shopping, yet?

W：Not quite. I'm still having trouble trying to decide what to buy my niece.

M：How about something for home entertainment?

W：I thought about that, and it's a good idea. Still, I'm thinking about something to wear.

M：I used to hate it when I got clothes for a New Year's present.

W：That's because you were a boy. It's different for girls.

M：Oh, yeah. I forgot.

W：The problem is: what kind of clothes do you buy for a 16-year-old girl?

M：Clothes are too hard to choose. I would play it safe and just buy some jewelry.

W：Jewelry? Now why didn't I think of that? The problem is her mother said she needs clothes and that's what I'm going to buy.

◎中譯

男士：妳完成年貨採購了嗎？

女士：還剩一些，我還在苦惱要買什麼給我的姪女。

男士：不如買家庭娛樂用品？

女士：這是個好主意，我有想過。不過我在考慮買衣服。

男士：我以前最討厭新年禮物收到衣服。

女士：因為你是男生，女生可就不一樣。

男士：噢，也對，我忘了這點。

女士：問題是，十六歲的女孩適合買什麼樣的衣服？

男士：服飾太難選購了。避免出錯的話，我會買珠寶首飾。

女士：珠寶首飾？我之前怎麼沒想到？問題是她媽媽說她需要衣服，我才打算去買的。

1.1

◎解答

b）Gift ideas for New Year.
（新年送禮的點子。）

◎聽力原文

What are the speakers talking about?

◎中譯

兩人在討論什麼？

a）這位女士的購物經驗。

b）新年送禮的點子。

c）這位女士的姪女。

d）珠寶店。

◎解析

從對話中提到的 shopping、New Year's present 等關鍵字，可知兩人是在討論如何挑選新年禮物，所以選 b）Gift ideas for New Year（新年送禮的點子）。

1.2

◎解答

c）Clothes.（衣服。）

◎聽力原文

What is the woman going to buy her niece?

◎中譯

這位女士要買什麼送給她的姪女？

a）家庭娛樂設備。

b）珠寶首飾。

c）衣服。

d）化妝品。

◎解析

女士在最後一句提到 ...she needs clothes and that's what I'm going to buy... ，可知答案應選 c）Clothes（衣服）。

2

◎解答

a）Tom.

◎聽力原文

W：Did you pick out a gift for Tom's birthday?

M：No. I have no idea what would be good.

W：Well, I know that he likes John Miller novels.

Who is going to receive a gift?

◎中譯

女士：Tom 的生日禮物你挑好了嗎？

男士：還沒，我不知道挑什麼好。

女士：嗯，我知道他喜歡 John Miller 的小說。

誰將會收到禮物？

a）Tom

b）這位男士

c）John

d）這位女士

◎解析

第一句提到 a gift for Tom's birthday，可知兩人在討論要挑甚麼禮物給 Tom，所以選 a）Tom。

3

◎解答

c）He looks forward to his birthday.

（他期待著他的生日。）

◎聽力原文

W：Boy, Joshua sure looks happy. What happened?

M：Nothing. His birthday's coming up and he's expecting a lot of presents, you know.

W：Uh-oh. I better hurry up and get him one!

Why does Joshua look happy?

◎中譯

女士：哇，Joshua 看起來非常開心。怎麼了？

男士：沒什麼。他的生日快到了，他期待會收到很多禮物，你知道的。

女士：糟了。我最好趕快準備禮物給他！

為什麼 Joshua 看起來很開心？

a）這位女士買給他很棒的禮物。

b）他收到許多禮物。

c）他期待著他的生日。

d）他準備迎接一個男嬰。

◎解析

男子在第二句提到，Joshua 期待在生日當天收到很多禮物，所以答案應選 c）。

簡短對話

考試及課業

🎧 學習重點

考試（take a test）是學生共同的生活經驗，當某人通過某項測驗（pass the test）或資格考試（qualification test）時，旁人總是感到羨慕，也希望能夠分享準備考試的經驗，因而有如下的對話。

🎧 情境介紹及導引

Theresa and Victor received the results of a qualification test they took recently. The test is considered difficult because many people had to take it several times before they passed. Theresa was very pleased with her score. When Victor came to congratulate her, Theresa told him about the preparation guidebook she used and how she managed her time beforehand.

  C-07

在簡短對話裡，你會聽到兩個人（通常是一男一女）的交談，接著再依據談話內容，找出女士達成什麼事情。

M：How did you ever do it? Some people take it five or six times before they pass.

W：I had a good preparation guidebook and I studied every day for two weeks beforehand.

M：That's great. Congratulations. You're sure to get a good job.

What has the woman accomplished?（這位女士達成了什麼事情？）

_____

a) She has taken the exam 5 times.（她參加了五次考試。）

b) She has passed a test.（她通過了測驗。）

c) She has gotten a good job.（她得到了一份好工作。）

d) She has managed to get a good book.（她設法得到了一本好書。）

答案：b)

🎧 說明

a. Information Focus

問題的重點是「達成什麼事情」，從對話中的句子 " Some people take it five or six times before they pass. "，及其他關鍵字 preparation guidebook, studied 得知女士是通過了某項測驗。

b. Language Skills

重點字彙：qualification test（資格考試）、guidebook（「測驗」指南）、beforehand（事先）、congratulations（祝賀）、manage to（設法；勉強）。

特定詞組：take ＋ 測驗／考試

c. Tips for Listening

以 What 為首的問句重點是問「事情」；問句中的 " has...accomplished " 表示已經完成某件事，請注意 has 及 accomplished 的發音。

 練習題　C-08

請聽以下的對話題，並回答相關的問題。

1 _____

a) Tidy up his desk.　　　　　　b) Make better plans.

c) Be aware of the deadline.　　d) Get a daily planner.

2 _____

a) The man finished the report on time.　b) The man didn't meet the deadline.

c) The man is lazy.　　　　　　　　　d) The man didn't keep his word.

3 _____

a) The man did not explain it.　　b) It was too complicated.

c) She didn't read it.　　　　　　d) The diagrams were missing.

4 詳解

1

◎解答

b）Make better plans.

（計畫得更完善。）

◎聽力原文

M：I don't think I'll be able to finish this report by tomorrow's deadline.

W：You need to start planning your schedule better. This happened last month.

M：I know. Next month, I'll be better organized.

What does the woman advise the man to do?

◎中譯

男士：我不認為我能在明天期限之前，完成這份報告。

女士：你必須更妥善地規畫你的時間表。這種情形上個月也發生過一次。。

男士：我知道。下個月我會更有效率。

這位女士奉勸這位男士做什麼？

a）清理他的桌面。

b）計畫得更完善。

c）注意截止期限。

d）準備一個行事曆。

◎解析

女士建議男士：...planning your schedule better（更妥善規畫時間），以免再犯同樣錯誤，所以 b）是最適合的答案。

2

◎解答

b）The man didn't meet the deadline.

（這位男士沒有趕上繳交期限。）

◎聽力原文

M：I'm sorry, but I need more time to write the report.

W：You have really disappointed me this time.

M：I promise it will never happen again.

Why is the woman upset?

◎中譯

男士：對不起，但我需要更多的時間來寫這份報告。

女士：你這次真的讓我很失望。

男士：我保證下不為例。

這位女士為了什麼事不開心？

a）這位男士準時完成報告。

b）這位男士沒有趕上繳交期限。

c）這位男士個性懶惰。

d）這位男士沒有信守承諾。

◎解析

從兩人對話得知，男士需要更多時間來完成報告，是女士感到失望的原因，故選 b）這位男士沒有趕上繳交期限。

3

◎解答

d) The diagrams were missing.

（圖表不見了。）

◎聽力原文

W : I don't understand this report at all. Can you explain it to me?

M : Well, it looks like the charts and graphs are missing. Here they are.

W : Oh, now it makes sense. Please be more careful next time.

Why didn't the woman understand the report?

◎中譯

女士：我完全看不懂這報告。你能說明一下嗎？

男士：嗯，看來報告中的圖表不見了。圖表在這兒！

女士：噢，這樣看起來合理多了。下次請更細心一點。

為何這位女士無法理解這份報告？

a) 這位男士沒有向她解釋。

b) 報告太過複雜。

c) 女士沒有讀過報告。

d) 圖表不見了。

◎解析

在對話中男士提到：...charts and graphs are missing（圖表不見了），可以知道選項 d) 最恰當。chart、graph 和 diagram 皆指「圖表」。

簡短對話 5

寵物飼養

學習重點

許多家庭喜歡飼養寵物（keep a pet），寵物種類很多，包括貓、狗、兔子（rabbit）、倉鼠（hamster）、鸚鵡（parrot）等；至於哪種寵物較合適，就得看飼主的喜好，或其他客觀條件，例如居住的公寓很小（The apartment is small.），可能就不能養氣味很重（smell quite a bit）的寵物。

情境介紹及導引

Ava is looking to keep a pet. Ava asks Zack for advice and tells him that her ideal pet would be one that is cute and cuddly. Because Ava has a small apartment, she also needs a pet that does not smell too much or require a lot of space. Zack suggests birds, rabbits, mice, or a cat.

範例 C-09

在簡短對話裡，你會聽到兩個人（通常是一男一女）的交談，接著再依據談話內容，找出女士想養的寵物。

M：You should get a rabbit! They're cuddly and quiet.

W：I agree, they are cute. But they smell quite a bit and my apartment is small. I think I'm going to get a pair of hamsters. They can keep each other company while I'm at work.

M：What about a cat? They don't make a lot of noise and kittens are just so cute.

W：I thought about that too.

What pet will the woman probably keep?（這位女士可能會養哪種寵物？）

a) A mouse or cat（老鼠或貓）

b) A rabbit or hamster（兔子或倉鼠）

c) A bird or mouse（鳥或老鼠）

d) A rabbit or cat（兔子或貓）

答案：a)

🎧 說明

a. Information Focus

問題的重點是「會養什麼寵物」，從對話中的句子 "I think I'm going to get a pair of hamsters..."、"What about a cat?...I thought about that too."，得知她可能會養老鼠或貓。

b. Language Skills

重點字彙：cuddly（討人喜愛的）、keep each other company（彼此作伴）、kitten（小貓）、cute（可愛的）。

c. Tips for Listening

I think I'm going to ＋ V 這類句法表示打算做某事，V 所代表的就是要做的事。

熟悉一些寵物名稱的單字讀音，如 pet, rabbit, hamster, cat, kitten 等。

練習題 C-10

請聽以下的對話題，並回答相關的問題。

1 ＿＿＿＿＿＿＿＿

a) Bird.   b) Cat.

c) Dog.   d) Mouse.

2.1 ＿＿＿＿＿＿＿ 請聽對話 **2**，回答以下 2 題。

a) Bird.   b) Turtle.

c) Rabbit.   d) Fish.

2.2 ＿＿＿＿＿＿＿

a) He is dead.   b) Someone stole him.

c) He flew away.   d) He is sick.

5 詳解

1

◎解答

c）Dog.（狗。）

◎聽力原文

M：Is it true that you adopted three more puppies?

W：Yes. My cousin's dog gave birth to six puppies, and she can't afford to keep all of them.

M：But you already have four dogs and two cats!

What kind of pet did the woman adopt from her cousin?

◎中譯

男士：妳另外多收養了三隻小狗是真的嗎？

女士：是啊。我表妹的狗生了六隻小狗，但她沒有辦法全部都養。

男士：但妳已經有四隻狗和兩隻貓了耶！

這位小姐從她表妹那裡收養了哪種寵物？

a）鳥

b）貓

c）狗

d）老鼠

◎解析

對話中表妹的狗生了六隻小狗（puppies），所以正確答案選 c）。

2

◎聽力原文

M：Why do you look so depressed?

W：Do you remember Petey, my parrot?

M：Sure I do! He repeated everything anyone said and made awful noises whenever he was hungry.

W：Well, you won't be hearing anything from him anymore...

M：Oh, no! What happened? Did he die?

W：Don't say such a thing! I just accidentally left my window open and he got out.

M：Maybe he just wanted to take the sightseeing bus tour of the city.

W：Very funny. I'm hoping to get him back by putting out some of his favorite food.

◎中譯

男士：你怎麼看起來如此沮喪？

女士：你還記得我的鸚鵡 Petey 嗎？

男士：當然記得啊！牠會重複任何人說過的任何事情，而且每當牠餓的時候還會製造難聽的噪音。

女士：嗯，你再也不會聽到牠製造的任何聲音了。

男士：天啊，不會吧！發生什麼事了？牠死了嗎？

女士：別這麼說！我只是不小心窗戶沒關，牠就飛出去了。

男士：也許牠只是想搭個市區觀光巴士逛逛。

女士：不好笑。我倒希望能放些牠愛吃的東西讓牠回來。

2.1

◎解答

a）Bird.（鳥）

◎聽力原文

What kind of pet does the woman
keep?

◎中譯

這位女士養哪種寵物？
a）鳥
b）烏龜
c）兔子
d）魚

◎解析

女士在對話中提到鸚鵡（parrot），可知她
的寵物是鳥類，所以選 a）。

2.2

◎解答

c）He flew away.
　（牠飛走了。）

◎聽力原文

What happened to the woman's pet?

◎中譯

這位女士的寵物發生了什麼事？
a）牠死了。
b）某人把牠偷走了。
c）牠飛走了。
d）牠生病了。

◎解析

對話中提到 ... left my window open and
he got out（窗戶沒關，牠就飛出去了），
故選 c）。

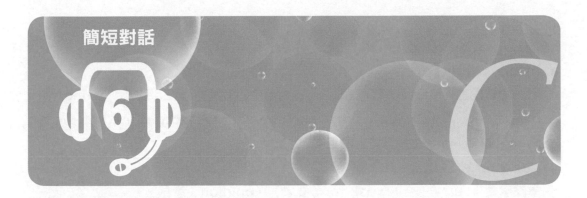

朋友之間的相處

 學習重點

朋友相處時難免會因為對方心情不佳,而有意見相左(disagreement)的情況,例如剛與男友分手(break up)的 Mary 詢問朋友有關穿著的問題,因為心情敏感易怒(sensitive),與友人發生爭執,而引發以下的對話。

 情境介紹及導引

Fred is telling his wife about their friend Mary, who recently broke up with her boyfriend. Mary has been in a bad mood and gets overly sensitive about other people's comments. Today Mary wore a new dress and asked Fred how she looked. Fred was surprised when Mary got mad at him.

範例 🎧 C-11

在簡短對話裡,你會聽到兩個人(通常是一男一女)的交談,接著再依據談話內容,找出 Mary 做了什麼事情。

M:What was wrong with my saying that Mary's dress didn't suit her?

W:You know how sensitive she's been since John broke up with her.

M:Well, she asked for my honest opinion. I don't think she should have gotten mad at me for that.

What did Mary do?(Mary 做了什麼事?)

_____

a)Broke up with the man.(跟這位男士分手了。)

b)Agreed with the man's comment.(同意男士的意見。)

c)Got angry at the man.(生這位男士的氣。)

d)Complained about the woman.(抱怨這位女士。)

答案:c)

a. Information Focus

問題的重點是「Mary 做了什麼事」，從對話中的關鍵句 "What was wrong with my saying…"、"I don't think she should have gotten mad at me for that." 得知 Mary 生這位男士的氣。

b. Language Skills

重點字彙：suit（適合）、ask for（要求）、opinion（意見）。

說明某件事情有誤：something ＋ is / was ＋ wrong with ＋ 事物

認為某人不應如此作為：I don't think ＋ 人 ＋ should have ＋ V-p.p.

c. Tips for Listening

在英文對話中提到人名（如 Mary），後面的內容通常會以代名詞（she, her）來替代，尤其非母語人士對於代名詞性別常會混淆（如 he or she, his or her），熟悉一些外國人名及其代表的性別，有助於聽懂談話內容。

🎧 練習題　C-12

請聽以下的對話題，並回答相關的問題。

1 _____

a) She is kind.　　　　　　　　b) She is polite.

c) She works very hard.　　　　d) She talks too much.

2 _____

a) He reads the news on the Internet.

b) He subscribes to the newspaper.

c) He reads news magazines.

d) He watches the morning and evening news.

3 _____

a) He almost never studied.　　　b) He was a hard-working student.

c) He was an important person.　 d) He always read novels.

詳解

1

◎解答

d) She talks too much.
（她太多話了。）

◎聽力原文

M : I know you aren't getting along with Lucy, but please don't be so obvious about it.

W : It's really hard to be polite when she is so talkative and I'm buried in my work.

M : I understand. I'll talk to her this afternoon about it.

How does the woman feel about Lucy?

◎中譯

男士：我知道你和 Lucy 處不來，但也請不要那麼明顯嘛。

女士：當我埋首忙於工作而她講話卻滔滔不絕時，要對她有禮貌真的很難。

男士：我了解，今天下午我會找她談談這個問題。

這位女士對 Lucy 的看法為何？
a) 她很和善。
b) 她很有禮貌。
c) 她工作很努力。
d) 她太多話了。

◎解析

關鍵句為 ... It's really hard to be polite when she is so talkative and I'm buried in work ... ，可知 Lucy 讓人受不了的地方是她太多話，故答案選 d ）。

2

◎解答

a) He reads the news on the Internet.
（他在網路上看新聞。）

◎聽力原文

W : Mike is really up on things. He always seems to know what's going on.

M : He must read the newspaper every day or at least read some magazines.

W : Actually, he told me he goes to a website every night and every morning. It gives him all he needs.

How does Mike keep up with current events?

◎中譯

女士：Mike 真的很熟悉各種事物。他似乎總是知道發生了什麼狀況。

男士：他一定是每天看報紙，不然至少看了一些雜誌。

女士：事實上，他告訴我他每天晚上和早上都會瀏覽網頁，提供他所需的所有資訊。

Mike 是如何得知時事？
a) 他在網路上看新聞。
b) 他訂閱報紙。
c) 他閱讀新聞雜誌。
d) 他看晨間和夜間的電視新聞。

◎解析

關鍵句為 ...he goes to a website every night and every morning... ，表示 Mike 透過網路得知各種最新資訊，不是透過報紙或雜誌、電視等其他媒體，故答案選 a ）最貼切。

3

◎解答

b) He was a hard-working student.

（他是個用功的學生。）

◎聽力原文

M : I wonder whatever happened to my college friend George?

W : Isn't he the one who we called "The Bookman" because he never stopped studying?

M : Yeah, him. He must be somebody important by now.

Why did the man's friend have a nickname?

◎中譯

男士：我在想我的大學同學 George 現在不知道如何了？

女士：他不就是那個以前那個不停念書，被我們稱作「書蟲」的人嗎？

男士：是啊，就是他。他現在應該是個重要的大人物了。

為什麼這位男士的朋友有個綽號？

a) 他幾乎不曾讀書。

b) 他是個用功的學生。

c) 他曾經是個大人物。

d) 他總是讀小說。

◎解析

關鍵句是 ...The one who we called "The Bookman" because he never stopped studying...，可知那位朋友因為愛念書而有「書蟲」的綽號，表示他很用功（hard-working），所以選 b ）。

參加課程、社團或競賽

🎧 學習重點

在學校常有機會參加各種社團（club）或是競賽（tournament），以參加競賽為例，通常都會有參加規定（entry requirements），想參加且符合規定的人必須報名登記（sign up），如此才方便主辦單位統計人數、規畫賽程（competition schedule）。

🎧 情境介紹及導引

Darren and Elsie are officers of the school tennis club and responsible for planning this year's tennis tournament. Two weeks before the event, only three people have signed up. Darren is wondering whether the new, strict entry requirements have turned off potential players.

在簡短對話裡，你會聽到兩個人（通常是一男一女）的交談，接著再依據談話的內容，找出登記人數很少的原因。

M：Last time I checked, there were only three people who had signed up for the tennis tournament next month.

W：Is that so? Don't worry. There will be more people signing up this weekend and a lot more the next weekend.

M：I think a lot of people are turned off by the new, stricter entry requirements.

Why does the man think only three people signed up?
（這位男士為何認為只有三個人報名登記？）

a) The tournament isn't free.（這項比賽並非免費的。）

b) It's too late to enter.（來不及參加。）

c) It's their turn.（這回輪到他們了。）

d) The entry rules are tougher.（參加規則更嚴格了。）　　答案：d)

🎧 說明

a. Information Focus

問題的重點是「男士認為登記人數很少的原因」，從男士的對話 "I think a lot of people are turned off by the new, stricter entry requirements." 得知是因為參賽規則變嚴格了。

b. Language Skills

其他字彙：tennis tournament（網球錦標賽）、be turned off（在此意指「被刷掉」參賽資格）、strict / tough（嚴格的）、potential player（可能的參賽選手）。

c. Tips for Listening

此題目的是問 "why"，正確的回應是說明原因及理由；請注意題目與答案中相同字義的字彙，如 strict 與 tough，rule 與 requirement。

 練習題　🎧C-14

請聽以下的對話題，並回答相關的問題。

1 _____

a) So he can use his old computer.　　b) He has a lot of time.

c) He is having trouble with his computer.　　d) The new computer is free.

2 _____

a) She thinks it is too difficult.　　b) She can't speak Spanish.

c) She does not have enough time.　　d) She thinks it is fun.

3 _____

a) He is afraid of meeting new people.　　b) Dancing is too complicated.

c) He hasn't danced in a long time.　　d) Dance lessons are so expensive.

詳解

1

◎解答

c) He is having trouble with his computer.（他有電腦上的問題。）

◎聽力原文

M：This new computer is really hard to use. I like the old one better.

W：Why don't you sign up for one of the free computer classes? They're very helpful.

M：I'd like to, but I just don't have the time.

For what reason should the man take computer classes?

◎中譯

男士：這臺新電腦真的很不順手。我比較喜歡舊的那臺。

女士：何不報名一堂免費的電腦課呢？那些課程很有幫助喔！

男士：我很想啊，只是沒有時間。

為什麼這位男士必須上電腦課？

a) 如此他可以使用他的舊電腦。

b) 他有很多時間。

c) 他有電腦上的問題。

d) 新電腦是免費的。

◎解析

由對話內容可知，男士抱怨新電腦不好用，所以要上電腦課學習新電腦的使用方式，故選 c)。

2

◎解答

a) She thinks it is too difficult.（她認為太困難了。）

◎聽力原文

M：Why don't we take a Spanish class together? There is one being offered at the community center.

W：I'd like to, but I heard it's really hard, and there is a lot of studying. Those things put me off.

M：Really? From what I heard, it's fun and not too hard at all.

Why is the woman reluctant to take the class?

◎中譯

男士：我們何不一起去上西班牙文課？社區中心現在有開班。

女士：我很想，但我聽說那真的很難，而且功課很重。那會讓我卻步。

男士：真的嗎？但我聽說很有趣，而且一點也不難學啊。

為什麼這位女士不願意去上課？

a) 她認為太困難了。

b) 她不會說西班牙文。

c) 她沒有足夠的時間。

d) 她認為很有趣。

◎解析

根據女士提到的 really hard（很困難）、a lot of studying（功課很重），可知不願意參加的原因是聽說課程太難，故選 a)。

◎解答

c) He hasn't danced in a long time.

（他很久沒有跳了。）

◎聽力原文

M : You want me to take dance lessons? You must be crazy. I haven't danced in years!

W : Relax. This is a perfect chance for you to meet new people.

M : Well. OK. I'll take some lessons.

Why is the man hesitant?

◎中譯

男士：你要我去上舞蹈課？你一定是瘋了。 我好幾年沒跳舞了！

女士：放輕鬆。這是個讓你認識新朋友的絕 佳機會。

男士：嗯，好吧。我會上幾堂課看看。

這位男士為何遲疑？

a) 他害怕認識新朋友。

b) 跳舞實在太複雜了。

c) 他很久沒有跳了。

d) 舞蹈課程太昂貴。

◎解析

關鍵在第一段最後的 ...I haven't danced in years...，可以知道男士感到猶豫的原因 是 c)。

喜歡的童年活動

 學習重點

許多人喜歡的童年回憶（favorite childhood memory）通常都是跟家人一起度過的（spend time with the family），不過有的人比較喜歡獨處或跟朋友在一起（alone by oneself or with one's friends），以下的對話就是探討這個主題。

 情境介紹及導引

On their first date, Joy and Ivan went to see a movie about childhood memories. To make conversations after the movie, Ivan decided to ask Joy about the things she enjoyed doing when she was young. Remembering the past and sharing their favorite memories will help them get to know each other better.

範例 C-15

在簡短對話裡，你會聽到兩個人（通常是一男一女）的交談，接著再依據談話的內容，找出男士喜愛的童年時光。

M：What's your favorite childhood memory?

W：I remember that my favorite times as a child were just being with my family.

M：I love my family, but when I was young, the best times I had were alone by myself or with my friends.

W：Yeah, I guess boys will always be boys. Not me though. There was nothing I would rather do than get in the car and go somewhere and spend the whole day with my family.

M：We used to do that a lot, too. We'd also have barbecues.

W:Well, we used to enjoy our family cookouts as well, but that was nothing compared to the fun we had at the beach. I can't think of anywhere I liked to go more when I was growing up.

What were the best times for the man in his childhood?
（何者是男士童年中最好的時光？）

_____

a）When he was with his family.（他與家人在一起的時候。）
b）When he went to the movies.（他去看電影的時候。）
c）When he was alone.（他獨處的時候。）
d）When he was in the car.（他在車子裡的時候。）　　　　答案：c）

🎧 說明

a. Information Focus

問題的重點是「男士童年裡最好的時光」，從男士的對話 "...when I was young, the best times I had were alone by myself..." 得知答案是獨處的時候。

b. Language Skills

重點字彙：favorite（特別喜歡的）、childhood（童年時期）、memory（回憶）、remember（記得）、alone by myself（獨處）。

c. Tips for Listening

本段對話的聽力重點是「最喜歡的事物」：favorite / best ＋ 事物。

 練習題　C-16

請聽以下的對話題，並回答相關的問題。

1.1 _____　承接範例題，再聽一次，回答以下 2 題。

a）Their family members.
b）Their favorite dishes.
c）Their favorite childhood memories.
d）Their hobbies.

1.2 _____

a) At barbecue restaurants.

b) At the beach.

c) In her father's car.

d) At the man's house.

2.1 _____ 請聽對話 **2**，回答以下 2 題。

a) A movie.

b) Their teacher in high school.

c) A dance drama.

d) Their childhood dreams.

2.2 _____

a) A ballerina.

b) A nurse.

c) A teacher.

d) An actress.

1

◎聽力原文

M : What's your favorite childhood memory?

W : I remember that my favorite times as a child were just being with my family.

M : I love my family, but when I was young, the best times I had were alone by myself or with my friends.

W : Yeah, I guess boys will always be boys. Not me though. There was nothing I would rather do than get in the car and go somewhere and spend the whole day with my family.

M : We used to do that a lot, too. We'd also have barbecues.

W : Well, we used to enjoy our family cookouts as well, but that was nothing compared to the fun we had at the beach. I can't think of anywhere I liked to go more when I was growing up.

◎中譯

男士：什麼事情是你最美好的童年回憶？

女士：我記得小時候最美好的時光就是和家人相處的時刻。

男士：我愛我的家人，但年輕的時候，我擁有過最好的時光是獨處或和朋友在一起。

女士：是啊，我想男孩永遠是男孩。我卻相反。對我來說，沒有比坐車到某個地方，然後花一整天時間跟家人在一起

更棒的了。

男士：我們以前也經常那樣，甚至還會烤肉。

女士：我們以前也很喜歡家庭戶外野炊，但比不上去海灘好玩。我想不出從小還有什麼是比海灘讓我更喜歡去的地方。

1.1

◎解答

c) Their favorite childhood memories.（他們最喜歡的童年回憶。）

◎聽力原文

What are the speakers talking about?

◎中譯

說話者在談論什麼？

a) 他們的家庭成員。

b) 他們最愛的料理。

c) 他們最喜歡的童年回憶。

d) 他們的嗜好。

◎解析

關鍵句在第一句 ...What's your favorite childhood memory?...，詢問的是最喜歡的童年回憶，所以選 c)。

1.2

◎解答

b) At the beach.（在海邊。）

◎聽力原文

Where did the woman have the most fun?

◎中譯

女士在哪裡玩得最開心？

a) 在烤肉餐廳。

b) 在海邊。

c）在她父親的車裡。

d）在男士的家中。

◎解析

對話的關鍵句是 ...but that was nothing compared to the fun we had at the beach...，強調海邊是她認為最好玩的地方，故選 b）。

2

◎聽力原文

M：What did you want to be when you were a little girl? A ballerina?

W：Not all girls want to do that. I didn't anyway.

M：I just said that because most little girls want to be ballerinas or nurses or actresses.

W：I did think about entertainment, but I mostly wanted to work with children.

M：You mean like teaching them to read and write and watching them learn?

W：Exactly. I would have loved to teach.

◎中譯

男士：當妳還是小女孩的時候，妳最想成為什麼樣的人？一位芭蕾舞者嗎？

女士：並不是每個女孩都想當芭蕾舞者。我就不想。

男士：我會這麼說，是因為多數的女孩不是想當芭蕾舞者，就是想當護士或女演員。

女士：我確實想過娛樂事業，但我還是比較傾向從事和兒童有關的工作。

男士：妳是指像教他們讀書寫字、看著他們學習的工作嗎？

女士：沒錯！我喜歡教書。

2.1

◎解答

d）Their childhood dreams.

（他們童年的夢想。）

◎聽力原文

What are the speakers talking about?

◎中譯

說話者在談論什麼？

a）一部電影。

b）他們的高中老師。

c）一部歌舞劇。

d）他們童年的夢想。

◎解析

關鍵在開頭的問句 What did you want to be when you were a little girl?，兩人接著討論女士小時候夢想成為的人，所以答案選 d）。

2.2

◎解答

c）A teacher.（一位老師。）

◎聽力原文

What most likely did the woman want to be when she was small?

◎中譯

這位女士小時候最希望成為什麼？

a）一位芭蕾舞者。

b）一位護士。

c）一位老師。

d）一位女演員。

◎解析

關鍵在最後一句，女士提到 ...I would have loved to teach...（我喜歡教書），所以答案選 c）最適當。

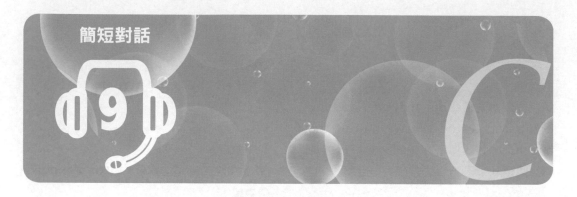

簡短對話

師長之間的對話

 學習重點

學校師長之間的對話主題通常都圍繞在所教授的課程（courses）、學生的課業（schoolwork）、上大學（go on to college）、或是自己的研究及著作（research & writing），例如某人詢問一位校長有關學校升學的狀況，而有以下對話。

 情境介紹及導引

Kevin and Lynette ran into each other at a party. As they were catching up, Lynette learned that Kevin runs a high school known for its advanced courses and impressive records of college admission.

範 例 C-17

在簡短對話裡，你會聽到兩個人（通常是一男一女）的交談，接著再依據談話的內容，找出男士的身分。

W：How many of your students are going on to college?

M：Nearly half of them.

W：That's impressive. You run a good school.

What is the man's occupation?（這位男士的職業為何？）

_____

a）High school principal.（高中校長。）

b）High school teacher.（高中教師。）

c）College dean.（大學教務長。）

d）University president.（大學校長。）

答案：a）

a. Information Focus

問題的重點是「男士的職業」，從對話裡的 "...your students are going on to college?"、" You run a good school. " 得知男士是高中校長。

b. Language Skills

重點字彙：college（大學，學院）、run（經營）、impressive（令人印象深刻的）、principal / president（校長）、dean（教務長，院長）、admission（進入許可）。

c. Tips for Listening

通常從對話中的第一句可以大致判別出雙方的身分或關係，例如本題的第一句話，大致可以知道這位男士是學校的老師或校長；但是從女士的回應（ "You run a good school." ）才能判斷出這位男士是校長。

🎧 練習題　C-18

請聽以下的對話題，並回答相關的問題。

1 _____

a) Become the athletic director.   b) Coach a football team.

c) Take a vacation.   d) Become the basketball coach.

2 _____

a) He can't think of a good opening.

b) He is too busy to write a book.

c) He is having a hard time with the ending.

d) He is stuck in the office finishing work.

3 _____

a) It helps the students learn about science.

b) It is required for getting accepted to university.

c) It is a great way to learn English.

d) It is a skill they will need in college.

1

◎解答

d）Become the basketball coach.
（當籃球教練。）

◎聽力原文

W：I hear you will coach the girl's basketball team this season.

M：Yeah. I usually coach football, but the old coach just quit and the athletic director begged me to help out this year.

W：That's really nice of you because I know you were planning to take a long vacation this year.

What is the man going to do?

◎中譯

女士：我聽說你這一季會擔任女籃隊的教練。

男士：是啊。我通常都是帶足球隊。但因為之前的教練請辭，所以體育主任請我今年先幫忙。

女士：你人真好啊！據我所知，你原本打算今年要休長假的。

男士將要做什麼？

a）成為體育主任。

b）當足球教練。

c）休假。

d）當籃球教練。

◎解析

開頭女士對男士說 I hear you will coach the girl's basketball team.，而男士給予肯定的回應，所以應選 d）。

2

◎解答

c）He is having a hard time with the ending.
（他在結尾部份遇到困難。）

◎聽力原文

W：How is that book you are writing coming along?

M：I've gotten most of it finished, but I'm stuck on how to finish it.

W：I can read what you have so far and help you with the rest.

What is the man's problem?

◎中譯

女士：你正在寫的書進展如何？

男士：大部份已經完成，但是卡在不知道該如何結尾。

女士：讓我先讀目前你已經完成的部份，然後幫你完成其餘的部份。

男士的問題是什麼？

a）他不知道如何起頭。

b）他忙得沒有時間寫書。

c）他在結尾部份遇到困難。

d）他守在辦公室裡把工作完成。

◎解析

選項 c）的 have a hard time with（遇到……的困難）對應了對話中的 be stuck on（困住）；the ending（結尾）則對應 finish（完成），因此 c）最符合題意。

◎解答

d）It is a skill they will need in college.

（是學生在大學時必需用到的技能。）

◎聽力原文

M：Are the students learning to write research papers OK?

W：Yes, they are. Only they don't see the importance of it.

M：Wait until they go to college, then they'll know.

Why does the man think learning to write research papers is important?

◎中譯

男士：學生們正在學習寫研究報告，沒問題吧？

女士：是的，沒問題。只是他們還不了解寫報告的重要性。

男士：等到上了大學，他們就會明白了。

為何男士認為學習寫研究報告是很重要的事？

a）可幫助學生在科學方面的學習。

b）是學生取得大學入學許可時必備的。

c）是學習英文的好方法。

d）是學生在大學時必需用到的技能。

◎解析

對於女士提到學生不了解寫報告的重要性，男士回應 "Wait until they go to college, then they'll know."，可知 d）是正確答案。

簡短對話

選擇餐廳

 學習重點

選擇去那裡用餐,通常是依照個人的喜好而定,例如有的人偏愛牛排(steak),有的人喜歡素食(vegetarian cuisine),或是印度咖哩(Indian curry)。

情境介紹及導引

When people go out for dinner, they usually discuss what they want to eat before deciding where to go. Some people like to eat steak while others prefer vegetarian cuisine. If curry is among your personal favorites, you can choose between Indian and Japanese restaurants.

範例   C-19

在簡短對話裡,你會聽到兩個人(通常是一男一女)的交談,接著再依據談話的內容,找出晚餐的地點。

M:Want to go out for dinner tonight?

W:That sounds great.

M:What do you want to eat?

W:I haven't had steak in a while.

M:But I don't like meat.

W:Well, what about Indian food?

M:Yeah, I like Indian food.

W:There is a great curry house nearby.

M:But isn't that Japanese curry?

W:No, it's an Indian curry restaurant.

M:Really? That sounds delicious. Just lead the way.

Where will they eat dinner tonight?（他們今晚會在哪吃飯？）

_____

a）At home.（在家裡。）
b）At a Japanese eatery.（在日本飯館。）
c）At a steak house.（在牛排館。）
d）At an Indian restaurant.（在印度餐廳。）   答案：d）

🎧 說明

a. Information Focus
問題的重點是「晚餐的地點」，從對話裡的 "it's an Indian curry restaurant...
That sounds delicious. Just lead the way." 得知他們會去印度餐廳。

b. Language Skills
其他字彙：in a while（有一段時間）、delicious（美味的）、lead the way（帶
　　　　　路）。

c. Tips for Listening
在對話中有些字彙是表示語氣的轉折，例如 but, well, yeah, no，通常是表達贊
同或否定的看法。

 練習題　C-20

請聽以下的對話題，並回答相關的問題。

1.1 _____　請聽對話 ❶，回答以下 2 題。

a）The restaurant was not open yet.
b）It went out of business.
c）It was under renovation.
d）It changed its menu.

1.2 _____

a）At a Mexican restaurant.
b）At a Chinese restaurant.
c）At an American restaurant.
d）At a hot dog stand.

2 _____

a) In their room.

b) At Antonio's.

c) At a Russian restaurant.

d) At a Chinese restaurant.

3 _____

a) She doesn't like spicy food.

b) She likes eating at home.

c) The food is too oily.

d) The restaurant is too expensive.

詳解

1

◎聽力原文

W：We'd better decide which restaurant we're going to before lunchtime.

M：OK, I vote for hot dogs. We can go to the hot dog stand near the park.

W：No, that place closed down. Let's go have a hamburger.

M：So you want to eat fast food, huh? Let's go have Mexican food.

W：Mexican food always gives me an upset stomach.

M：Would you like to have Chinese?

W：Why don't we go to an American restaurant?

M：That sounds fine to me.

◎中譯

女士：我們最好在午休時間以前決定要去哪間餐廳？

男士：沒問題，我投熱狗一票。我們可以去公園附近的熱狗攤。

女士：不，那個地方關門大吉了。我們改吃漢堡吧。

男士：所以，你是想吃速食？那我們去吃墨西哥料理吧。

女士：墨西哥食物總是讓我肚子不舒服。

男士：那你想吃中國菜嗎？

女士：我們何不去美式餐廳？

男士：聽來還不錯。

1.1

◎解答

b）It went out of business.
（它倒閉了。）

◎聽力原文

What happened to the hot dog stand?

◎中譯

熱狗攤怎麼了？

a）那間餐廳尚未開幕。

b）它倒閉了。

c）它正在裝修中。

d）它換菜單了。

◎解析

由女士的回答 "No, that place closed down" 可知，那間餐廳已經關門大吉，故選 b）。

1.2

◎解答

c）At an American restaurant.
（美式餐廳。）

◎聽力原文

Where do they want to have lunch?

◎中譯

他們想去哪裡吃午餐？

a）墨西哥餐廳。

b）中國餐館。

c）美式餐廳。

d）熱狗攤。

◎解析

對話最後兩句中，女士提議去美式餐廳，男士也給予正面回應，所以結論是 c）。

2

◎解答

b）At Antonio's.
（在安東尼奧餐廳。）

M：The guidebook recommends we go to Antonio's if we want Italian.

W：That's fine with me, unless you want to get Chinese or order some room service.

M：I'm not really in the mood for Chinese, and I want to go out tonight.

Where are they likely to have dinner?

◎中譯

男士：旅遊書建議我們如果想吃義大利菜的話，可以到安東尼奧餐廳。

女士：我可以啊，除非你想點中國菜或是叫客房服務的餐點。

男士：我不是很想吃中國菜，而且今晚我想出去吃。

他們可能會去哪裡吃晚餐？

a）在房間內。

b）在安東尼奧餐廳。

c）在俄羅斯餐廳。

d）在中國餐館。

◎解析

男士一開始便提議去旅遊書推薦的義大利餐廳，又提到想外出用餐，但不想吃中國菜，所以答案選 b）。

3

◎解答

d）The restaurant is too expensive.（那間餐廳太貴了。）

◎聽力原文

M：Do you have any ideas about where we should eat tonight? I was thinking about El Taco Grande, if you don't mind spicy food.

W：I like the place, but it's a little pricey. Is there any other place you can think of?

M：We could order a pizza. That's all I can think of for now.

Why does the woman NOT want to go to the restaurant?

◎中譯

男士：對於我們今晚要去哪吃飯，妳有沒有什麼想法呢？我在考慮去 El Taco Grande，如果你不介意辣的食物。

女士：我喜歡那個地方，但有點貴。你想得到其他的地方嗎？

男士：我們可以叫比薩。我現在只能想到這個。

為什麼女士不想去那間餐廳？

a）她不喜歡辣的食物。

b）她喜歡在家吃。

c）那家食物太油。

d）那間餐廳太貴了。

◎解析

由對話中女士的回答 "I like the place, but it's a little pricey." 可知，她不想去的原因是那家餐廳消費太高了，故答案選 d）。選項 a）的 spicy 和 pricey 發音相近，勿混淆。

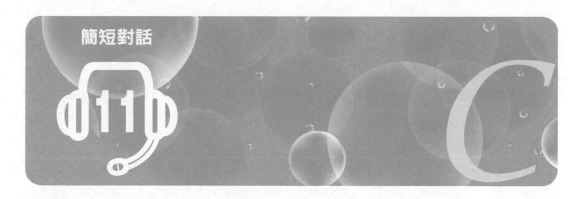

C

點餐

 學習重點

外出用餐總是需要先點餐（order a meal），通常在較正式的餐廳會有侍者（waiter）服務客人，餐點的種類包括開胃菜（appetizer）、主菜（main course）、附菜（side order），有時還會加上飲料（drink/ beverage）或甜點（dessert）。

 情境介紹及導引

A Western meal usually consists of several courses. To start, diners order a drink and an appetizer plate which may contain seafood, such as shrimp, crab, or calamari, and finger food such as cheese or nachos. After the main course, desserts are served to complete the meal.

範 例 C-21

在簡短對話裡，你會聽到兩個人（通常是一男一女）的交談，接著再依據談話的內容，找出女士在做什麼。

M：Would you like to start with an order of nachos?

W：Sounds good, but today we're thinking of the calamari.

M：Good choice, and might I also recommend the potato skins?

What is the woman doing?（這位女士在做什麼？）

_____

a）Ordering a meal.（點餐。）

b）Cooking.（烹飪。）

c）Eating.（用餐。）

d）Buying cookbooks.（買烹飪書。）

答案：a）

a. Information Focus

問題的重點是「女士在做什麼」，從對話裡的 "...start with an order..."、 "...recommend the potato skins." 得知女士是在餐廳點菜。

b. Language Skills

重點字彙：order（「點」餐）、nacho（墨西哥玉米片）、calamari（花枝）、 choice（選擇）、recommend（推薦）。

客氣的詢問對方是否要做某事：Would you like to ＋ V

c. Tips for Listening

對話中的 nachos 及 calamari 屬於較陌生的字彙，即使聽不懂仍然可以從 would you like, might I recommend 等客氣用語，及重點字彙如 start with an order, potato，推知這是餐廳中服務生與客人的對話。

🎧 練習題　C-22

請聽以下的對話題，並回答相關的問題。

1 ＿＿＿＿＿＿＿

a) Waiting in a restaurant.

b) Buying airplane tickets.

c) Sitting in a movie theater lobby.

d) Smoking a cigarette.

2 ＿＿＿＿＿＿＿

a) If the chef has any experience.

b) If there are dishes that contain meat and vegetables.

c) If there are any daily specials.

d) If the chef can make a dish with no meat.

3 ＿＿＿＿＿＿＿

a) His driving was bad.

b) He was very rude.

c) He was late.

d) He brought the wrong pizza.

11 詳解

1

◎解答

a）Waiting in a restaurant.
（在餐廳等候。）

◎聽力原文

M：I wonder what's taking so long. We've been waiting for half an hour.

W：The headwaiter said it would take a little longer if we wanted to sit in the nonsmoking section.

M：I hope it's worth the wait.

What are the man and woman doing?

◎中譯

男士：我很疑惑為什麼要這麼久。我們已經等了半小時了耶。

女士：領班服務生說，如果我們想坐在非吸菸區就得等稍微久一點。

男士：我希望這個等待是值得的。

這位男士和女士在做什麼？

a）在餐廳等候。

b）在買機票。

c）坐在電影院的大廳。

d）在抽菸。

◎解析

對話中的 waiting （等待）、headwaiter（領班服務生）和 nonsmoking section（非吸菸區）等關鍵字，可以得知答案應選 a）。

2

◎解答

d）If the chef can make a dish with no meat.
（主廚是否能做一道不含肉的餐點。）

◎聽力原文

M：Excuse me. I'm a vegetarian, and there doesn't seem to be anything on the menu that...

W：If you could wait one moment, I'll go ask the chef what he can do for you.

M：I'd appreciate that.

What will the woman ask the chef?

◎中譯

男士：抱歉，我吃素，但這菜單上似乎沒有任何素餐……

女士：如果您可以稍候一下，我馬上去問主廚看他能為您做什麼餐點。

男士：喔，謝謝。

這位女士會問主廚什麼問題？

a）主廚是否有任何經驗。

b）是否有葷素皆含的菜色。

c）是否有每日特餐。

d）主廚是否能做一道素菜。

◎解析

男士一開始便說自己是 vegetarian（素食者），所以女士會為他詢問主廚能否製作素食的餐點，故答案選 d）。

◎解答

c）He was late.

（他遲到了。）

◎聽力原文

M：Hello, did someone order a large pepperoni pizza?

W：Yes, I did. Frankly, I thought it would be here a while ago.

M：I'm sorry. There was a traffic accident a few blocks away.

Why did the woman complain to the man?

◎中譯

男士：您好，請問有人點了一份大的義大利香腸比薩嗎？

女士：有，是我點的。坦白說，我還以為老早之前就會送到的。

男士：抱歉，因為幾個街區外發生了交通事故。

為何這位女士要向男士抱怨？

a）他的開車技術欠佳。

b）他非常粗魯無禮。

c）他遲到了。

d）他送錯比薩。

◎解析

從女士抱怨的關鍵句 "I thought it would be here a while ago."（我還以為老早之前就會送到的），以及男士的道歉及原因說明，可知答案為 c）。

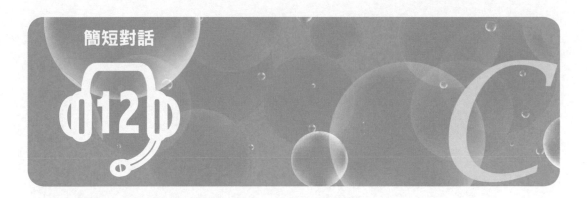

簡短對話 12

喜愛的娛樂活動

 學習重點

許多人喜愛去遊樂園或主題公園（amusement park/ theme park），乘坐驚險刺激的遊樂設施（thrill rides），例如像是摩天輪（Ferris wheel）、雲霄飛車（roller coaster）、自由落體（freefall）、碰碰車（bumper cars）等。

 情境介紹及導引

Most people, young and old alike, enjoy going to amusement parks. The parks provide many attractions from thrill rides such as freefall and roller coasters, to rides for young children such as Ferris wheels, carousels, and bumper cars. For a scary experience, don't miss the haunted house.

範例 **C-23**

在簡短對話裡，你會聽到兩個人（通常是一男一女）的交談，接著再依據談話的內容，找出談話的主題。

M : What's that you've got there?

W : These are the pictures from my trip to the amusement park.

M : I guess you had a good time.

W : It was great. I rode my favorite ride.

M : Oh, so you like the thrill rides, do you?

W : No, they're so scary.

M : Well, how about the carousel?

W : OK, I did like the carousel when I was a little girl, but now I like the Ferris wheel much better.

M：Oh? Why is that?

W：Well, you can see the whole park, and at night, the lights are really pretty.

What is this talk mainly about?（這段對話主要在談什麼？）

_____

a）The woman's photography skills.（女士的攝影技術。）

b）A thrilling movie.（一部恐怖片。）

c）Amusement rides.（遊樂園的遊樂設施。）

d）Horse riding experiences.（騎馬經驗。）

答案：c）

 說明

a. Information Focus

問題的重點是「談話的主題」，從對話的關鍵字 amusement park、favorite ride、thrill rides、carousel 得知他們是在談論遊樂園的遊樂設施。

b. Language Skills

其他字彙：favorite（鍾愛的）、scary（可怕的）、carousel（旋轉木馬）、haunted house（鬼屋）。

c. Tips for Listening

本段聽力以遊樂園為談論主題，跟遊樂園相關的字彙如 amusement park, ride, carousel, Ferris wheel，都需要熟悉其發音。

練習題　C-24

請聽以下的對話題，並回答相關的問題。

1 _____ 承接範例題，再聽一次，回答以下問題。

a）Carousel.

b）Horseback riding.

c）Thrill rides.

d）Ferris wheel.

2 _____

a) Swimming is not good for knees.

b) Yoga is a good way to keep in shape.

c) The woman doesn't exercise at the moment.

d) Jogging works well, depending on the person.

3 _____

a) He wants to get work done in the morning.

b) He doesn't like late sleepers.

c) He wants to wake up more easily.

d) He likes to work out before his job.

範 例 & 1

◎聽力原文

M：What's that you've got there?

W：These are the pictures from my trip to the amusement park.

M：I guess you had a good time.

W：It was great. I rode my favorite ride.

M：Oh, so you like the thrill rides, do you?

W：No, they're so scary.

M：Well, how about the carousel?

W：Ok, I did like the carousel when I was a little girl, but now I like the Ferris wheel much better.

M：Oh? Why is that?

W：Well, you can see the whole park, and at night, the lights are really pretty.

◎中譯

男士：妳拿的是什麼？

女士：這些是我去遊樂園玩的照片。

男士：我想妳一定玩得很開心吧。

女士：是啊，超開心的！我坐了我最愛的遊樂設施。

男士：喔，所以說妳喜歡驚險刺激的遊樂設施，對吧？

女士：才不是，那超恐怖的！

男士：嗯……，那旋轉木馬如何？

女士：當我還是個小女孩時我的確很喜歡旋轉木馬，但現在比較喜歡摩天輪。

男士：喔？為什麼呢？

女士：因為可以看到整個遊樂園，而且到了晚上，那些燈光真好漂亮！

1

◎解答

d）Ferris wheel.（摩天輪）

◎聽力原文

Which ride does the woman prefer?

◎中譯

這位女士偏好哪一種遊樂設施呢？

a）旋轉木馬

b）騎馬

c）刺激的遊樂設施

d）摩天輪

◎解析

由對話中女士的回答 ...but now I like the Ferris wheel much better... 可知，她最喜歡的是摩天輪。

2

◎解答

b）Yoga is a good way to keep in shape.（瑜珈是保持窈窕的好方法。）

◎聽力原文

M：You look great. Are you still jogging and swimming to stay in shape?

W：Actually, jogging made my knees sore, and I didn't like driving all the way to the pool so I started taking a yoga class. It's really working well for me.

M：I can tell. I heard that yoga was good exercise, and now I know it's true.

What did the man find out?

男士：嗯，我喜歡上班前做點運動。

為何男士要如此早起？

a）他希望早上就能把工作完成。

b）他不喜歡晚睡的人。

c）他希望更快醒過來。

d）他喜歡在上班前運動健身。

◎解析

work out 在此指「運動；健身」，意思同 exercise，男士最後一句話說明了早起的原因是，故答案選 d）。

◎中譯

男士：妳看起來很不賴喔。妳還是靠慢跑和游泳保持窈窕的好身材嗎？

女士：其實慢跑會讓我的膝蓋痠痛，而我也不喜歡一路開車到游泳池，所以我開始上瑜珈課，那真的對我很有幫助。

男士：我看得出來。聽說瑜珈是很好的運動，現在我才知道果真如此！

這位男士發現什麼？

a）游泳對膝蓋不好。

b）瑜珈是保持窈窕的好方法。

c）這位女士現在不做任何運動。

d）慢跑效果良好，但因人而異。

◎解析

對話中女士提到 yoga class「瑜伽課」，男士回應 ...I heard that yoga was good exercise, and now I know it's true...，所以 d）是正確描述。in shape 指「健康；體態良好」。

3

◎解答

d）He likes to work out before his job.（他喜歡在上班前運動健身。）

◎聽力原文

M : I usually wake up around 6:00 in the morning.

W : That is much too early for me.

M : Well, I like to exercise a bit before work.

Why does the man wake up so early?

◎中譯

男士：我通常早上六點起床。

女士：那對我來說有點太早了。

預約住宿、餐廳

學習重點

出外旅遊或用餐時常需要先預約（make a reservation），以旅館住宿為例，預約的主要事項包括登記預約的名字，房型種類（single or double），住宿天數（two nights），為了保險起見，住宿前一天最好再跟旅館確認一次（reconfirm）。

情境介紹及導引

John is in Las Vegas for a convention. A month ago, John asked the travel agent to make a hotel reservation for him. He needs a single room for two nights under the name of Grant. Yesterday, he called the hotel and confirmed his reservation. Now he is ready to check in.

範例 C-25

在簡短對話裡，你會聽到兩個人（通常是一男一女）的交談，接著再依據談話的內容，找出男士做了什麼樣的預約。

M : I have a reservation for Grant; a single, for two nights.

W : I'm sorry sir, but I have no reservation under the name of Grant.

M : Are you sure? I just called and reconfirmed my reservations yesterday.

What did the man reserve?（男士預約了什麼？）

_____

a）A car.（一輛車。）

b）A seat on a plane.（機位。）

c）A table at a restaurant.（餐廳位子。）

d）A hotel room.（旅館房間。） 答案：d）

a. Information Focus

問題的重點是「預約的項目」，從對話的關鍵字 a single、two nights 得知，只有旅館住宿才會提到這類字彙。

b. Language Skills

重點字彙：reservation（預約）、single（單人房）、under the name of（在某人的名下）、reconfirm（再確認）、check in（投宿登記）。

c. Tips for Listening

跟預約住宿有關的字彙及句法如 have / make a reservation for ＋ 人名、single / double、confirm、reconfirm，都需要熟悉其發音，由其是 confirm 這個字，很多人都會跟 conform（符合、一致）混淆。

練習題　C-26

請聽以下的對話題，並回答相關的問題。

1 _____

a) On a Monday or Tuesday.

b) In the middle of the week.

c) On a Friday or Saturday.

d) At the beginning of the month.

2 _____

a) As soon as possible.

b) During the busy season.

c) They haven't decided.

d) During off-season.

3 _____

a) Drink alone.

b) Wait outside.

c) Wait in her car.

d) Go to the bar.

詳解

1

◎解答

c) On a Friday or Saturday.

（在週五或週六。）

◎聽力原文

M 1： Good evening, sir. What name is your reservation under?

M 2： We don't have a reservation. Is that a problem?

M 1： I'm sorry. We require reservations on weekends since we are extremely busy.

When is this conversation taking place?

◎中譯

男士一： 先生晚安。請問您是用誰的名字預約呢？

男士二： 我們沒有預訂，那會有問題嗎？

男士一： 抱歉，因為適逢週末特別忙碌，所以需要預約。

這段對話是發生的時間是？

a) 在週一或週二。

b) 在週間。

c) 在週五或週六。

d) 在月初的時候。

◎解析

第二位男士提到 We require reservations on weekends since we are extremely busy. 「因為適逢週末特別忙碌，所以需要事先預約」，可推知對話發生在週五晚到週日的週末時段。

2

◎解答

b) During the busy season.

（正當旺季的時候。）

◎聽力原文

W： When should I book our hotel room for our trip?

M： The sooner, the better. I've heard that it gets really busy that time of the year there.

W： I better get right on it!

When are they taking their trip?

◎中譯

女士： 我什麼時候該為我們的旅行預訂飯店呢？

男士： 愈快愈好。我聽說每年的那時候會是旺季。

女士： 那麼我最好馬上進行。

他們何時要啟程旅行？

a) 盡可能愈快愈好。

b) 正當旺季的時候。

c) 他們尚未決定。

d) 適逢淡季的時候。

◎解析

關鍵句為男士提到的 ...it gets really busy that time of the year there...，可推知是在旺季時去旅行，故選 b)。busy season 「旺季」（反義為 off season 「淡季」）。

❸

◎解答

d) Go to the bar.（去吧檯等。）

◎聽力原文

W : How long will the wait be for a party of four?

M : I'm sorry. Unless you have a reservation, you'll have to wait about an hour.

W : That's fine. We'll just wait at the bar.

What is the woman going to do?

◎中譯

女士：四個人的座位要等多久？

男士：不好意思，除非你們有先預訂，不然可能要等上一個小時。

女士：沒關係，我們可以在吧檯等。

這位女士打算做什麼？

a) 獨自喝酒。

b) 在外面等候。

c) 回她車上等。

d) 去吧檯等。

◎解析

題目的關鍵句是最後一句 ...We'll just wait at the bar...，所以答案選 d) 最恰當。名詞 party 在此指「一群人，一行人」。

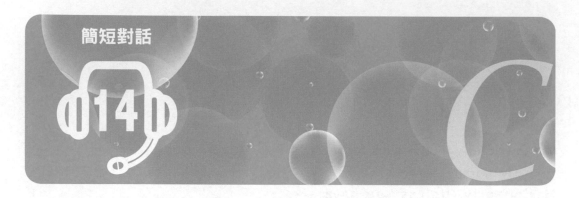

簡短對話

14

談論音樂

 學習重點

一般人閱讀時會喜歡找個安靜的角落（a quiet corner），泡一杯好茶（make a good cup of tea），翻開書本，聆聽自己喜歡的音樂（listen to your favorite music），通常會選擇聽柔的音樂（soft music），例如古典樂曲（classical music）。

 情境介紹及導引

We all like music. Some people enjoy classical music, while others prefer jazz, rock, or popular music. Some music, such as symphonies and piano concertos, may require listeners to concentrate, but certain soft music is ideal as background music for reading or enjoying a cup of tea.

範例 🎧 C-27

在簡短對話裡，你會聽到兩個人（通常是一男一女）的交談，接著再依據談話的內容，找出他們對話的主題。

M：What are your plans for tonight?

W：I'm just going to stay home and read a book, or maybe I'll put on some music.

M：I also like to listen to soft music when I'm reading.

W：Yeah, it's hard to concentrate when there is loud, heavy music playing.

M：I like classical music for reading. My favorite is Beethoven's 9th symphony.

W : Symphonies are great, but when I'm reading a book, nothing is better than a piano concerto.

M : Piano? That makes me sleepy.

What are the speakers talking about?（他們在談論些什麼？）

_____

a) Their favorite novels.（他們最喜愛的小說。）

b) A musician's biography.（一位音樂家的生平。）

c) Music they listen to while reading.（看書時聽的音樂。）

d) Noise in their neighborhood.（居家附近的噪音。） 答案：c)

 說明

a. Information Focus

問題的重點是「對話的主題」，從文中 "...read a book, and maybe I'll put on some music." 及字彙 soft music, classical music 等，得知他們是在談論閱讀時聽的音樂。

b. Language Skills

其他字彙：concentrate（專注）、symphony（交響樂）、piano concerto（鋼琴協奏曲）、nothing is better than（沒有比……更好的）。

c. Tips for Listening

跟音樂有關的字彙如 music, classical, piano, concerto, symphony 都須熟悉其發音。

 練習題 C-28

請聽以下的對話題，並回答相關的問題。

1 _____ 承接範例題，請再聽一次，回答以下問題。

a) Loud and heavy music.

b) Jazz music.

c) A symphony.

d) A piano concerto.

2 _____

a) Jazz.

b) Rock 'n' roll.

c) Classical.

d) Heavy metal.

3 _____

a) Memorize the first part.

b) Wash the car.

c) Write the music.

d) Drive in reverse.

14 詳解

範例 & 1

◎聽力原文

M：What are your plans for tonight?

W：I'm just going to stay home and read a book, or maybe I'll put on some music.

M：I also like to listen to soft music when I'm reading.

W：Yeah, it's hard to concentrate when there is loud, heavy music playing.

M：I like classical music for reading. My favorite is Beethoven's 9th symphony.

W：Symphonies are great, but when I'm reading a book, nothing is better than a piano concerto.

M：Piano? That makes me sleepy.

◎中譯

男士：今晚有沒有什麼計畫？

女士：我只打算待在家看點書，或許放點音樂來聽。

男士：我看書的時候，也愛聽輕音樂。

女士：是啊，聽到播放吵鬧的重搖滾樂實在很難令人專心。

男士：看書時我喜歡聽古典音樂，最愛的就是貝多芬的第九號交響曲。

女士：交響曲很棒，但看書的時候，我覺得聽鋼琴協奏曲是最好的！

男士：鋼琴曲？那令我昏昏欲睡。

1

◎解答

d）A piano concerto.

（鋼琴協奏曲）

◎聽力原文

What is the woman's favorite music?

◎中譯

這位女士最喜歡的音樂是什麼？

a）吵鬧的重搖滾樂。

b）爵士音樂。

c）交響樂。

d）鋼琴協奏曲。

◎解析

女士最後一句提到 …nothing is better than a piano concerto…，因此可知女士的最愛是鋼琴協奏曲。

2

◎解答

a）Jazz.（爵士樂。）

◎聽力原文

W：Thanks for the CD. I really like jazz.

M：Do you know the group?

W：I do. I heard them perform at the JazzFest in 2009.

What kind of music does the woman like?

◎中譯

女士：謝謝你的 CD，我真的很喜歡爵士樂。

男士：妳知道這個團體嗎？

女士：知道啊！我聽過他們在 2009 年爵士音樂節的演出。

這位女士喜歡哪一種音樂？

a）爵士樂。

b）搖滾樂。

c）古典音樂。

d）重金屬樂。

◎解析

女士第一句提到 ...I really like jazz... 「我真的很喜歡爵士樂」，故答案選 a)。

3

◎解答

a) Memorize the first part.
（記住第一部份。）

◎聽力原文

M：Did you memorize the music?

W：I memorized everything except the last verse.

M：We can practice at home.

What did the woman do?

◎中譯

男士：妳記下這段音樂了嗎？。

女士：我記得所有音樂，除了最後那一段。

男士：我們可以在家練習。

這位女士做了什麼？
a) 記住第一部份。
b) 洗車。
c) 作曲。
d) 倒車。

◎解析

由對話中女士的回答 ...I memorized everything except the last verse... 判斷，答案為 a) 最恰當。名詞 verse 是指「（歌曲的）主歌旋律」，介系詞 except 則指「除了……之外」。

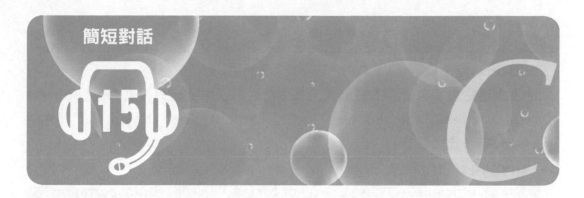

簡短對話

通勤問題

🎧 學習重點

因為就學及工作必須每天通勤（commute）的人，通常會遇到的問題包括選擇交通工具（choose your mode of transportation），行車路線（routes），路況（road conditions），有時不同的路線還得搭配不同的交通工具（subway / car / bus / bike），才不會遲到。

🎧 情境介紹及導引

Christina just started college in a new city. To get from her dormitory to classes, she rides a bicycle, or walks if the weather is good. On the weekends, Christina takes the bus to the supermarket to buy food, or rides the subway to the downtown area.

 範例 C-29

在簡短對話裡，你會聽到兩個人（通常是一男一女）的交談，接著再依據談話的內容，找出男士的主要通勤工具。

M：Have you been able to find your way around the city?

W：It's not been a problem. The subway system is really efficient here.

M：Isn't it? I use it all the time, except for really short trips.

What mode of transportation does the man use most often?

――――――――――――――

a）His bicycle.（他的腳踏車。） b）His car.（他的車子。）

c）The bus.（巴士。） d）The subway.（地鐵。）　答案：d）

a. Information Focus

問題的重點是「男士的主要通勤工具」，從對話中女士先提到 "The subway system is really efficient here."，男士回應 "I use it all the time,..." 得知他主要是搭乘地鐵。

b. Language Skills

重點字彙：efficient（有效率的）、except for（除了…之外）、transportation（交通）。

c. Tips for Listening

聽力的重點是與通勤有關的字彙，如 subway, bike, efficient, transportation；以及跟「頻率」有關的字彙，如 all the time, most often。

練習題　C-30

請聽以下的對話題，並回答相關的問題。

① ＿＿＿＿＿＿

a) He must ride the train.

b) He won't have any means of transportation.

c) He has to wait for the next one.

d) The man will drive him.

② ＿＿＿＿＿＿

a) Construction will begin.

b) Pearl Street will be closed off.

c) Going downtown will be easier.

d) Trips downtown will be slower.

③ ＿＿＿＿＿＿

a) The neighbors are noisy.

b) There isn't enough space.

c) It takes a long time to get to work.

d) The faucets are always running.

1

◎解答

b）He won't have any means of transportation.

（他將沒有任何交通工具可搭。）

◎聽力原文

W：Why does Adam have to wake up so early in the morning?

M：He's got to catch the bus. If he misses it, he won't have a ride.

W：Poor guy, I guess that means he goes to bed pretty early.

What will happen if Adam misses the bus?

◎中譯

女士：為什麼 Adam 要如此早起？

男士：因為他得趕公車，如果錯過就搭不到了。

女士：可憐的傢伙，我猜那表示他都很早就寢吧。

如果 Adam 錯過了公車會如何？

a）他必須改搭火車。

b）他將沒有任何交通工具可搭。

c）他必須等下一班。

d）男士會載他一程。

◎解析

男士在對話中提到 "If he misses it, he won't have a ride."，ride 在此指「交通接送」，means of transportation 則指「交通工具」，故答案選 b）。

2

◎解答

c）Going downtown will be easier.

（去市中心將更便捷。）

◎聽力原文

W：The construction on Pearl Street is really annoying!

M：I know. For the next three months, it's going to take an hour and a half just to get downtown.

W：On the plus side, though, we'll be able to get there much faster after it's all done.

What is going to happen in three months?

◎中譯

女士：珍珠街正在進行的建設工程真的很惱人！

男士：我知道。往後的三個月，我們得花一個半小時才能抵達市中心。

女士：雖然如此，但往好處想，等它完工後我們就可以更快抵達市中心。

三個月之後會是什麼樣的狀況？

a）建設工程將開始。

b）珍珠街將會封閉。

c）去市中心將更便捷。

d）到市中心的交通會更加緩慢。

◎解析

題目是問三個月之後的情況，根據對話內容，可知工程完工後去市中心就會更方便迅速，所以答案選 c）

3

c) It takes a long time to get to work.

（去上班要花很長的時間。）

W : How do you like your new house?

M : It's spacious and the neighborhood is really quiet. The only problem is the long commute.

W : It seems like a fair exchange in the long run.

What does the man complain about?

女士： 你喜歡你的新家嗎？

男士： 房子很寬敞而且環境很清幽，唯一的困擾是通勤時間很長。

女士： 長期來看這似乎是個很划算的犧牲啊。

這位男士在抱怨什麼問題？

a) 鄰居們很吵。

b) 沒有足夠的空間。

c) 去上班要花很長的時間。

d) 水龍頭一直漏水。

男士在對話中提到 ...the only problem is the long commute.，可知唯一不滿的是通勤時間較長，所以答案選 c)。commute 在此為名詞「通勤」之意。

簡短對話

16

與家人的活動

 學習重點

週末通常是家庭聚會（family get-together）的時機，尤其是生活在外地（living away from home）的人們，返家與父母相聚，常成為最美好的時光與回憶。

 情境介紹及導引

Vera and Justin are good friends and they usually find something to do together over the weekends. For this coming weekend, Vera has to turn down an invitation to the beach because she will visit her parents, who are owners of a small inn.

範例 C-31

在簡短對話裡，你會聽到兩個人（通常是一男一女）的交談，接著再依據談話的內容，找出對話的主題。

M: Do you want to go to the ocean with me this weekend?

W: I'm sorry. I promised my family I would visit them this weekend.

M: Can't you visit your parents anytime?

W: No, they are so busy running their business.

M: What do they do?

W: They run a small inn in the mountains.

M: So what will you do with your parents this weekend?

W: We have plans to pick berries and make jam.

M: That sounds great.

W: Yeah, I love spending time with my parents.

What are the speakers discussing?（請問他們在談些什麼？）

_____
a) An ocean surf trip（衝浪旅遊）

b) A jam recipe（果醬食譜）

c) Weekend activities（週末的活動）

d) A very special inn（一間很特殊的旅店） 答案：c)

🎧 說明

a. Information Focus

問題的重點是「對話的主題」，從第一句男士邀約女士週末去海邊，女士婉拒並說明將與家人共度週末，得知他們是在談論週末的活動（weekend activities）。

b. Language Skills

重點字彙：run a business（經營商家）、inn（小旅館）、berry（莓果）。

c. Tips for Listening

本段聽力的重點是事件的時間點（this weekend）、活動內容（go to the ocean, visit one's parents, pick berries, make jam）、以及地點（in the mountains）。

 練習題　C-32

請聽以下的對話題，並回答相關的問題。

1 _____ 承接範例題，再聽一次，回答以下問題。

a) Take over her parents' business.　b) Go to the ocean.

c) Spend time with her parents.　d) Visit a jam factory.

2 _____

a) He will go to the mountains.　b) He will take a boat trip.

c) He will buy a new house.　d) He will go to a lake.

3 _____

a) For a business trip.　b) To visit family.

c) To drink beer.　d) For a ski trip.

範例 & 1

◎聽力原文

M：Do you want to go to the ocean with me this weekend?

W：I'm sorry. I promised my family I would visit them this weekend.

M：Can't you visit your parents anytime?

W：No, they are so busy running their business.

M：What do they do?

W：They run a small inn in the mountains.

M：So what will you do with your parents this weekend?

W：We have plans to pick berries and make jam.

M：That sounds great.

W：Yeah, I love spending time with my parents.

◎中譯

男士：這週末想跟我一起去海邊嗎？

女士：很抱歉，我已經答應家人這週末會回家。

男士：你不能改天再回家探望父母嗎？

女士：不行，他們經營事業很忙。

男士：他們從事什麼行業？

女士：他們在山中經營一間小旅館。

男士：所以你這週末打算和父母一起從事什麼活動？

女士：我們計劃去採莓果製成果醬。

男士：聽來很不賴。

女士：是啊，我喜歡和父母共處的時光。

1

◎解答

c）Spend time with her parents.
（陪伴父母。）

◎聽力原文

What does the woman plan to do this weekend?

◎中譯

女士這週末計畫做什麼？

a）接手父母的事業。

b）去海邊。

c）陪伴父母。

d）參觀果醬工廠。

◎解析

女士一開始提到...I would visit them this weekend，最後又說 I love spending time with my parents...，可知答案選 c）最恰當。

2

◎解答

d）He will go to a lake.
（他會去湖邊。）

◎聽力原文

W：Jim, are you going to the mountains again for your vacation this summer?

M：Actually, we've rented a house on the lake for the whole family. What about you, Sheila?

W：We're going to take a white-water rafting trip for a week down the Colorado River.

How will the man spend his vacation?

◎中譯

女士：Jim，今年夏天你打算再去山裡渡假
　　　嗎？。

男士：其實我們已經為全家人租了一間湖濱
　　　小屋。那妳有何打算，Sheila？

女士：我們整個星期都要去參加科羅拉多河
　　　急流泛舟之旅。

男士將如何度過他的假期？
a）他會去山裡。
b）他會參加划船之旅。
c）他將買新房子。
d）他會去湖邊。

◎解析

對話中男士提到 rented a house on the
lake（租了湖濱小屋），故答案選 d）。

❸

◎解答

b）To visit family.
　（去探訪家人。）

◎聽力原文

M：What will you do for summer
　 vacation?

W：I think I'll go visit my relatives in
　 Germany.

M：Sounds great. Bring me back some
　 beer, OK?

Why is the woman going to Germany?

◎中譯

男士：暑假你打算做什麼呢？

女士：我想我會去探望住在德國的親戚。

男士：聽起來很不錯耶，幫我帶些啤酒回來
　　　好嗎？

女士為何要去德國？
a）為了商務洽公。
b）去探訪家人。
c）去喝啤酒。
d）為了滑雪之旅。

◎解析

由女士的回答 ...I think I'll go visit my
relatives in Germany.，可知她去德國拜
訪親戚，所以選 b）。relative 為名詞「親
戚」，visit 是動詞「拜訪」。

 簡短對話

抱怨

學習重點

人難免會生氣（upset），例如功課太多（too much homework）、噪音太吵不能專心（too noisy to concentrate）、等人時對方未出現（hasn't shown up），都會讓人生氣。

情境介紹及導引

Julia and her husband, Joe, work for the same company but in different departments. They usually drive home together. On this evening, Julia has been waiting for Joe for an hour. Then she runs into Joe's colleague, who tells her that Joe is tied up at work.

範例　〔C-33〕

在簡短對話裡，你會聽到兩個人（通常是一男一女）的交談，接著再依據談話的內容，找出女士生氣的原因。

M : You look upset. What's wrong?

W : Joe said he would pick me up an hour ago, but he hasn't shown up yet.

M : Oh, I just talked to him. He will need another hour at least.

Why is the woman angry?（女士為何生氣？）

_____

a) She needs to pick up Joe.（她需要去載 Joe。）

b) Joe hasn't come yet.（Joe 還沒到。）

c) She is scared of Joe.（她怕 Joe。）

d) Joe is angry.（Joe 在生氣。）

答案：b)

 說明

a. Information Focus

問題的重點是「女士生氣的原因」,從對話中的 "Joe said he would pick me up an hour ago, but he hasn't shown up yet." 得知她是因對方未出現感到懊惱。

b. Language Skills

重點字彙:upset(苦惱)、show up(出現)、scare(恐懼)。

c. Tips for Listening

以 why 開頭的疑問句是問「生氣的理由」,因此需要注意表示情緒的字詞,如 upset, angry,及引起說話者情緒的原因。

 練習題　C-34

請聽以下的對話題,並回答相關的問題。

1 _____

a) To work hard.

b) To tell something again.

c) To be on time.

d) To take lecture notes.

2 _____

a) The teacher was unreasonable.

b) It was easy to finish the assignment.

c) There was too much homework.

d) They should work faster.

3 _____

a) Shut the door.

b) Study at the library.

c) Make some noise.

d) Sing loudly.

17 詳解

1

◎解答

c）To be on time.

（要準時）

◎聽力原文

W：I'm sorry, Ted. I'm late.

M：I hate to bring it up, Sandra. But I do not have to tell you again that punctuality is really important.

W：I know, I know. No more lectures, please.

What does the man want the woman to do?

◎中譯

女士：Ted，抱歉，我遲到了。

男士：Sandra，我不想老調重彈。但我不得不再說一次，準時是很重要的。

女士：我知道，我知道。拜託不要再說教了。

這位男士希望女士怎麼做？

a）認真工作。

b）重述某件事。

c）要準時。

d）做演講筆記。

◎解析

男士在對話中向女士強調 punctuality is really important（準時是很重要的），故答案選 c）。片語 on time 是指「準時」的意思。

2

◎解答

b）It was easy to finish the assignment.（完成作業很容易。）

◎聽力原文

M：The teacher gave us too much homework this week.

W：I disagree. I still had free time after I finished it.

M：I don't know how you did it so fast.

What does the woman mean?

◎中譯

男士：這星期老師給我們太多作業了。

女士：我不同意，我寫完作業後還有空閒時間。

男士：我不知道妳怎麼可以寫得這麼快。

這位女士的意思是？

a）老師不講理。

b）完成作業很容易。

c）作業太多了。

d）他們動作應該快一點。

◎解析

男士在對話提到 too much homework，但女士持相反意見，表示做完後還有空閒時間，可知選項 b）為正確描述。assignment 為名詞「功課；作業」（＝homework）。

3

◎解答

b）Study at the library.

（去圖書館念書。）

◎聽力原文

W：It's no use. I can't concentrate on my studies because of the noise.

M：Why don't you go to the library?

W：I think I will. It's much quieter there.

What will the woman do?

◎中譯

女士：真的沒辦法。因為噪音導致我無法集中精神用功念書。

男士：為什麼不乾脆去圖書館呢？

女士：我想我會。那邊安靜多了。

這位女士打算怎樣做？

a）關門。

b）去圖書館念書。

c）製造噪音。

d）大聲唱歌。

◎解析

對話中男士建議女士 go to the library（去圖書館），女士也正面回答 ...I think I will（我想我會），故答案選 b）。

簡短對話

18

聰明購物

 學習重點

對於在外地就學或就業的人來說，住宿是個重要的議題，尤其是預算很緊的人（live on a tight budget），就算是買個家具也得精打細算（squeeze every penny）。

 情境介紹及導引

Mandy is moving to an apartment near work. Her new place is unfurnished, so she will need to buy some furniture. A sofa bed is a useful item to have, because underneath the seats it has a metal frame and mattress that can be unfolded into a bed.

範例 C-35

在簡短對話裡，你會聽到兩個人（通常是一男一女）的交談，接著再依據談話的內容，找出談話的主題。

M：When are you moving into your new apartment?

W：Next week. It's a nice apartment, but I don't have any furniture.

M：So what are you going to buy?

W：That's hard to decide. You see, I don't have very much money.

M：I suggest you start with the basics, like a bed.

W：I was thinking about that, but people need a couch to sit on and I can sleep on one, too.

M：How about a couch that is also a bed?

W：That's it! I need a couch that is also a bed. I'll get a sofa bed.

a) House repairs.（房屋修繕。）

b) The woman's financial status.（女士的財務狀況。）

c) A piece of furniture.（一件家具。）

d) A TV program.（電視節目。） 答案：c)

🎧 說明

a. Information Focus

問題的重點是「談話的主題」，從對話中的關鍵字彙 furniture, couch, sofa, bed，得知他們是在討論跟家具有關的話題。

b. Language Skills

重點字彙：apartment（公寓）、furniture（家具）、sofa bed（沙發床）、unfurnished（無家具設備的）、unfold（展開）。

c. Tips for Listening

本段談話是關於購物前聽取他人意見，因此聽力重點是跟「建議、考慮」有關的字詞，如 S + suggest (that) S + V，how about + 建議的物品，S + be thinking about + 物品。

🎧 練習題  C-36

請聽以下的對話題，並回答相關的問題。

1 _____ 承接範例題，再聽一次，回答以下問題。

a) A new apartment.   b) A car.

c) A table.   d) A sofa bed.

2 _____

a) Call a manager.   b) Lower the price.

c) Buy him a coat.   d) Lend him some money.

3 _____

a) As soon as possible.   b) In three months.

c) Next month.   d) When she has enough money.

範例 & 1

◎聽力原文

M: When are you moving into your new apartment?

W: Next week. It's a nice apartment, but I don't have any furniture.

M: So what are you going to buy?

W: That's hard to decide. You see, I don't have very much money.

M: I suggest you start with the basics, like a bed.

W: I was thinking about that, but people need a couch to sit on and I can sleep on one, too.

M: How about a couch that is also a bed?

W: That's it! I need a couch that is also a bed. I'll get a sofa bed.

◎中譯

男士：妳何時要搬進新公寓？

女士：下星期，那間公寓不錯，但我沒有任何家具。

男士：那麼妳打算買些什麼呢？

女士：那真是難以決定。你知道的，我的預算不太多。

男士：我建議妳從基本的必備品開始，像是床之類的。

女士：我有在考慮，但客人需要張可坐的沙發，而我也需要一張可以睡的床。

男士：那買張沙發床如何？

女士：就是那個了！我需要一張可坐也可睡的沙發。我要去買張沙發床。

1

◎解答

d) A sofa bed.

（一張沙發床。）

◎聽力原文

What is the woman going to buy?

◎中譯

女士打算買什麼？

a) 一間新公寓。

b) 一輛汽車。

c) 一張桌子。

d) 一張沙發床。

◎解析

由女士最後說的 ...I'll get a sofa bed... 可知，女士打算買張沙發床，故選 d)。

2

◎解答

b) Lower the price.

（降低價格。）

◎聽力原文

W: That looks really good on you, sir.

M: I really like this coat, but it's a little expensive.

W: Well, let me ask my manager if we can get you a discount.

What is the woman going to try to do for the man?

◎中譯

女士：先生，那看來真的很適合你。

男士：我真的很喜歡這件外套，但它有點貴。

女士：這樣的話，讓我問經理看看是否能給你一些折扣。

這位女士打算幫男士什麼忙？

a）請經理來。

b）降低價格。

c）替他買外套。

d）借錢給他。

◎解析

關鍵是對話最後 ...if we can get you a discount...，表示要詢問經理能否給男士一些折扣，故答案選 b）。discount 是名詞「折扣」，lower 則是動詞「降低」。

③

◎解答

c）Next month.

（下個月。）

◎聽力原文

M：Are you sure you want to buy a new desktop computer now?

W：I've had my eye on this model for three months. Why?

M：Because there's going to be a sale next month when the new models are released.

According to the man, when should the woman buy a new computer?

◎中譯

男士：妳確定現在要買臺新的桌上型電腦？

女士：我注意這款電腦有三個月之久了，怎麼了？

男士：因為下個月新機型上市後將有一波大降價。

依據男士指出，女士應該何時去買新電腦？

a）愈快買愈好。

b）三個月內。

c）下個月。

d）當她有足夠的錢。

◎解析

關鍵是最後一句 ...there's going to be a sale next month...（下個月將有一波大降價），故選 c）。

簡短對話

環境保護

 學習重點

由於人為破壞（man-made destruction），造成對地球環境的衝擊（environmental impact），許多動物瀕臨滅絕（extinction），因此許多人志願承擔動物保育（animal conservation）的工作。

 情境介紹及導引

Steve is looking to participate in an ecological rescue project this summer as a volunteer. He has heard about an eco-friendly resort in Mexico in which the volunteers gather sea turtle eggs on the beach before they fall prey to predators.

範例　C-37

在簡短對話裡，你會聽到兩個人（通常是一男一女）的交談，接著再依據談話的內容，找出男士將會做的事情。

W：What particular type of volunteer work would you like to do?

M：I'd like to participate in projects involving ecological rescue.

W：A sea turtle conservation program is available in Mexico.

What will the man probably do?（男士將會做什麼事情？）

_____

a）Save sea turtles.（拯救海龜。）

b）Study Ecology.（研究生態學。）

c）Teach English.（教英語。）

d）Travel around Mexico.（旅遊墨西哥。）　　　　答案：a）

說明

a. Information Focus

問題的重點是「男士將會做的事情」，從對話中的關鍵字 ecological rescue, A sea turtle conservation program，得知男士將會從事海龜保育工作。

b. Language Skills

重點字彙：volunteer（志工）、participate in（參與）、involve（與……有關）、ecological（生態的）、rescue（救援）、conservation（保育）、available（可利用的）、prey（被捕食者）、predator（掠食動物）。

c. Tips for Listening

以 what 開頭的疑問句是問「要做什麼」，因此回應的動詞 participate in 以及接續的名詞 projects involving ecological rescue 就成為聽力重點；選項 b）ecology 是對話中的 ecological 的名詞，選項 d）的 Mexico 是重覆對話裡的地點，都是混淆聽者的判斷。

 練習題 C-38

請聽以下的對話題，並回答相關的問題。

1 _____

a）Cut down the tree.　　　　b）Plant new trees.
c）Landscape her yard.　　　　d）Take a photo.

2 _____

a）A good deed.　　　　b）Wildlife protection.
c）Property damage.　　　　d）Traffic regulations.

3 _____

a）In isolated areas.
b）On mountain peaks.
c）In the new park additions.
d）In preserved areas.

詳解

1

◎解答

d）Take a photo.
（拍張照片。）

◎聽力原文

W：The old tree down the street will be cut down.

M：Yes. A landscape crew is coming later today.

W：I want to take a picture before that happens.

What will the woman probably do?

◎中譯

女士：街尾的那棵老樹會被砍除。

男士：是啊，景觀團隊今天稍晚就會過來。

女士：我想在老樹被砍之前先拍張照。

這位女士可能採取什麼行動？

a）砍倒樹木。

b）種植新的樹木。

c）美化她的庭院。

d）拍張照片。

◎解析

對話中女士最後一句提到 I want to take a picture，表示想趁景觀設計團隊砍樹前先拍照，故答案選 d）。選項 c）中的 landscape 為動詞「景觀美化」，而對話中的名詞 landscape 不同。

2

◎解答

b）Wildlife protection.
（保護野生動物。）

◎聽力原文

W：It's against the regulations to feed the wildlife.

M：I thought I was doing a kind deed by giving them something to eat.

W：This behavior may lead to property damage and human injury.

What are the speakers discussing?

◎中譯

女士：餵食野生動物是違反規定的。

男士：我以為餵牠們東西吃是在做善事。

女士：這種行為可能會導致財物損失並影響人身安全。

說話者在討論什麼？

a）一項善行。

b）保護野生動物。

c）財物損失。

d）交通規則。

◎解析

對話中女士提到 feed the wildlife（餵食野生動物）是 against the regulations（違法行為），並且試圖阻止男士的餵食行為，可知兩人在談論餵食野生動物產生的問題，故答案選 b）最恰當。

3

◎解答

c) In the new park additions.

（在公園的新規畫區內。）

◎聽力原文

M : Hunting is prohibited at the park, isn't it?

W : It's allowed in the new additions, but you mustn't go into the preserved areas.

M : OK, I'll follow the park rules.

Where can the man go hunting?

◎中譯

男士：國家公園是禁止打獵，對嗎？

女士：在新增建區可以，但你不能進入保護區。

男士：沒問題，我會遵守國家公園的規定。

這位男士可以到哪裡打獵？

a) 到隔離區域。

b) 到山頂。

c) 在公園的新規畫區內。

d) 在保護區。

◎解析

對話中第二句提到 ...It's allowed in the new additions...，可知新增建區內是允許打獵的，故答案選 c)。

飲食健康

學習重點

有句話是這麼說的：吃什麼像什麼 "You are what you eat."，健康意識（health consciousness）的覺醒，讓人們越來越重視飲食（diet）；例如在大熱天時，有些人會忍不住大口喝冷飲（cold drink），這時總會有人提醒這樣對健康是不好的（bad for the health）。

情境介紹及導引

Cold drinks can be good or bad for your health. The healthiest cold drink is just plain water. During exercising, drinking cold water allows your body to absorb water faster. Of course, drinking lots of sugary drinks remains unhealthy, whether they are served chilled, or at room temperature.

  範例

在簡短對話裡，你會聽到兩個人（通常是一男一女）的交談，接著再依據談話的內容，找出女士對冰啤酒的看法。

M：Wow, I can't believe how hot it is. This must be the hottest day of the year.

W：I agree. We should have brought something to drink with us.

M：I feel like having an ice-cold beer. That would be perfect.

W：I heard beer and other alcoholic drinks are bad for you on a hot day.

M：So what is your choice?

W：I feel like having a cola, but I don't need all the caffeine.

M : Then why don't you just get water? You find something wrong with everything else.

W : That just might be the best choice.

What is the woman's opinion on ice-cold beer?

_____

a) It cools your body down quickly.（它可以迅速冷卻你的身體。）

b) It is bad for your health when you are sweaty and hot.
（燥熱流汗時，對健康不好。）

c) It is easy to carry in summer.（夏天時攜帶方便。）

d) It is perfect to drink on a hot day.（天熱時的最佳飲料。）   答案：b）

🎧 說明

a. Information Focus
問題的重點是「女士對冷飲的看法」，從對話中的 "I heard beer and other alcoholic drinks are bad for you on a hot day." 得知她認為這對健康有害。

b. Language Skills
重點字彙：feel like ＋ V-ing（想要做……）、alcoholic（含酒精的）、ice-cold（冰鎮的）

c. Tips for Listening
本段對話的內容跟健康與飲料有關，請熟悉相關字彙的發音，如 drink, ice-cold, beer, alcoholic, health；對話的關鍵字句 "bad for you"，其中 bad 的發音是非母語人士較不擅長的部份。

🎧 練習題  C-40

請聽以下的對話題，並回答相關的問題。

1 _____ 承接範例題，再聽一次，回答以下問題。

a) Ice-cold beer.

b) Other alcoholic drinks.

c) Water.

d) Ice cubes.

2 _____

a) Find a new way to lose weight.

b) Change the kinds of food she eats.

c) Make an appointment with her doctor.

d) Buy a cookbook.

3 _____

a) He should eat less take-out food.

b) He should order healthier food.

c) He should eat his food very quickly.

d) He should work less so he has time to cook.

範例 & 1

◎聽力原文

M : Wow, I can't believe how hot it is. This must be the hottest day of the year.

W : I agree. We should have brought something to drink with us.

M : I feel like having an ice-cold beer. That would be perfect.

W : I heard beer and other alcoholic drinks are bad for you on a hot day.

M : So what is your choice?

W : I feel like having a cola, but I don't need all the caffeine.

M : Then why don't you just get water? You find something wrong with everything else.

W : That just might be the best choice.

◎中譯

男士：哇，真不敢相信今天這麼熱。這大概是今年最熱的一天了吧！

女士：對啊，我們應該帶些東西來喝才對。

男士：我想來杯冰涼的啤酒，那真是棒呆了！

女士：聽說啤酒和其他酒精性飲料不適合在大熱天飲用，對身體不太好。

男士：那妳會喝什麼呢？

女士：我想來杯可樂，卻又不想喝進那些咖啡因。

男士：既然如此，何不喝水就好？妳會發現其他飲料也都不太適合。

女士：那大概是最好的選擇了吧！

1

◎解答

c）Water.（開水。）

◎聽力原文

What is probably the best choice for the woman?

◎中譯

哪種飲料可能是女士的最佳選擇？

a）冰涼的啤酒。

b）其他酒精性飲料。

c）開水。

d）冰塊。

◎解析

對話最後男士建議女士 ...why don't you just get water?（何不喝水就好？），女士則回應 That just might be the best choice（那大概是最好的選擇了吧！），故答案選 c）。

2

◎解答

b）Change the kinds of food she eats.（改變飲食攝取的種類。）

◎聽力原文

W : What seems to be the problem?

M : Well, it looks like you're lacking in protein, but that can be fixed.

W : I guess I'll have to change my diet.

What will the woman probably do next?

◎中譯

女士：可能是什麼問題？

男士：嗯，看來妳似乎是缺乏蛋白質，不過這是可以治療的。

女士：我想我應該要改變飲食習慣。

這位女士接下來可能會怎麼做？

a）尋找新的減肥方法。

b）改變飲食攝取的種類。

c）和醫生預約。

d）買本烹飪書。

◎解析

女士對話最後提到 ...I guess I'll have to change my diet...，可知女士覺得自己應該改變飲食習慣，故答案選 b）最恰當。此處的 diet 是指「飲食」，非「減肥」。

3

◎解答

b）He should order healthier food.
（他應該點些較健康的食物。）

◎聽力原文

W: You're eating fast food again! That stuff has so many calories in it.

M: But I'm so busy at work. I never have time to cook.

W: You should at least order something with a little less fat.

What suggestion does the woman give the man?

◎中譯

女士：你又在吃速食了！那些食物熱量很高。

男士：但我忙於工作，根本沒時間作飯。

女士：你至少應該點些較不油膩的食物。

這位女士提供男士什麼建議？

a）他應該少吃外食。

b）他應該點些較健康的食物。

c）他應該吃快一點。

d）他應該減少工作量好空出下廚的時間。

◎解析

對話最後一句女士提到 ...You should at least order something with a little less fat...，建議男士應該點較不油膩的食物，故答案選 b）。

短文聽解

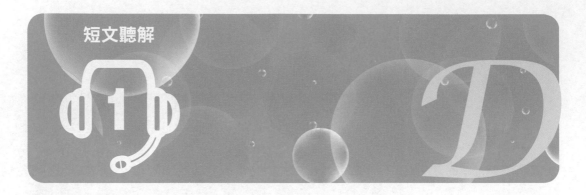

賣場廣播

 學習重點

去商店或賣場逛街採購時常會聽到各類廣播（announcement）內容，包括介紹賣場設施（facilities）、限時搶購（time-limited offers）、尋人（物）啟示（lost and found）、打烊通知等。

 情境介紹及導引

Amy is shopping at D. B. Mathews, a department store. With a daytime job, she only has time to shop in the evenings. Today, Amy is looking for a new party dress. Amy tries on several dresses and, as she decides, she hears the following announcement.

範例 D-01

在以下資訊中，你會聽到一段廣播，請注意廣播的地點。

Where is the announcement being heard?（這段廣播是在哪裡聽到的？）

_____

a）In a theater.（在劇院。）
b）In an office.（在辦公室。）
c）In a clothing store.（在服飾店。）
d）In a museum.（在博物館。）

答案：c）

（聽力原文請見詳解）

說明

a. Information Focus

問題的重點是「廣播的地點」，從文中的關鍵字 shoppers, dress, purchase，得知這是間服飾店。

b. Language Skills

重點字彙：attention（注意）、shopper（顧客）、dress（衣服）、purchase（購買）、register（收銀機）。

c. Tips for Listening

廣播常用的開頭語是 " Attention " 或 " Your attention, please. "，目的是請大家注意，後面接續的文字通常就是說話的重點。

練習題 D-02

1 ＿＿＿＿＿＿ 承接範例題，請再聽一次並作答。

When will D. B. Mathews be open tomorrow?

a) It will be closed.

b) At the regular time.

c) From 9:00 a.m. to 5:00 p.m.

d) Only in the morning.

2.1 ＿＿＿＿＿＿ 請聽短文 **2** ，回答以下 2 題。

What kind of place might this be?

a) A museum.

b) An amusement park.

c) A sports stadium.

d) A zoo.

2.2 ＿＿＿＿＿＿

What is the purpose of this announcement?

a) A lost notice.

b) An advertisement.

c) A meeting notice.

d) A closure notice.

範例 & 1

◎聽力原文

Attention, shoppers. D. B. Mathews will be closing in 20 minutes. Please bring the clothes you wish to purchase to the nearest register. Registers are located on every floor. We accept cash, checks, all major credit cards and, of course, the D. B. Mathews charge card. We will be open tomorrow from 10:00 a.m. until 8:00 p.m. as usual.

◎中譯

親愛的顧客，請注意。D. B. Mathews 將在 20 分鐘內打烊。請帶著你欲購買的服飾前往最近的收銀台。我們所有的樓層都有收銀台。我們接受現金、支票、各大銀行信用卡，當然，還有 D. B. Mathews 的簽帳卡。本店明天如同往常，從早上 10:00 營業至晚間 8:00。

1

◎解答

b）At the regular time.
（跟平常一樣。）

◎中譯

D. B. Mathews 明天何時開始營業？
a）明天不營業。
b）跟平常一樣。
c）從上午九時營業至下午五點。
d）只有早上營業。

◎解析

廣播裡最後一句提到：We will be open tomorrow from 10:00 a.m. until 8:00 p.m. as usual，指出明日的營業時間跟平常一樣，沒有特別更動，因此應選擇 b）。

2

◎聽力原文

Attention, please. We have a lost child at the main entrance. I repeat; lost child at the main entrance. Her name is Jocelyn, she is five years old and she is wearing white shoes, blue pants and a brown coat. Would her parents please come pick her up at the main entrance? The main entrance is located directly south of the Ferris wheel.

◎中譯

請注意。正門口有一位走失的孩童。再重複一次，正門口有一位走失的孩童。她的名字是 Jocelyn， 5 歲，穿著白鞋，藍色褲子和棕色外套。麻煩她的家長來正門口接她？正門口位於摩天輪的南邊。

2.1

◎解答

b）An amusement park.
（遊樂園。）

◎中譯

這裡可能是什麼地方？
a）博物館。
b）遊樂園。
c）體育館。
d）動物園。

◎解析

關鍵在於最後一句話中的 Ferris wheel（摩天輪），整段文章只有此處提供線索，所以正確答案為 b）an amusement park（遊樂園）。

2.2

◎解答

a）A lost notice.
　（尋人通知。）

◎中譯

這則廣播的目的是什麼？
a）尋人通知
b）一則廣告
c）一則會議通知
d）打烊提醒

◎解析

廣播內容是在通知家長來認領走失的小孩，所以正確答案為 a）。

短文聽解 2

機艙廣播

 學習重點

搭乘飛機時，常會聽到各類廣播，包括即將起飛時的安全規定（safety regulations）、飛航高度（altitude）、餐點（meal）、亂流（turbulence）、惡劣天候（bad weather）、即將下降（descend）等內容。

 情境介紹及導引

Matt is flying to Ellis County for a visit. Before the airplane took off, he watched a short video about safety regulations. As the plane rose to the desired altitude, a meal was served. All was well until right before the plane was about to descend. The plane began to shake violently from turbulence and bad weather.

範例 D-03

在以下資訊中，你會聽到一段廣播，注意廣播的原因。

Why is this announcement being made?（為何做此廣播？）

_____

a）To announce a landing delay due to an accident.
（宣布因意外事故延後降落。）

b）To announce a landing delay due to bad weather.
（宣布因惡劣天候延後降落。）

c）To announce that the plane is about to descend.（宣布飛機即將下降。）

d）To announce that meals are going to be served.（宣布即將供應餐點。）

（聽力原文請見詳解）   答案：b）

說明

a. Information Focus

問題的重點是「廣播的原因」，從文中的關鍵字 delay、heavy thunderstorms，得知原因是惡劣的天候導致降落時間延後。

b. Language Skills

重點字彙：captain（機長）、scheduled arrival time（原定到達時間）、delay（延後）、heavy thunderstorms（大雷雨）、due to（由於）。

說明原因：結果 ＋ is / are ＋ due to ＋ 原因

c. Tips for Listening

負責廣播的人通常會在 "May I have your attention, please?" 之後說明自己的身分，所用的句法是 "This is ＋ 身分 / 姓名 ＋ speaking."。

練習題　D-04

1 ＿＿＿＿＿＿＿＿＿　承接範例題，請再聽一次並作答。

Which is the correct description of the situation on the plane?

a) All passengers are probably in their seats.

b) All passengers are carrying their suitcases.

c) All passengers are probably confused.

d) Flight attendants are in the aisles.

2.1 ＿＿＿＿＿＿＿＿　請聽短文 **2**，回答以下 2 題。

Why is it important to remember your bus number?

a) To avoid getting on the wrong bus.

b) To claim your luggage in Denver.

c) To report it if the bus breaks down.

d) To get a ticket refund if needed.

2.2 ＿＿＿＿＿＿＿＿

Where can a passenger smoke on the bus?

a) The bathroom.

b) In their seat, at certain times.

c) Anywhere on the bus.

d) Nowhere on the bus.

a）所有乘客大概都待在自己座位上。
b）所有旅客都帶著他們的行李箱。
c）所有乘客可能都很困惑。
d）空服員們在走道上。

◎解析

文中提到安全帶警示燈亮起，機長也要求乘客坐在座位上並繫上安全帶。所以乘客應是在座位上，所以應該選 a）All passengers are probably in their seats.（所有乘客大概都待在自己座位上。）

範例 & 1

◎聽力原文

May I have your attention, please? This is your captain speaking. Our scheduled arrival time for Ellis County Airport will be delayed a bit as the area is experiencing heavy thunderstorms. We will be in a holding pattern as we wait for the thunderstorms to pass. As we may run into some turbulence, please note that the seat belt sign is now turned on. Please remain seated with your seat belts fastened. We expect we'll be on the ground within half an hour to 45 minutes.

◎中譯

各位請注意，我是機長。我們的預定到達 Ellis County 機場的時間將會延遲，因為該地區正發生大雷雨。我們將會保持在等待航線直到雷雨結束。由於我們可能會通過一些亂流，請注意安全帶警示已經亮燈。請您留在座位上並將安全帶繫上。我們預計將在半小時至 45 分鐘內著陸。

1

◎解答

a）All passengers are probably in their seats.
（所有乘客大概都待在自己座位上。）

◎中譯

關於飛機上的情況，下列哪一項描述為是？

2

◎聽力原文

Good afternoon passengers, and welcome aboard Basset Hound Bus Lines. This is bus 4304 from Chicago to Denver. If at any time we stop for a break at an area with other buses, just remember to get back on bus 4304, and you won't end up in the wrong city. Before we depart, please note that this is a non-smoking bus, and smoking will be permitted in no part of the bus, not even the bathroom.

◎中譯

午安，各位乘客，歡迎搭乘 Basset Hound 的客運路線。這是從芝加哥到丹佛的 4304 號客運。如果我們停車休息，而附近有其他客運時，請記得回到 4304 號車，以免被帶往錯誤的目的地。在我們啟程前，請注意本車禁煙，在車上的任何角落都不准吸菸，包括洗手間在內。

2.1

◎解答

a）To avoid getting on the wrong bus.（為了避免上錯車。）

◎中譯

為什麼記住車號很重要？

a）為了避免上錯車。

b）為了在丹佛領取你的行李。

c）為了公車故障時能夠呈報。

d）需要時可以辦理退票。

◎解析

文中第三句話指出，為了避免與其他暫停的公車混淆，要看清車號上車，才能到達正確的目的地，所以 a）To avoid getting on the wrong bus.（為了避免上錯車）是最適合的答案。

2.2

◎解答

d）Nowhere on the bus.

（公車上都不能抽。）

◎中譯

車上哪裡可供乘客吸菸？

a）洗手間。

b）在自己座位上的某個時段。

c）公車上的任何地方。

d）公車上都不能抽。

◎解析

廣播中已表明這是一輛禁菸公車，全車都不能吸菸，所以應該選 d）Nowhere on the bus.（公車上都不能抽。）

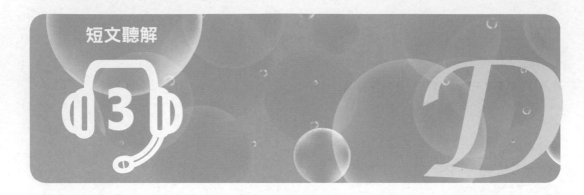

短文聽解

 3

球賽廣播

學習重點

觀賞球賽時會聽到以下類似的廣播，包括球賽地點（Sparrow Stadium）、地主隊名稱（Sparrows）、客隊名稱（Jamestown Dolphins），及球隊狀況的介紹。

情境介紹及導引

Owen is a fan of the Sparrows, who are taking on the Jamestown Dolphins in the Sparrow Stadium tonight. Owen has been attending the games for several seasons and seldom misses one. He loves the excitement, great energy, and thrills. Since today is the opening day, both teams are determined to win.

範例　D-05

在以下資訊中，你會聽到一段廣播，請注意球賽舉行的時間。

What part of the season does this game take place in?
（這場球賽是在一季裡的什麼時間舉行的？）

_____

a) The beginning.（開頭。）
b) The middle.（中段。）
c) The end.（季末。）
d) The post-season.（季後。）

答案：a ）

（聽力原文請見詳解）

a. Information Focus

問題的重點是「球季的時段」，從文中第一句 "...welcome to the opening day of this year's baseball season..." 得知本場球賽是在球季的開頭舉行。

b. Language Skills

重點字彙：folks（「稱呼」各位）、opening day（開幕日）、 stadium（體育場）、 take on（對壘）、team（隊）、energy（活力）、thrilling（刺激的）。

c. Tips for Listening

廣播中的第一句經常會提出內容的重點，如 "...welcome to the opening day...", 聽懂第一句話，才能掌握短文的主題。

練習題　D-06

1 ＿＿＿＿＿＿＿　承接範例題，請再聽一次並作答。

Why does the announcer think it will be a thrilling game?

a) Because many players have been in all-star game.

b) Because the fans for these teams are very energetic.

c) Because both teams were energetic during training.

d) Because the two teams have been rivals for many years.

2 ＿＿＿＿＿＿＿

Who are Tracy and Louis Ellen?

a) Football players.

b) Hairdressers.

c) Tennis players.

d) Gymnasts.

3 ＿＿＿＿＿＿＿

Where will the sports team practice?

a) In the field.

b) By the beach.

c) At a club.

d) In the gym.

範例 & 1

◎聽力原文

Good evening folks and welcome to the opening day of this year's baseball season here at Sparrow Stadium. Tonight the Sparrows will be taking on the Jamestown Dolphins. Both teams have had great energy in spring training so I'm sure it will be a thrilling game. The Sparrows are hoping to get off to a good start this season after coming close but not quite making it into the playoffs last season.

◎中譯

晚安，歡迎各位來到 Sparrow 體育館參加今年棒球季的開幕賽。今晚 Sparrows（麻雀隊）將對上 Jamestown Dolphins（詹姆斯城海豚隊）。兩支球隊在春訓時都鬥志高昂，所以這肯定會是場精采的比賽。在上個賽季只差臨門一腳就挺進季後賽的麻雀隊，期待本賽季能旗開得勝。

1

◎解答

c) Because both teams were energetic during training.
（因為兩支球隊在訓練中鬥志高昂。）

◎中譯

為何廣播員認為這會是場精采的比賽？
a) 因為有許多球員參加過明星賽。
b) 因為兩支球隊的球迷都非常熱情。
c) 因為兩支球隊在訓練中都鬥志高昂。
d) 因為兩支球隊互為敵手已經多年。

◎解析

文中提到 "both teams have had great energy in spring training"（兩支球隊在春訓時都鬥志高昂），可知原因為 c)。

2

◎解答

c) Tennis players.
（網球選手。）

◎聽力原文

Fifteen-love, Louise Ellen serving. From where I'm sitting, that looks like a net ball. Net. This is her second serve. Tracy returns it. And Louise Ellen comes to the net. What a rally this is. It's deep left, and she pushes Tracy all the way into the alley. Return...and it's out. Thirty-love.

◎中譯

十五比零，Louise Ellen 發球。從我這兒看起來像是個擦網球。觸網。這是她第二次發球。Tracy 回擊。Louise Ellen 來到網邊。這是一記偏左深球，將 Tracy 一路逼向角落。一個回擊……出界。三十比零。

Tracy 和 Louis Ellen 是什麼身分？
a) 足球員。
b) 美髮師 。
c) 網球選手。
d) 體操運動員。

◎解析

文中可知這是來回對打的雙人競賽，因此只有 c) Tennis players（網球選手）符合。

3

◎解答

d) In the gym.

（體育館裡。）

◎聽力原文

The field team will meet in the gym today. Attention field team members: Your practice will be in the gymnasium this afternoon due to the thunder showers.

◎中譯

田賽隊今天改在體育館集合。田賽隊隊員請注意：因為雷雨關係，今天下午的練習改在體育館進行。

運動員們將在哪裡練習？

a) 田賽場。

b) 沙灘旁。

c) 在俱樂部。

d) 體育館裡。

◎解析

從 attention（注意）之後的句子可知練習場地移至室內體育館，因此選 d) In the gym（體育館裡）。

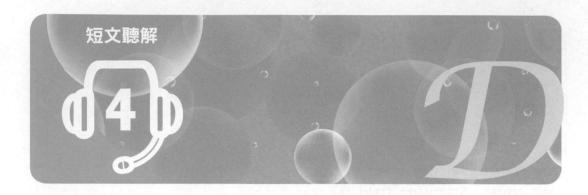

短文聽解

劇院廣播

 學習重點

常見的藝文活動之一是到劇院（theater）觀賞表演（performance），在開演前常會聽到一段廣播，主要是介紹演出內容、節目流程、以及注意事項。

 情境介紹及導引

Kenny and Jane arrive at the Clairmont Theater to see a play. They are offered free programs at the entrance. Both of them are surprised to see a packed house tonight and quickly find their seats in the theater. Before the play begins, they hear the following announcement.

範例 **D-07**

在以下資訊中，你會聽到一段廣播，請注意廣播的地點。

Where is the announcement being heard?（這段廣播是在哪裡聽到的？）

_____

a）In a hospital.（在醫院。）
b）In a theater.（在劇院。）
c）In an office.（在辦公室。）
d）In a gym.（在健身房。）

答案：b）

（聽力原文請見詳解）

🎧 說明

a. Information Focus

問題的重點是「廣播的地點」，從文中的關鍵字彙 theater, performance, show，得知廣播地點是劇院。

b. Language Skills

重點字彙：entrance（入口）、packed house（客滿）、act（幕）、present（呈現）、intermission（中場休息）、film（錄影）、photography（拍照）、allow（允許）、cooperation（合作）。

c. Tips for Listening

廣播第一句為內容的重點 "...welcome to the Clairmont Theater."，接續的句子則是細節說明。

 練習題 D-08

1 ＿＿＿＿＿＿＿＿ 承接範例題，請再聽一次並作答。

What is not allowed during the performance?

a) Watching the show quietly.

b) Taking a break during the interval.

c) Taking pictures of the performers onstage.

d) Reading the theater program.

2.1 ＿＿＿＿＿＿＿＿ 請聽短文 **2**，回答以下 2 題。

What will Director Alicia Stone be doing at the theater tonight?

a) Signing autographs.

b) Introducing the film.

c) Narrating the film.

d) Speaking after the film.

2.2 ＿＿＿＿＿＿＿＿

What is the film about?

a) New York politicians.

b) The director's childhood.

c) Children in New York.

d) Drug dealers in New York.

範例 & 1

◎聽力原文

Ladies and gentlemen, welcome to the Clairmont Theater. Tonight's performance will be presented in four acts, with a short intermission. Filming or photography is not allowed during the performance. Thank you for your kind cooperation. We hope you will enjoy the show.

◎中譯

先生女士們，歡迎蒞臨 Clairmont 劇院。今晚的表演分為四幕，會有一次短暫的中場休息。表演中禁止攝影和拍照。謝謝您的配合。希望您能盡情享受此次的演出。

1

◎解答

c) Taking pictures of the performers onstage.

（拍攝舞臺上的演員們。）

◎中譯

表演中不能做什麼？

a) 安靜的觀賞演出。

b) 在中場時稍作休息。

c) 拍攝舞臺上的演員們。

d) 閱讀劇院的節目表。

◎解析

廣播中提及：...filming or photography is not allowed（禁止攝影和拍照），因此 c) 是最適合的答案。

2

◎聽力原文

Welcome everyone to the Downtown Cinema. Tonight's feature is the latest film by director Alicia Stone, entitled *I Walk the Streets*, about two young orphans in New York City. We have the special honor of having Ms. Stone with us tonight, and she will be answering questions from the audience after the showing of the film.

◎中譯

歡迎各位光臨 Downtown 電影院。今晚放映的是導演 Alicia Stone 的最新力作《漫步街頭》，內容是關於紐約市兩名孤兒的故事。今晚我們很榮幸能邀請到 Stone 女士出席，在電影放映完畢後，Stone 女士會回答觀眾的提問。

2.1

◎解答

d) Speaking after the film.

（在電影結束後發言。）

◎中譯

今晚導演 Alicia Stone 會在電影院裡做什麼？

a) 親筆簽名。

b) 介紹這部電影。

c) 為這部電影配旁白。

d) 在電影結束後發言。

◎解析

從廣播中得知，導演在電影結束後會回答觀眾提問，因此 d) 是最合適的選項。

2.2

◎解答

c）Children in New York.

（紐約的孩童。）

◎中譯

這部電影的內容是關於什麼？

a）紐約的政客們。

b）導演的童年生活。

c）紐約的孩童。

d）紐約的毒販。

◎解析

廣播中提及這部電影是關於：...two young orphans in New York City（紐約市的兩名孤兒），所以應選 c）。

短文聽解

動物園、遊樂場所廣播

🎧 學習重點

到動物園等遊樂場所時,常會聽到的廣播內容是請遊客遵守園規,例如禁止餵食(do not feed the animals),即使開放可以餵食的動物,也必須是園內正式核准販賣的食物(official feed sold by the zoo)。

🎧 情境介紹及導引

Abby and Bernie are very excited about their class field trip to the zoo. On their way there, the teacher told them that the most important rule is not to feed the animals. Exceptions can be made, however, during the feeding time arranged by the zoo keepers, but only with official feed sold by the zoo.

  D-09

在以下資訊中,你會聽到一段廣播,請注意最重要的遊園規則。

Which is the most important rule?(什麼是最重要的規則?)

_____

a) Not to take feathers home.(不要拿羽毛回家。)
b) Not to run in the zoo.(不要在園內奔跑。)
c) Not to feed the animals.(不要餵食動物。)
d) To buy food only at the zoo.(只能在園內購買食品。)

答案:c)

(聽力原文請見詳解)

說明

a. Information Focus

問題的重點是「最重要的規則」，從短文中的句子"First and most important — do not feed the animals!"，得知不要餵食動物是正確的選項。

b. Language Skills

重點字彙：reminder（提醒的事情）、acceptable（可接受的）、exhibit（展覽）、
exception（例外）、official（官方的，正式的）。

c. Tips for Listening

廣播內容的重點通常在第一句就會告知："...a reminder to...visitors of the zoo about...acceptable and...unacceptable"，聽懂第一句的關鍵字彙，即可掌握內容的重點。

 練習題 D-10

1 ＿＿＿＿＿＿＿＿ 承接範例題，請再聽一次並作答。

Why are visitors asked NOT to run?

a) Because it bothers the elephants.

b) Because there are many exhibits.

c) Because people could get hurt.

d) Because there are injured animals.

2.1 ＿＿＿＿＿＿＿＿ 請聽短文 **2**，回答以下 2 題。

Where does this announcement take place?

a) At a swimming pool.

b) In a hotel.

c) At a public beach.

d) By a harbor.

2.2 ＿＿＿＿＿＿＿＿

When does this announcement take place?

a) At sunset.

b) At lunchtime.

c) In the morning.

d) Late at night.

範例 & ①

◎聽力原文

This is a reminder to all visitors of the zoo about which activities are acceptable and which activities are unacceptable while observing the various animal exhibits.

First and most important—do not feed the animals! The only exception to this rule is that feeding the elephants is permitted, but only with official feed sold by the zoo outside the elephant exhibit. No animal-related materials may be removed from the zoo, including feathers or hair. We also ask that you do not run within the zoo grounds, as injuries may result.

◎中譯

以下是要提醒所有動物園的遊客，哪些活動是在參觀不同動物展示區時可以進行，而哪些活動是被禁止的。首先最重要的是：請勿餵食動物！這條規定唯一例外的是可餵食的大象，但僅限餵食動物園大象展示區外園方販售的飼料。請勿將動物相關物品帶出動物園，包含羽毛或毛髮。我們也請各位勿在動物園內奔跑，恐有受傷之虞。

①

◎解答

c）Because people could get hurt.
（因為人們可能會受傷。）

◎中譯

為何遊客被要求不能奔跑？
a）因為會驚擾到大象。
b）因為有很多展示區。
c）因為人們可能會受傷。
d）因為有受傷的動物。

◎解析

題目最後一句 ...as injuries may result（恐有受傷之虞）提到禁止遊客在園內奔跑的原因，故答案為 c）。

②

◎聽力原文

Your attention, please. The Ponte Verde Beach Lifeguard Service will be closing now. We ask all swimmers to come out of the water. We also advise all surfers to come out of the water. The darker conditions make it difficult to see. Lifeguard service will resume at 9:00 tomorrow morning. Thank you and good night.

◎中譯

各位請注意，Ponte Verde 海灘的救生服務即將結束。請所有泳客都回到岸邊。同時也請衝浪的遊客上岸，因為較暗的天色會導致視線不清。救生服務將於明早九點恢復。謝謝大家，晚安。

2.1

◎解答

c）At a public beach.
（在公共海灘。）

◎中譯

這段廣播的地點為何？
a）在游泳池。

b）在飯店。

c）在公共海灘。

d）在港口邊。

◎解析

本題重點是「廣播地點」，從文中的 Ponte
Verde Beach（海灘）、swimmers（泳
客），surfers（衝浪客）得知地點是海灘，
故選 c）。

2.2

◎解答

a）At sunset.
　（日落時。）

◎中譯

這段內容是在何時廣播？

a）日落時。

b）午餐時。

c）上午時。

d）深夜時。

◎解析

本題問的是「廣播時間」，從文中的 "The
darker conditions make it difficult to
see." 、 "...good night" 可推知時間應是
接近黃昏時分，答案為 a）。

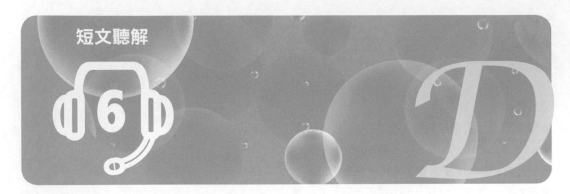

短文聽解 6

旅遊導覽

 學習重點

參加旅遊活動時，每到一個景點（scenic spot），導遊通常會介紹該處的特色（feature）、歷史沿革（past history of a place）等，例如後文介紹的 St. Monique，因為有許多藝術家聚集於此從事創作活動，畫室（studio）及藝廊（art gallery）林立其間，成為該社區的主要特色。

 情境介紹及導引

Elsie is visiting the St. Monique district this weekend. Before her trip, Elsie read up on the history and scenic spots of the area. The main attraction of the district is an arts community where visitors can shop at art galleries and see artists at work in their studios. When Elsie arrives at the entrance of the community, she hears a tour guide make the following announcement.

範例 D-11

在以下資訊中，你會聽到一段導覽，請注意 St. Monique 的現狀。

What is the current situation in St. Monique?（St. Monique 的現狀如何？）

_____

a）There is no artist around the place.（這地方沒有藝術家。）

b）There are both art galleries and studios in this place.
（這裡有藝廊及畫室。）

c）There is a very big art museum.（有間很大的藝術博物館。）

d）A shopping mall is under construction.（購物中心在興建中。）

（聽力原文請見詳解）   答案：b）

說明

a. Information Focus

問題的重點是「St. Monique 的現況」，從短文中的句子 "...still at work in some studios..."、"...former studios have now been converted into small art galleries." 得知這裡有藝廊及畫室。

b. Language Skills

其它字彙：district（行政區域）、community（社區）、convert（轉換）。

事物之間的轉換：事物 1 ＋ be converted into ＋ 事物 2

c. Tips for Listening

注意與藝術有關的名詞，如 studio, art gallery，及一些動作的表達用語，如 still at work（仍然在工作）。

練習題　D-12

1 _____ 承接範例題，請再聽一次並作答。

Where are they heading to next?

a) To a museum.

b) To a coffee house.

c) To a coffee plant.

d) To an art studio.

2.1 _____ 請聽短文 **2**，回答以下 2 題。

What is the purpose of the talk?

a) To explain security procedures.

b) To introduce an extraordinary artist.

c) To teach visitors how to paint pictures.

d) To sell some modern art pieces.

2.2 _____

What is on display at the museum?

a) Photographs.

b) Sculptures.

c) Paintings.

d) Machines.

範例 & 1

◎聽力原文

To your left, we are coming up on the St. Monique district. This is the famous artists' community. As you can see, there are artists—many painters, in fact—still at work in some studios along this street. Even so, many of these former studios have now been converted into small art galleries.

Now, follow me as we are going to stop and have some coffee at one of the cafés that many of the famous artists frequented.

◎中譯

在您的左方，我們來到 St. Monique 區。這裡是知名的藝術家社區。如您所見，仍然有藝術家—實際上，很多是畫家—在這條街上的畫室創作。即使如此，許多以前的畫室已經改成小藝廊。

現在，請跟著我到一間許多知名藝術家經常光顧的咖啡店駐足，喝杯咖啡吧。

◎解答

b) To a coffeehouse.
（去咖啡廳。）

◎中譯

他們接下來要去哪裡？
a) 去博物館。
b) 去咖啡廳。

c) 去咖啡工廠。
d) 去一間畫室。

◎解析

關鍵句為最後一句 ...we are going to stop and have some coffee at one of the cafés...，所以可知他們要去咖啡廳喝咖啡。

◎聽力原文

Welcome to the modern art exhibition in the Metropolitan Gallery, featuring paintings by the most well-known artists of the twentieth century. Top of the list is Pablo Picasso. His art as well as his life continue to surprise people in many ways. He died when he was ninety-two years old. Pablo Picasso produced thousands of paintings which are exhibited all over the world.

◎中譯

歡迎來到大都會畫廊的當代藝術展，展覽展出幾位二十世紀最著名的畫家所繪的畫作。其中最有名的就是 Pablo Picasso。他的創作和人生持續以不同方式驚艷著人們。他 92 歲那年過世。他創作的數千幅的作品在世界各地展出。

◎解答

b) To introduce an extraordinary artist.
（介紹一位非凡的藝術家。）

◎中譯

這段話的目的是什麼？

a）解釋安全程序。

b）介紹一位非凡的藝術家。

c）教觀眾如何畫畫。

d）銷售一些當代藝術作品。

◎解析

從 the most well-known artists （ 最
著名的畫家 ）、Top of the list is Pablo
Picasso.（其中最有名的就是畢卡索）可得
知，這段話主要在介紹畫廊目前展出的畢卡
索作品，所以答案選 b ）。

 2.2

◎解答

c）Paintings.

　（繪畫。）

◎中譯

博物館現在正在展覽什麼？

a）攝影照片。

b）雕塑。

c）繪畫。

d）機器。

◎解析

由開頭的 ...featuring paintings... 可以得
知，博物館目前的展覽以「繪畫」為主，所
以選 c ）。

課堂知識

學習重點

在學校上課時常可獲得各類資訊及知識，例如在課堂中探討研究人員（researcher）為了增進巴西的養蜂業（beekeeping），而引進非洲蜂與當地蜜蜂雜交（hybridize），而後產生了在美洲為害甚鉅的殺人蜂（killer bees）。

情境介紹及導引

Fanny and her classmates are visiting the Natural Science Museum, which is famous for their research on bees. In the museum, there are displays about the history of beekeeping and hybridization. During the museum orientation, Fanny hears the following introduction to a special kind of honeybee.

範例 D-13

在以下資訊中，你會聽到一段有關生物的資訊，請注意內容的主題。

What is this talk mainly about?（這段談話主要是關於什麼？）

_____

a) Human origins in Africa.（人類在非洲的起源。）
b) Honey products in Brazil.（巴西的蜂蜜產品。）
c) The origin of the Africanized honeybees.（非洲化蜜蜂的起源。）
d) The hybrid cars in South America.（南美洲的油電混合車。）　　答案：c)

（聽力原文請見詳解）

說明

a. Information Focus

問題的重點是「這段談話的重點」，從短文中的關鍵句子 "...imported honeybees from Africa to Brazil..."、"Hence, the name "Africanized" honeybees." 得知是在探討非洲化蜜蜂的起源。

b. Language Skills

重點字彙：import（引進）、improve（改善）、suit（使適應）、colonize（殖民）、hybridize（使雜交）、orientation（導覽）。

c. Tips for Listening

聽取知識性的資訊請注意每句話之間的承接字彙，如第一句的 honeybees from Africa 與第二句的 These African bees；第二句的 hybridizing with European honeybees 與第三句的 "Africanized" honeybees。

練習題 D-14

1 _____ 承接範例題，請再聽一次並作答。

Where were African honeybees first introduced to the Americas?

a) In countries having no bee populations.

b) In every country in South and Central America.

c) In Brazil.

d) In areas with no livestock.

2.1 _____ 請聽短文 **2**，回答以下 2 題。

What is this talk mainly about?

a) Different species of butterflies.

b) The migration of butterflies.

c) The habitat of butterflies.

d) The life span of butterflies.

2.2 _____

According to this talk, which animal has a similar behavior pattern?

a) Monkeys.　　　　　　　b) Bats.

c) Birds.　　　　　　　　d) Flies.

範例 & 1

◎聽力原文

In 1956, researchers imported honeybees from Africa to Brazil in an effort to improve beekeeping in that region. These African bees were well suited to conditions in Brazil, and they began colonizing South America by hybridizing with European honeybees. Hence, the name "Africanized" honeybees. Compared to docile European honeybees, Africanized honeybees are extremely defensive. Large numbers of them may sting people and livestock with little provocation. Because of these bees' aggressive behavior, many beekeepers abandoned beekeeping and the media widely publicized these so-called "killer bees".

◎中譯

1956 年，研究人員從非洲引進蜜蜂到巴西，致力促進該地區的養蜂業。這些非洲蜜蜂十分適應巴西的環境，便開始和歐洲蜜蜂混種並遍佈南美洲，因此有「混種非洲蜂」一名。相較於溫馴的歐洲蜜蜂，混種非洲蜂防禦性極強。只要稍微挑釁，蜂群就會集體叮咬人類及家畜。由於這些蜜蜂具攻擊性的行為，許多養蜂人放棄養蜂，而媒體也大肆報導這些所謂的「殺人蜂」。

1

◎解答

c）In Brazil.（巴西。）

◎中譯

非洲蜜蜂首次被引進美洲的哪個地方？

a）那些沒有蜜蜂的國家。

b）南美洲和中美洲的每個國家。

c）巴西。

d）沒有牲畜的地區。

◎解析

第一句即點出引進蜜蜂的地區 ...from Africa to Brazil （從非洲到巴西），所以答案選 c）。

2

◎聽力原文

We all like butterflies, but do you know how far a butterfly can fly? Some butterflies live long enough to make amazing migratory trips. Like birds, they fly south and stay in warm places in winter. When spring comes, they fly back home. Some species can fly as far as 2,000 miles (or 3,200 kilometers).

◎中譯

我們都喜歡蝴蝶，但你知道蝴蝶可以飛多遠嗎？有些蝴蝶活得夠久，得以進行驚人的遷徙旅程。像鳥類一樣，牠們往南飛、在溫暖的地方過冬。春天來臨時，牠們便飛回原居地。有些種類的蝴蝶可以飛行長達 2,000 英里（或 3,200 公里）遠。

2.1

◎解答

b) The migration of butterflies.

（蝴蝶的遷徙。）

◎中譯

這段談話的主旨是關於什麼？

a) 不同種類的蝴蝶。

b) 蝴蝶的遷徙。

c) 蝴蝶的棲息地。

d) 蝴蝶的壽命。

◎解析

關鍵為第二句 ...Some butterflies...make amazing migratory trips...，可知是關於「蝴蝶的遷徙」，所以選 b)。

2.2

◎解答

c) Birds.（鳥。）

◎中譯

根據這段談話，哪一種動物有相似的行為模式？

a) 猴子

b) 蝙蝠

c) 鳥

d) 蒼蠅

◎解析

從關鍵句提到的 ...Like birds, they fly south...，可得知蝴蝶和鳥類有相似的遷徙模式，故答案為 c)。

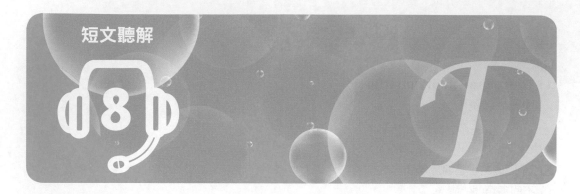

短文聽解

圖書館介紹

學習重點

規模較大的圖書館通常都會有解說員導覽（guided tour），會介紹館史（history）、館內設施（facilities）、藏書（holdings），以及其他服務（services）。

情境介紹及導引

Jane moved to a new apartment and was walking around the neighborhood when she saw a public library. Jane went in and noticed a small crowd gathering near the entrance for the guided tour. Jane saw the head librarian coming toward them, ready to give her tour.

  範例 D-15

在以下資訊中，你會聽到一段圖書館的介紹，請注意這段談話的目的。

What is the purpose of the talk?（本段談話的目的為何？）

_____

a) To promote a new product.（促銷新產品。）
b) To announce a new borrowing policy.（宣布新的借閱政策。）
c) To introduce resources in the library.（介紹圖書館的資源。）
d) To collect more books.（蒐集更多圖書。）

答案：c）

（聽力原文請見詳解）

說明

a. Information Focus

問題的重點是「這段談話的目的」，從短文中的關鍵字彙 Library guided tour（圖書館解說員導覽）、current collection（現有收藏）等得知是在介紹圖書館的資源。

b. Language Skills

其他字彙：entrance（入口）、approximately（大約）、periodicals（期刊）、reference（參考文獻）、index（文獻索引）。

c. Tips for Listening

本則聽力的重點在於第一句 "Welcome to...Library guided tour."，接續的文句就是 "introduce resources in the library"。

練習題 D-16

1 _____ 承接範例題，請再聽一次並作答。

What are the new facilities in this library?

a) New book shelves.

b) New rare books collection.

c) The new third floor.

d) The new computer lab.

2.1 _____ 請聽短文 **2**，回答以下 2 題。

What is the purpose of the talk?

a) To introduce the exhibition content.

b) To sell carved ivory.

c) To announce the opening of a new cafeteria.

d) To tell the story behind a rare stamp.

2.2 _____

When did they start to show the African stamps?

a) In the 19th century.

b) At 3:50.

c) A few minutes ago.

d) At ten minutes to 8:00.

8 詳解 D

範例 & 1

◎聽力原文

Welcome to the Parson City Public Library guided tour. The tour begins at the first floor north entrance and should take approximately 30 minutes. The Parson City Public Library first opened in 1974 and covers 40,000 square feet on three floors. Our current collection numbers over 250,000 titles. These holdings include books, periodicals, and reference and index volumes. On your left, you'll find the new Library Computer Lab. Our new networked computer lab has 30 fully functioning public workstations which give access to the computer catalogue, local and online databases and word processing software.

◎中譯

歡迎蒞臨 Parson 市立圖書館的解說導覽。導覽將在一樓北邊入口處開始，歷時約 30 分鐘。Parson 市立圖書館在 1974 年啟用，佔地 40,000 平方英呎，共三層樓高。我們目前的館藏超過 250,000 冊。這些收藏包括了書籍、期刊、參考書及索引目錄。在你的左手邊，你會看到新的圖書館電腦室。我們的新網路電腦室有 30 個功能完整的公共工作站，提供查閱電子目錄、區域和線上資料庫，以及文書處理軟體。

1

◎解答

d）The new computer lab.
（新電腦室。）

◎中譯

哪些是這間圖書館的新設備？

a） 新書架。

b） 新典藏的稀有書籍。

c） 新的三樓空間。

d） 新電腦室。

◎解析

後半段提到 new Library Computer Lab（新電腦室）及 public workstations（公共工作站）等新電腦設備，可以知道答案應選 d）。

2

◎聽力原文

Stamp Collectors, listen up! The Association of African Stamp Collectors has just opened its new exhibit. With stamps from Zaire, the Ivory Coast, South Africa, Morocco, some rare stamps date back to the 19th century. The African Stamp Collectors' table is Number 35. Booth Number 35, near the cafeteria entrance. African Stamps has just opened its display.

◎中譯

集郵的夥伴們，注意聽好！非洲集郵協會的新展覽剛剛開始。有來自薩伊、象牙海岸、南非、摩洛哥各地，以及一些罕見的 19 世紀郵票。非洲集郵者的桌號是 35 號，攤位號碼 35，靠近自助餐廳的入口。非洲集郵的展示才剛剛開始。

2.1

◎解答

a）To introduce the exhibition
content.
（介紹展覽的內容。）

◎中譯

這段談話的目的為何？

a）介紹展覽的內容。

b）販售雕刻的象牙。

c）宣布新自助餐廳開幕。

d）訴說珍稀郵票背後的故事。

◎解析

開頭第二句即提到非洲集郵協會的新展覽
（new exhibit），接著介紹展出的郵票，
故答案選 a）。

2.2

◎解答

c）A few minutes ago.
（幾分鐘前。）

◎中譯

他們何時開始展示非洲的郵票？

a）19 世紀。

b）3 點 50 分。

c）幾分鐘前。

d）7 點 50 分。

◎解析

關鍵句為最後一句 ...African Stamps has
just opened its display...，可得知展覽
在才剛剛開始，文中並沒有提到確切的時
間，故答案選 c）。

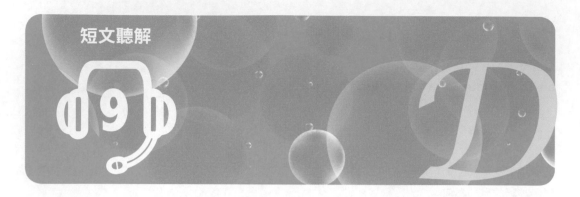

短文聽解

婚禮致詞

 學習重點

在一般的婚禮宴會（wedding reception）中，與會的親友會舉杯敬酒（toast），同時雙方家長或好友也會致詞（give / deliver a speech）祝福新人。

 情境介紹及導引

Tim and Mark were college buddies. Today is a big day for Tim because he is marrying Cindy, Mark's high school classmate. Naturally, Mark is going to be the best man. He feels honored and privileged to be the one to give a speech and the first toast at the wedding reception.

範例 🎧 D-17

在以下資訊中，你會聽到一段致詞，請注意致詞的場合。

What kind of occasion is this?（這是怎樣的場合？）

_____

a）A business lunch.（商業午餐。）

b）A cocktail party.（雞尾酒會。）

c）A wedding reception.（婚宴。）

d）An anniversary.（周年紀念日。）

答案：c）

（聽力原文請見詳解）

a. Information Focus

問題的重點是「談話的場合」，從短文中的第一句 "it is my honor and privilege to make the first toast to Tim and Cindy as husband and wife." 得知這是在婚禮中的致詞。

b. Language Skills

重點字彙：honor（榮幸）、privilege（殊榮）、best man（伴郎）、special（特殊的）。

很榮幸做某事：it is my honor ＋ to V

c. Tips for Listening

公開場合的致詞，通常第一句話都會以客套的語氣說明致詞的目的，如本聽力內容的 "it is my honor ＋ to V"；或是先表明身分 "As ＋ 身分, I want to ＋ V"，後面接續的動詞就是致詞的目的。

練習題 D-18

1 _____ 承接範例題，請再聽一次並作答。

When does this speech take place?

a) Morning.   b) Midday.

c) Afternoon.   d) Evening.

2.1 _____ 請聽短文 **2**，回答以下 2 題。

What did the bride say about her father giving a speech?

a) She was opposed at first, but allowed it anyway.

b) She expected nothing less than a speech from her father.

c) She wanted her father to do what he wanted.

d) She invited all the guests only in order to have them hear her father's speech.

2.2 _____

What does the father think about his daughter's new husband?

a) He thinks the husband doesn't speak enough.

b) He is completely satisfied with him.

c) He has mixed feelings about the man.

d) He only cares that the man pleases his daughter.

範例 & 1

◎聽力原文

Tonight it is my honor and privilege to make the first toast to Tim and Cindy as husband and wife. As the best man, I wanted to say that I've know them both for such a long time that they've grown to be special friends of mine. And though it seems like so much time has passed, this ceremony tonight is really only the beginning of a long and happy life together. May that life be filled with love and laughter. May their joys be many and their troubles be few. Congratulations.

◎中譯

今晚我十分榮幸，成為第一位向 Tim 和 Cindy 這對夫婦敬酒的人。身為他們的伴郎，我想說的是，認識他們兩人已經很長一段時間，他們已經成為我生命中特別的朋友。雖然好像已經交往了很久，今晚的儀式其實只是你們將永遠幸福生活在一起的起點。希望你們生活中充滿愛和歡笑，開心多過於煩惱。恭禧你們。

1

◎解答

d) Evening.
　（傍晚。）

◎中譯

這段發言在何時發表？

a) 早上。
b) 中午。
c) 下午。
d) 晚間。

◎解析

由第一句話開頭的 Tonight 可得知，說話時間是在晚上。

2

◎聽力原文

Ladies and gentlemen, I know that as the father of the bride, I am expected to give a speech. However, I am not a slave to custom, and so first I asked Kelly if she honestly wanted me to give a speech or not. She told me that if I had something I wanted to say to everyone, then she would be honored to have all of the guests she invited listen to my words. I have only a few words to say, and that is that I couldn't be happier with my new son-in-law and that I think these two are perfect for each other. Thank you.

◎中譯

各位女士先生們，我知道身為新娘的父親，大家都期待我致詞。但因為我不是一個拘泥於禮數的人，先前我也問過我的女兒 Kelly，是不是真的希望我致詞。而她告訴我，如果我有一些話想和今晚所應邀的嘉賓分享，她會感到非常榮幸。我只有幾句簡短的話，有了這麼一位新女婿，是再開心不過的事了，我相信他們倆是天作之合。謝謝。

2.1

◎解答

c) She wanted her father to do what he wanted.

（她希望父親想怎麼做，就怎麼做。）

◎中譯

對於父親致詞，新娘有什麼說法？

a) 她先是反對，後來同意了。

b) 她預期到父親會致詞。

c) 她希望父親想怎麼做，就怎麼做。

d) 她邀請所有賓客只是為了聽她父親致詞。

◎解析

由 第 三 句 提 到 的 ...She told me that if I had something I wanted to say to everyone, then she will be honored...，可得知新娘希望父親致詞、但不強迫，故答案選 c)。

2.2

◎解答

b) He is completely satisfied with him.

（他對女婿非常滿意。）

◎中譯

關於女兒的丈夫，父親有什麼想法？

a) 他認為女婿話說得不夠多。

b) 他對女婿非常滿意。

c) 他對女婿的感覺很複雜。

d) 他只在乎女婿是否會讓女兒開心。

◎解析

父親最後說 ...I couldn't be happier with my new son-in-law... 來表達對女婿滿意的程度，所以答案選 b)。

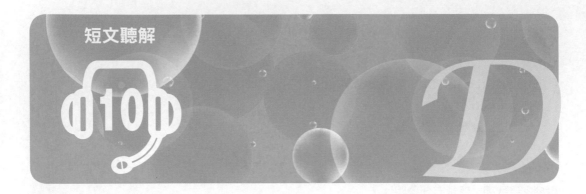

短文聽解

對師長的謝詞

🎧 學習重點

在某些場合，如畢業典禮（graduation）、師長的退休宴（retirement parties）、或是其他主題派對（theme parties），通常會對師長致謝詞（acknowledgment）。

🎧 情境介紹及導引

At graduation or teacher's retirement parties, a student is usually asked to speak on behalf of all students. In the speech, the speaker talks about the important lessons he learned from the teacher. When Coach Woodley retired, Howard was asked to say a few words to acknowledge the coach's contribution.

 範 例   D-19

在以下資訊中，你會聽到一段致詞，請注意說話者的身分。

Who is giving this speech?（誰在致詞？）

_____

a）A basketball coach.（籃球教練。）
b）The coach's son.（教練的兒子。）
c）A basketball sportscaster.（籃球播報員。）
d）A basketball player.（籃球隊員。）

答案：d）

（聽力原文請見詳解）

說明

a. Information Focus

問題的重點是「致詞者的身份」，從談話中的 "...on behalf of all his players."、"Coach Woodley didn't just teach us the game of basketball..." 得知他是籃球隊員。

b. Language Skills

重點字彙：coach（教練）、on behalf of（代表）、lesson（教訓）、pass on to（傳承）。

c. Tips for Listening

在正式場合中致謝詞，通常第一句就會表明說話者的身分（如 on behalf of...），後續的文字就是說明致謝對象的事蹟及貢獻。

練習題　D-20

1.1 _____ 承接範例題，請再聽一次並回答以下 2 題。

Why does the speaker admire Mr. Woodley?

a) His teams won many games.　　b) He was a great basketball player.

c) He coached for many years.　　d) He taught more than basketball.

1.2 _____

How did Mr. Woodley help the speaker when he was a freshman?

a) He loaned him some money.　　b) He helped him with homework.

c) He helped him feel confident.　　d) He taught him how to coach basketball.

2.1 _____ 請聽短文 ❷，回答以下 2 題。

Who is making this speech?

a) A freshman.　　b) A new boss.

c) A customer.　　d) A retiring employee.

2.2 _____

Why is the speaker thankful?

a) She received cooperation.　　b) She was well-paid.

c) She was promoted.　　d) She got a new job.

詳解

範例 & 1

◎聽力原文

I've been asked by coach Woodley to say a few words on behalf of all his players. Coach Woodley didn't just teach us the game of basketball, he also taught us many important lessons about life. These are lessons we still use today and that we can pass on to our children and other young people. I remember when I was a freshman. It was the first day of practice, and I was scared and nervous. Coach Woodley knew something was wrong. He put his arm around my shoulder and said, "Don't worry. We all know you can play." I've never forgotten how important that was for me.

◎中譯

我應 Woodley 教練的要求,代表所有的球員們來講幾句話。Woodley 教練不只教我們打籃球,也教導我們許多重要的人生道理。這些道理我們至今仍然受用,還可以傳承給我們的孩子及其他年輕人。我記得當我還是新人時,第一天練習的時候,我既害怕又緊張。Woodley 教練知道哪裡出了問題,便伸手環抱著我的肩膀說道:「別擔心。我們都知道你可以。」我從未忘記那句話對我有多麼重要。

1.1

◎解答

d)He taught more than basketball.

（因為他教了打籃球以外的知識。）

◎中譯

說話者為何欽佩 Woodley 先生?

a）因為他的隊伍贏得許多比賽。

b）因為他是一位偉大的籃球選手。

c）因為他指導了很多年。

d）因為他教了打籃球以外的知識。

◎解析

關鍵句是 ...he also taught us many important lessons about life.（也教導我們許多重要的人生道理）,所以 d）為正確答案。

1.2

◎解答

c)He helped him feel confident.

（他協助他獲得自信。）

◎中譯

當說話者還是個新人時,Woodley 先生如何協助他?

a）他借了些錢給他。

b）他教他功課。

c）他協助他獲得自信。

d）他教他如何指導籃球動作。

◎解析

後半段提到教練鼓勵他 ...Don't worry. We all know you can play,讓他獲得自信心,故 c）是正確答案。

2

◎聽力原文

Before I leave, I just want to tell you all how grateful I am for all the support you have given me these past few years. When I started here, I wasn't quite sure how all of you would take to me because I was an outsider to this company. But from the very start, all of you made me feel welcome and helped me. With such assistance, I could attend to my work here even when I faced obstacles. So it is with a heavy heart I say farewell and give each of you my heartfelt thanks.

◎中譯

在我離開前,我只想告訴各位,我有多麼感激大家在過去幾年間給予我的支持與鼓勵。剛開始到這裡工作時,我不確定大家會如何看待我,因為我對這間公司而言還是個外人。不過從一開始,所有人就讓我感受到歡迎之意且樂意幫忙。有了這些協助,即使當我面對阻礙時,仍能致力於我的工作。所以我是帶著沉重的心情道別,並對每個人獻上最誠摯的謝意。

◎解答

d) A retiring employee.
（一位即將退休的員工。）

◎中譯

發表致詞的人是誰?
a) 一位新鮮人。
b) 一位新老闆。
c) 一位顧客。
d) 一位即將退休的員工。

◎解析

從第一句的 before I leave,或最後一句的 I say farewell 等關鍵字詞,可推知致詞者是即將離職的員工,故答案選 d)。

◎解答

a) She received cooperation.
（她受到協助。）

◎中譯

為什麼說話者充滿感激?
a) 她受到協助。
b) 她獲得不錯的薪水。
c) 她被升遷。
d) 她得到一份新工作。

◎解析

由 第 三 句 ...all of you made me feel welcome and helped me... 可知,她因受到大家的協助而充滿感激,故答案選 a)。

短文聽解

電話語音或留言

 學習重點

一般商家或機構的電話常會有語音信箱服務（voicemail service），方便來電者了解商品種類或服務項目，來電者可依照個人需求選取按鍵，將電話轉接（transfer）到其他分機（extension），由專人服務；在無人接聽的情形下，也可以利用留言訊息（message），方便後續處理。

 情境介紹及導引

In today's service calls, it is common for us to hear a voicemail message, asking us to enter an extension or select from the service menu. Our calls are then transferred accordingly. When Kim calls the service hot line of a computer company, she hears the following message.

範例 D-21

在以下資訊中，你會聽到一段電話語音訊息，請注意內容的主旨。

What does the message say?（此段訊息在說什麼？）

_____

a) The business has changed its opening hours.（商店已變更營業時間。）

b) The business is closed.（商店已打烊。）

c) The business has moved.（商店已搬遷。）

d) The business is having a sale.（商店正舉行特賣。）

答案：b）

（聽力原文請見詳解）

a. Information Focus

問題的重點是「訊息內容為何」，從電話語音中的 "At the moment, no one is here to take your call." 得知該商家已打烊。

b. Language Skills

重點字彙：take your call（接聽您的電話）、regular business hours（一般營業時間）

c. Tips for Listening

電話語音的開頭常用語：Thank you for calling ＋ 打電話的對象／電話號碼，後面接續的話語通常就是語音內容的主旨，如商品服務介紹、分機號碼轉接或目前已打烊的訊息。

練習題　D-22

1.1 ＿＿＿＿＿＿＿　請聽短文 **1**，回答以下 2 題。

What are Frank and Stella going to do this weekend?

a) Go to a barbecue party.　　b) Go camping.

c) Go to a concert.　　d) Go to a beach party.

1.2 ＿＿＿＿＿＿＿

How will Frank receive this message from Stella?

a) From an answering machine.　　b) By P.A. announcement.

c) From a friend.　　d) In person.

2.1 ＿＿＿＿＿＿＿　請聽短文 **2**，回答以下 2 題。

What is this message about?

a) About a funny movie.　　b) About a city tour.

c) About family stories.　　d) About foot maintenance.

2.2 ＿＿＿＿＿＿＿

How can you get the current schedule?

a) In person.　　b) By filling out a form.

c) Through online information.　　d) By fax.

範例
◎聽力原文

Thank you for calling Top Computers. At the moment, no one is here to take your call. Please call back during our regular business hours: Monday to Friday, 9:00 a.m. to 5:00 p.m. Thank you.

◎中譯

感謝您來電 Top Computers，現在是下班時間，請於我們正常營業時間，週一至週五上午九點至下午五點來電。謝謝您。

1
◎聽力原文

Hello Frank, this is Stella. I'm sorry I couldn't talk to you personally. I got the tickets for the Saturday concert as you asked. The orchestra seats were all sold out, but the saleslady told me the box seats were better for sound and that we could bring binoculars. I'm thinking we could have a meal in the parking lot before the show. Call me back as soon as you get this message. Thanks, bye.

◎中譯

哈囉，Frank，我是 Stella。很抱歉我不能親自跟你說。我已經買到你要的週六音樂會門票了。正廳前方的座位已經銷售一空，但售票小姐告訴我包廂座位的音效較好，我們可以帶望遠鏡去。我在想開演前我們可以先

在停車場吃飯。聽到留言請盡快回電給我，謝了，再見。

1.1
◎解答

c）Go to a concert.
（去音樂會。）

◎中譯

Frank 和 Stella 週末打算去做什麼？
a）去烤肉派對。
b）去露營。
c）去音樂會。
d）去海灘派對。

◎解析

題目的關鍵句是：I got the tickets for the Saturday concert...（我已經買到週六音樂會的票），所以答案選 c）。

1.2
◎解答

a）From an answering machine.
（從答錄機。）

◎中譯

Frank 會從哪裡聽到 Stella 的留言？
a）從答錄機。
b）透過公共廣播。
c）透過一位朋友。
d）親自。

◎解析

開頭的 couldn't talk to you personally（不能親自跟你說），和最後的 call me back（回電給我）等關鍵字詞，可知這是一通電話答錄機留言，故選 a）。

❷

◎聽力原文

Hello and welcome to the City Tour by Foot hotline. City Tour by Foot presents the only free, tip-based tours of the city. These exciting and informative tours will take you throughout the city, entertaining you with stories and relevant information. Our expert guides will make the trip fun for everyone! The tour is free, and guides work for tips. For our current schedule, you may dial 1111 or check our webpage at www.CTBF.com. Thank you and enjoy the city.

◎中譯

您好,歡迎您撥打「徒步遊城」熱線。「徒步遊城」是唯一一家只收小費的免費市區旅遊。刺激又豐富的行程會帶您穿越整座城市,提供您許多有趣的故事和相關資訊。我們專業的導遊會讓每個人都有愉快的旅程。旅遊行程完全免費,導遊收入全靠小費。若要了解目前行程,您可以撥 1111 或是前往我們的網站 www.CTBF.com 查詢。謝謝您,並祝您享受這個城市!

2.1

◎解答

b) About a city tour.
　（關於城市旅遊。）

◎中譯

這則訊息是關於?
a)關於一部有趣的電影。
b)關於城市旅遊。
c)關於家庭的故事。
d)關於足部保養。

◎解析

由第一句的 welcome to the City Tour by Foot hotline,即可推測是和城市旅遊有關的訊息,故答案選 b)。

2.2

◎解答

c) Through online information.
　（透過網路查詢。）

◎中譯

如何取得目前的行程?
a)親自索取。
b)填寫表格。
c)透過網路查詢。
d)透過傳真。

◎解析

從倒數第二句的 ...For our current schedule, you may dial 1111 or check our webpage at...,清楚說明可撥打電話詢問或是上網查詢,故選 c)。

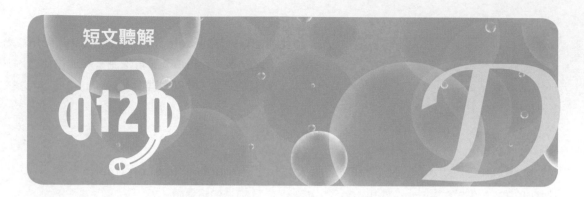

問題與處理

 學習重點

不論是個人或是團體，當遭遇到問題時，都會先找出原因（cause），並尋求解決方法（solution），例如一個遭受竊盜損失的店家，店長因此召開會議（call a meeting），告知員工發生的狀況及後續處理方式。

 情境介紹及導引

Work meetings usually involve some kinds of operation issues, such as low sales results, poor product quality, store theft, or personnel issues like poor service and low morale. Once the causes are identified, employees should work together to find a solution.

範例 ◖D-23◗

在以下資訊中，你會聽到一段會議主持人的說明，請注意召開會議的原因。

Why did the speaker call this meeting?（說話者為何召開會議？）

_____

a）The store received a big order.（該店接到一筆大訂單。）
b）The store is suffering theft loss.（該店遭受竊盜損失。）
c）Customers complain about poor service.（客戶抱怨服務不周。）
d）Some workers are late for work.（有些員工上班遲到。）

（聽力原文請見詳解）   答案：b）

說明

a. Information Focus

問題的重點是「開會的原因」，從短文的 "...our store has been losing over 100,000 dollars a month due to theft" 得知是因遭竊才需要開會解決。

b. Language Skills

重點字彙：due to（由於）、theft（竊盜）、figure（數字）、morale（士氣）。

特定詞組：receive an order（接到訂單）、suffer loss（遭受損失）、complain about（抱怨某事）、am / is / are + late for...（遲到）。

c. Tips for Listening

敘述原因的句法：S1 + V1 + because + S2 + V2

S + V + due to + 原因（如 theft）

Because 及 due to 句法不同，但後面都是說明原因，聽到這兩種字詞時，就需要特別留意後面接續的內容。

練習題　D-24

1　_____　承接範例題，請再聽一次並作答。

How did they deal with the situation?

a) They closed the business.

b) They contacted the police department.

c) They fired some workers.

d) They cancelled the orders.

2.1　_____　請聽短文 **2**，回答以下 2 題。

Who most likely is the speaker?

a) A bank manager.　　　　b) A doctor.

c) A school dean.　　　　　d) A police officer.

2.2　_____

What is the topic of this talk?

a) Student behavior.　　　　b) Medical complaints.

c) School anniversary activities.　　d) Teachers leaving their teaching jobs.

範例 & 1
◎聽力原文

I've called this meeting because, since the beginning of the year, our store has been losing over 100,000 dollars a month due to theft. Last month, this figure rose to nearly 150,000 dollars. We believe that a group of shoplifters has been operating in the building for the last few weeks and that this may explain the losses that occurred in September. We've been in touch with the police department, and they will be investigating the matter.

◎中譯

我召開這個會議是因為自從今年初開始,我們的店由於小偷偷竊,每月損失逾十萬元。上個月,失竊數字攀升至將近十五萬元。我們認為過去幾個禮拜有一個商店扒竊集團潛伏在這棟大樓內,或許可以說明發生在九月發生的幾起損失事件。我們已經和警方聯繫,而他們也將著手調查這起案件。

◎解答

b) They contacted the police
department.
（他們和警方聯繫。）

◎中譯
他們如何處理這個狀況?
a) 他們關閉這間店。
b) 他們和警方聯繫。

c) 他們開除了一些員工。
d) 他們取消了訂單。

◎解析
從對話中最後一句 ...We've been in touch with the police department... 可知他們已經報警,故答案選 b)。片語 in touch with 指「聯繫;聯絡」(= contact)。

2
◎聽力原文

Principal Kelly and I have called this meeting today because since last summer, we have lost over twelve teachers. Some have retired, but others have gone to the private sector. Accordingly, we want your ideas on how to make this a better place to work so that more of you will stay on. We have had differences in the past, but now this is your chance to express the things you think are important and what changes need to be made.

◎中譯

校長 Kelly 和我今天召開這個會議是因為從去年夏天開始,我們已經有 12 位教師離職。有些是退休了,有些則是到私立學校任教。因此,我們希望聽聽大家的意見,看如何讓這個學校成為更好的工作地點,讓大家更有意願繼續留任。過去我們理念或許不同,但各位可藉這個機會表達你覺得重要的意見,以及學校有哪些需要改進的地方。

2.1

◎解答
c) A school dean.
（學校系主任。）

◎中譯

說話者的身分最有可能是？

a）銀行經理。

b）醫生。

c）學校系主任。

d）警官。

◎解析

由開頭的關鍵句 ...Principal Kelly and I have called this meeting...，可判斷說話者的身分應是 c）。principal 通常指「校長」，dean 則指「系主任；院長」。

2.2

◎解答

d）Teachers leaving their teaching jobs.

（教師離職。）

◎中譯

這段談話的主旨為何？

a）學生表現。

b）醫療糾紛。

c）校慶活動。

d）教師離職。

◎解析

由開頭的第一句即點出召開會議的目的 ...because since last summer, we have lost over twelve teachers...，所以答案選 d）最合適。

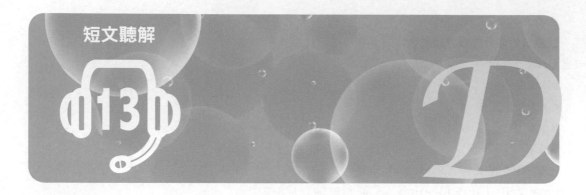

短文聽解

保健資訊

 學習重點

日常生活中常會聽到一些保健資訊，以皮膚保健為例，陽光是造成皮膚老化（aging）的元兇，因此避免日曬（exposure）、穿著防護衣物（protective clothing）是最基本及首要的措施。

 情境介紹及導引

Being in the sun too often for too long not only speeds up the natural aging process of our skin, but can also lead to skin cancer. To minimize skin damage from the sun, be wise about when you go out and protect yourself with sunscreen, hats, and sunglasses.

範例　ᐸ D-25 ᐳ

在以下資訊中，你會聽到一段有關健康的知識，請注意談話的主題。

What is the purpose of this talk?（此段談話目的為何？）

_____

a) To sell a new product.（銷售新產品。）

b) To learn how to slow down your voice.（學習如何放慢你的聲音。）

c) To learn how to protect your skin from the sun.
　　（學習如何保護皮膚免於日曬。）

d) To show how to choose sunglasses.（如何選購太陽眼鏡。）

（聽力原文請見詳解）　　　　　　　　　　　　　　　　　　　答案：c）

🎧 **說明**

a. Information Focus

問題的重點是「談話的主題」，從短文的 "To slow down the natural aging process of your skin, avoid sun exposure..." 得知談話主題是保護皮膚免於日曬。

b. Language Skills

重點字彙：aging process（老化過程）、avoid（避免）、sun's rays（陽光輻射線）、sunscreen（防曬產品）。

c. Tips for Listening

跟保健有關的內容通常會提到的重點包括保健的目的（slow down the skin's natural aging process）、避免做的事項（avoid sun exposure）、保護措施（wear protective clothing）。

🎧 **練習題** （D-26）

1 ＿＿＿＿＿＿＿ 承接範例題，請再聽一次並作答。

What type of sun protection is NOT mentioned as being recommended?

a) Hats.　　　　　　　　　　b) Sunscreen.

c) Bronzing lotions.　　　　　d) Protective clothing.

2.1 ＿＿＿＿＿＿＿ 請聽短文 **2**，回答以下 2 題。

Which disease does the speaker claim bananas can lower the risk of?

a) Heart disease.　　　　　　b) Flu.

c) Diabetes.　　　　　　　　d) Cancer.

2.2 ＿＿＿＿＿＿＿

What does the speaker recommend besides eating bananas?

a) Eating other fruits.　　　　b) Exercise.

c) Plenty of liquids.　　　　　d) Avoiding meats.

13 詳解

範例 & 1

◎聽力原文

To slow down the natural aging process of your skin, avoid sun exposure between 10:00 a.m. and 4:00 p.m., when the sun's rays are at their strongest. When you are in the sun, wear hats, sunglasses and other protective clothing. Use sunscreen with an SPF of 15 or greater. Apply sunscreen at least 30 minutes before you go out in the sun. Avoid sudden and strong sunlight exposure of skin that is normally covered. This type of exposure could increase your risk of getting skin cancer.

◎中譯

為了減緩您肌膚自然老化的過程，在早上十點到下午四點間陽光最強的時候，應避免曝曬。如果戶外，請戴上帽子、太陽眼鏡和穿著其他防護衣物。使用 SPF15 或防曬係數更高的防曬油，且至少在外出曬太陽之前的 30 分鐘就需塗上防曬油。避免讓平常受包覆的肌膚部位突然受到強烈陽光的照射，這類的曝曬可能會增加您罹患皮膚癌的風險。

1

◎解答

c) Bronzing lotions.
　　（助曬油。）

◎中譯

哪一種防曬方式未被推薦？

a) 戴帽子。
b) 防曬油。
c) 助曬油。
d) 防護衣物。

◎解析

談話中提到 wear hats, sunglasses and other protective clothing 以 及 use sunscreen 等防曬方法，僅答案 c) 未被提及。bronze 在此作動詞指「使曬黑，助曬」。

2

◎聽力原文

Did you know that bananas are a good source of vitamin C? Bananas are low in fat, and they are also an excellent source of fiber that can lower the risk of cancer. And for athletes like you, bananas replace body fluids that you burn during exercise. Do you want to keep in shape? Exercise often and eat bananas. Ready for your workout? Let's go!

◎中譯

你知道香蕉是豐富的維他命 C 來源嗎？香蕉的脂肪含量低，而且也是極佳的纖維質來源，可以降低罹癌風險。對於像你這樣的運動員，香蕉可補充你在運動時所燃燒的身體水分。你想維持良好的身材嗎？請經常運動和吃香蕉。準備好去健身了嗎？我們開始吧！

2.1

◎解答

d) Cancer.
　　（癌症。）

◎中譯

說話者宣稱香蕉可以降低哪一種疾病的風險？

a）心臟病。

b）流行性感冒。

c）糖尿病。

d）癌症。

◎解析

第二句後半提到的 ...can lower the risk of cancer...「可以降低罹癌風險」，所以選 d）。

2.2

◎解答

b）Exercise.

（做運動。）

◎中譯

除了建議吃香蕉之外，說話者還建議什麼？

a）吃其他的水果。

b）做運動。

c）充足的水分。

d）避免吃肉類。

◎解析

關鍵句在倒數第二句 ...Exercise often and eat bananas「請經常運動和吃香蕉」，所以可知答案應選 b）。

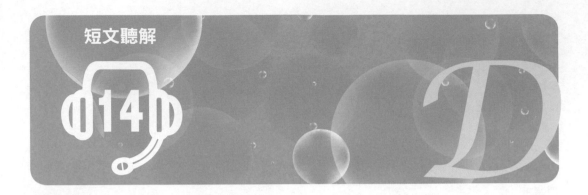

研習課程介紹

除了學校的正規課程外，我們常有機會參加各類機構主辦的研習營（workshop）或是專題研討會（seminar），這些課程都會邀請專家（expert / professional）主講，研討會的主題（topic）通常是大家感興趣的話題，例如網路約會（Internet dating）。

情境介紹及導引

Attending workshops and seminars is a great way to learn from the experts. It is where interesting ideas are exchanged. Some workshops address professional issues such as technological trends and investment opportunities; others may center on interesting topics such as creative writing or how to date online safely.

  D-27

在以下資訊中，你會聽到一段有關研討會的介紹，請注意談話的主題。

What is the seminar mainly about?（本研討會主要議題為何？）

_____

a）Road traffic regulations.（道路交通規則。）
b）Meeting people online.（網路交友。）
c）Social skills.（社交技巧。）
d）Internet software.（網路軟體。）

答案：b）

（聽力原文請見詳解）

說明

a. Information Focus

問題的重點是「研討的主題」，從短文中的 "...our topic will center on the problem of 'Internet dating.'" 得知主題是網路交友。

b. Language Skills

重點字彙：center on（集中）、advantages and disadvantages（利與弊）、professional（專業的）、issue（問題；爭議）、consider（考慮）、share（分享）。

c. Tips for Listening

研習課程的引言人或主講者，通常會先自我介紹（Phillip Olson），致歡迎詞 "It's my pleasure to welcome all of you to our monthly seminar."，接著介紹主題（Internet dating），以及要探討的問題 " What are its advantages and disadvantages? " 或課程的目標。

練習題　D-28

1 _____ 承接範例題，請再聽一次並作答。

Who is Phillip Olson?

a) A software engineer.
b) One of the audience.
c) The seminar speaker.
d) A policeman.

2.1 _____ 請聽短文 **2**，回答以下 2 題。

What is the topic of the course?

a) Financial management.
b) School bullying.
c) School admission information.
d) Emergency medical services.

2.2 _____

What will the audience learn from this course?

a) How to apply for a school.
b) How to save money.
c) How to deal with bullies.
d) How to do CPR.

範例 & 1

◎聽力原文

Good evening, everyone. I'm Phillip Olson. It's my pleasure to welcome all of you to our monthly seminar. Tonight, our topic will center on the problem of "Internet dating." Who enjoys dating online? Is it safe? What are its advantages and disadvantages? These are just a few issues we'll consider for now. As always, please feel free to ask questions or share your thoughts.

◎中譯

大家晚安！我是 Phillip Olson。很高興歡迎各位來參加本月的研討會。今天晚上我們主要是探討「網路約會」的議題。有哪些人喜歡網路約會？其安全性如何？又有何優缺點？這些只是我們要思考的一些問題。如同往常一樣，請大家踴躍提問或分享您的看法。

 1

◎解答

c) The seminar speaker.
（研討會的講者。）

◎中譯

Phillip Olson 的身分是？

a) 一位軟體工程師。
b) 其中一位觀眾。
c) 研討會的講者。
d) 一位警察。

◎解析

由開始的引言及之後介紹講題等內容可推知，Phillip Olson 是這場研討會的講者，故答案選 c)。

 2

◎聽力原文

Good morning and welcome to our course of "how to deal with school bullies." For parents with children in school, bullying is a major concern today. They want their children to fit in and be happy at school, but when their children come home upset and scared because they are being bullied, they feel very disappointed that such a thing could happen to them. This course will help parents better understand the problem of bullying and develop strategies for supporting their children to deal with school bullying.

◎中譯

各位早安，歡迎參加這門「如何面對校園霸凌事件」的課程。對於有小孩在學的家長們而言，校園霸凌是目前最令人憂心的問題。家長們希望孩子能適應並擁有愉快的校園生活，但當孩子們因為受到霸凌而沮喪且驚嚇地返家，家長們很難接受這樣的事情竟然發生在自己孩子身上。這門課將協助家長們對霸凌問題有更多認識，並提出策略來協助孩子們處理校園霸凌事件。

2.1

◎解答

b) School bullying.
（校園霸凌。）

◎中譯

這門課程的主題為何？

a）財務管理。

b）校園霸凌。

c）申請入學資訊。

d）緊急醫療服務。

◎解析

根據文章第一句中即提到 how to deal with school bullies，可知課程的主題是如何面對校園霸凌，所以答案選 b ）。

 2.2

◎解答

c）How to deal with bullies.

（如何處理霸凌問題。）

◎中譯

聽課者可以從這門課學到什麼？

a）如何申請學校。

b）如何省錢。

c）如何處理霸凌問題。

d）如何進行心肺復甦術。

◎解析

最後一句提到 ...develop strategies...to deal with school bullying...，說明協助家長去面對這個問題，所以答案選 c ）最合適。

短文聽解

提名與投票

 學習重點

在學校的公民教育（citizenship education）課程裡，會藉著實際的活動參與來教導學生公民的權利與義務（rights and duties），例如選舉投票（vote），以下是個有趣的實例。

 情境介紹及導引

For the school talent show, several students performed in comedy acts. Each performer either prepared a stand-up comedy routine or wrote a short, funny scene in which she and several friends acted. At the end of the show, the audience cast their votes to select a winner.

範例 D-29

在以下資訊中，你會聽到一段關於票選活動的介紹，請注意談話的主題。

What is the purpose of the talk?（本段談話的目的為何？）

_____

a) To learn how to make a comedy show.（學習如何製作喜劇。）

b) To vote for the funniest comic.（票選最佳喜劇演員。）

c) To learn how to color hair.（學習如何染髮。）

d) To remind students of the importance of good deeds.
   （提醒學生善行的重要性。）

答案：b)

（聽力原文請見詳解）

說明

a. Information Focus

問題的重點是「談話的主題」，從短文的第一句 "It's time to vote for your favorite comedian,... " 得知這是票選最佳喜劇演員的活動。

b. Language Skills

重點字彙：comedian/ comic（喜劇演員，comic 在口語中可解釋為喜劇演員）、
　　　　　　remind（提醒）、cast（投「票」）、ballot（選票）。

該是做某件事的時候：It's time to ＋ V

c. Tips for Listening

本段聽力的重點是跟票選活動有關的字彙，如 vote, choose, ballot；以及代表比較的字詞，如 favorite, best。

 練習題　D-30

1 _____ 承接範例題，請再聽一次並作答。

What will happen next?

a) People will go to color their hair.

b) People will pick out their favorite shoes.

c) People will cast their votes.

d) People will choose a car.

2.1 _____ 請聽短文 **2**，回答以下 2 題。

What is the purpose of the talk?

a) To introduce the nominees in a contest.

b) To welcome a union leader.

c) To tell the story of a Mexican hero.

d) To honor a mayor of an American city.

2.2 _____

Which statement about the speaker is true?

a) The speaker has been nominated.

b) The speaker will not announce the winner.

c) The speaker announced fewer people than he promised.

d) The speaker is the mayor of an American city.

15 詳解

範例 & 1

◎聽力原文

It's time to vote for your favorite comedian, and you can only vote for one. To remind you, we first heard Veronica on her mother's new car. Then we heard James on the price of sports shoes. And last was Susan, who told us about her unexpected hair color. These are three great young comics, but you have to choose the best one! Please take out your ballots.

◎中譯

現在是票選各位最喜愛的喜劇演員的時間，每個人只能投一票。提醒各位，第一位聽到的是 Veronica 介紹媽媽的新車；然後是 James 介紹運動鞋的標價。最後一位是 Susan，跟大家分享她意想不到的髮色。現有的三位傑出的年輕喜劇演員中，各位必須選出最棒的一位！請各位拿出你們的選票吧。

◎解答

c）People will cast their votes.
（人們會進行投票。）

◎中譯

接下來會發生什麼事？
a）人們會去染髮。
b）人們會挑出最喜歡的鞋款。

c）人們會進行投票。
d）人們會選一輛車。

◎解析

關鍵句是最後一句 ...Please take out your ballots...（請各位拿出你們的選票）。ballot 是名詞「選票」，cast one's vote 則指「投票」。

◎聽力原文

We have four nominees in the category of Best Actor. First, there is Roberto Gomez, for his starring role as the Mexican hero Emiliano Zapata. Second, we have Jeffrey Irons for his performance of Romeo in the latest production of Shakespeare's *Romeo and Juliet*. Next, Alex Rexroth was nominated for his outstanding work playing the mayor of an American city. And finally, Malik Jackson for his role as a labor union leader. Here is Sandra Clemens to announce the winner.

◎中譯

最佳男演員這個項目有四位提名者入圍。首先是由 Roberto Gomez 所飾演墨西哥的英雄 Emiliano Zapata 一角。其次是 Jeffrey Irons 在莎士比亞的最新改編作品《羅密歐與茱麗葉》中飾演羅密歐的角色。接下來是 Alex Rexroth 在劇中成功揣摩美國市長而受到提名。最後，Malik Jackson 則飾演一位勞工聯盟的領袖。現在將由 Sandra Clemens 來為我們揭曉得獎者。

2.1

◎解答

a) To introduce the nominees in a contest.

（介紹競賽中的被提名者。）

◎中譯

這段談話的主旨為何？

a) 介紹競賽中的被提名者。

b) 歡迎一位工會領袖。

c) 陳述一位墨西哥英雄的故事。

d) 表揚一位美國市長。

◎解析

由文章第一句關鍵句 ...We have four nominees in the category of Best Actor...，可推測談話的主要目的在介紹提名入圍者，故選 a) 最適合。

 2.2

◎解答

b) The speaker will not announce the winner.

（將不會由說話者揭曉得獎人。）

◎中譯

關於說話者的敘述下列哪一個正確？

a) 說話者已經被提名。

b) 將不會由說話者揭曉得獎人。

c) 說話者揭曉的人數比他承諾的少。

d) 說話者是美國某城市的市長。

◎解析

由文章最後一句關鍵句 ...Here is Sandra Clemens to announce the winner... 可知，得獎者將由 Sandra Clemens 來宣布，故答案選 b)。

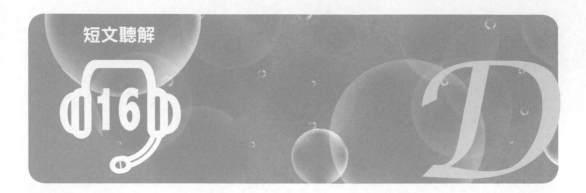

短文聽解

飼主與寵物

 學習重點

寵物已成為許多家庭的重要成員（an important member of the family），如何給予牠們適當的照顧及訓練（proper care and training），成為許多飼主必須學習的項目。

 情境介紹及導引

Denise got a puppy for her birthday. The small dog is very cute, but naughty. Denise is thinking of sending the puppy to a training school so he can develop good behavior patterns. With proper care and training, Denise hopes the puppy will become a happy member of the family.

範例 ◖D-31◗

> 在以下資訊中，你會聽到一段關於寵物飼養的資訊，請注意寵物受訓的原因。
>
> Why should owners take their dogs to obedience school?
> （飼主為何要帶他們的狗去訓練學校？）
>
> _____
>
> a）To teach them tricks.（教牠們一些特技。）
> b）To teach them proper table manners.（教牠們正確的用餐禮儀。）
> c）To learn how to discipline their dogs.（學習如何教導他們的狗。）
> d）To learn how to feed dogs.（學習如何餵食。）
>
> 答案：c）
>
> （聽力原文請見詳解）

說明

a. Information Focus

問題的重點是「寵物受訓的原因」，從短文的 "A professional will teach you how to give your dog commands and proper discipline." 得知是要學習如何教導他們的狗。

b. Language Skills

重點字彙：puppy（幼犬）、obedience（順從）、professional（專家）、command（命令）、discipline（訓練）。

c. Tips for Listening

熟悉與寵物飼養有關的字彙，如 owner, puppy, training, command；即使聽不懂 obedience, discipline 這些字，也可以從其他較為簡單的字彙（如 train, teach）推知其含意。

練習題  ﹙D-32﹚

1 ＿＿＿＿＿＿＿ 承接範例題，請再聽一次並作答。

How are obedience classes taught?

a) They are taught on a one-to-one basis.

b) The dogs' owners go to class without their dogs.

c) Dogs are taught without owners' participation.

d) They are taught along with other pets and their owners.

2.1 ＿＿＿＿＿＿＿ 請聽短文 **2**，回答以下 2 題。

What is the purpose of the talk?

a) To introduce a new dog breed.

b) To teach people how to adopt a pet.

c) To state the benefits of walking a dog.

d) To teach people how to jog in cold weather.

2.2 ＿＿＿＿＿＿＿

According to this passage, what does the government recommend?

a) Exercising on a regular basis.   b) Keeping 3–5 dogs at home.

c) Attending walking competitions.   d) Adopting shelter dogs.

16 詳解

範例 & ❶

◎聽力原文

Many new dog owners frequently ask me questions about how to give their puppies proper training, and my answer always is: The best way to train your dog is at an obedience school. A professional will teach you how to give your dog commands and proper discipline. Most obedience classes are taught along with other pets and their owners, so it's also a great opportunity to talk with other dog owners, as well as a chance for your dog to make new friends.

◎中譯

許多剛養狗的飼主常問我如何適當訓練幼犬，而我的答案總是：訓練狗兒的最佳方法就是送到「訓練學校」。專業訓練師會教導各位如何給予狗兒指令及適當紀律。多數的訓練課程是寵物與主人一同上課，所以這也是能和其他狗主人交流的好時機，同時給您的狗兒一個認識新朋友的機會。

❶

◎解答

d) They are taught along with other pets and their owners.
（和其他寵物及飼主一起上課。）

◎中譯

訓練課程如何進行？

a ）是採一對一教學。
b ）飼主不會帶狗一起上課。
c ）狗不會跟飼主一起上課。
d ）和其他寵物及飼主一起上課。

◎解析

文章最後有提到 ...classes are taught along with other pets and their owners，故答案選 d)。 along with 指「和……一起；隨同……」。

❷

◎聽力原文

A survey showed that having a dog to walk actually encourages regular exercise, with 60 percent of pet owners saying they always go for a walk with their dogs – even when time is precious. With increasing focus on leading an active, healthy lifestyle, it seems that owning a dog makes us healthier. The Government recommends 30 minutes of moderate exercise 3–5 times per week, and it's encouraging to see that dog walkers are exceeding this target and enjoying it at the same time.

◎中譯

一項調查顯示，遛狗事實上可促進規律運動，有六成的飼主表示，即使時間寶貴，他們總是會帶飼養的狗兒一起散步。隨著人們愈來愈注重積極、健康的生活型態，養狗似乎可以讓我們更健康。官方建議一週進行三到五次 30 分鐘的適度運動，而令人振奮的是，遛狗的人往往超過這個目標並且樂在其中。

2.1

◎解答

c）To state the benefits of walking a
dog.（說明遛狗的好處。）

◎中譯

這段談話的主旨為何？

a）介紹新狗種。

b）教人們如何認養寵物。

c）說明遛狗的好處。

d）教人們如何在冷天氣中從事慢跑。

◎解析

文章的關鍵句為第一句 ...having a dog
to walk actually encourages regular
exercise...，說明遛狗可以促進規律運動及
相關的益處，故答案選 c）。

2.2

◎解答

a）Exercising on a regular basis.
（規律運動。）

◎中譯

根據這段文章，官方提出什麼建議？

a）規律運動。

b）家中飼養三五隻狗。

c）參加競走比賽。

d）認養動物收容所的狗兒。

◎解析

由 最 後 的 關 鍵 句 ...The Government
recommends...moderate exercise 3-5
times per week... 可知，官方倡導規律且
適度的運動，故答案選 a）。on a regular
basis 指「規律地；定期地」。

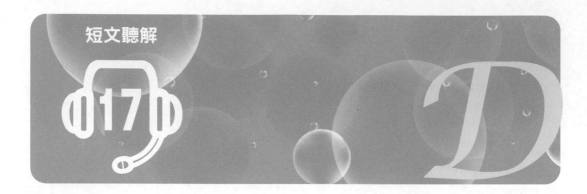

短文聽解

17

天氣預報

 學習重點

連續假期對很多人來說是度假的好時機,事先聽取氣象預報(weather forecast),依據天候狀況,選擇適當的旅遊方式,例如天氣好(good weather),就能去海灘(go to the beach),如果下雨可就得延期了(postpone)。

 情境介紹及導引

Today Daniel will go on a weekend trip with his classmates. He wakes up early to listen to the weather forecast so he will know what to pack. Daniel is hoping for good weather because they will go to the beach this afternoon and an amusement park tomorrow.

範例 🎧 D-33

> 在以下資訊中,你會聽到一段氣象預報的資訊,請注意今天的天氣概況。
>
> What is today's weather forecast?(今天天氣預報如何?)
>
> _____
>
> a) Sunny skies with highs in the low 70s.(晴朗,高溫大約為 70 度出頭。)
> b) Cloudy with a chance of rain.(陰天有雨。)
> c) Thunderstorms and strong winds.(強風雷雨。)
> d) Snowy with lows around zero.(下雪,低溫約為零度。)
>
> 答案:b)
>
> (聽力原文請見詳解)

a. Information Focus

問題的重點是「今天的天氣預報」，從短文的 "Today will be cloudy...light rain showers later tonight." 得知今天的天氣是陰天有雨。

b. Language Skills

重點字彙：high / low（在氣象中是指高低溫）、give way to（讓步：意指從某種狀況變成另一類狀況）。

c. Tips for Listening

聽取氣象報告的重點包括：天氣概況（如 sunny, cloudy, rainy, snowy, windy）、溫度（highs and lows）、天氣系統如高氣壓（high pressure system）、穿著建議等。

練習題　D-34

1 _____　承接範例題，請再聽一次並作答。

What advice is offered in this forecast?

a) That people stay indoors.

b) That people dress warmly.

c) That people carry an umbrella.

d) That people drive carefully.

2.1 _____　請聽短文 **2**，回答以下 2 題。

Why is this bad time for rainy conditions?

a) It's back-to-school time.

b) It's a three-day weekend.

c) There may be flooding.

d) There are several outdoor ceremonies.

2.2 _____

What is the weatherman's advice?

a) Carry an umbrella.　　　　　b) Stay indoors.

c) Dress warmly.　　　　　　　d) Avoid traveling.

17 詳解

範例 & 1

◎聽力原文

Here's the weather forecast for today and your holiday weekend. Today will be cloudy with highs in the low 90s. Those clouds will give way to light rain showers later tonight. The lows will be in the mid–70s. Those light rain showers are expected to become thunderstorms by tomorrow morning. It will be cloudy and rainy all day, so pack an umbrella and postpone your outdoor barbecue or picnic for Saturday or Sunday, as sunny skies are expected to return then.

◎中譯

以下是今日和本週末假期的氣象預報。今天為多雲陰天，高溫在華氏 90 度左右。夜間會由多雲轉為小雨，低溫約在華氏 75 度。預計到了明晨，陣雨將會轉為大雷雨，全天會是多雲有雨的天氣，請攜帶雨具出門，並延後您的戶外烤肉或野餐活動到週六或週日，天氣預計那時才會放晴。

1

◎解答

c）That people carry an umbrella.
（請大家攜帶雨具。）

◎中譯

氣象預報中提供什麼建議？
a）請大家待在室內。
b）請大家注意保暖。
c）請大家攜帶雨具。
d）請大家小心駕駛。

◎解析

關鍵句為最後一句 ...It will be cloudy and rainy all day, so pack an umbrella...，提醒民眾攜帶雨具外出，所以答案選 c）。

2

◎聽力原文

I wish I had good news for your holiday weekend forecast, but beginning today, the weather will be partly cloudy with isolated thunderstorms. Highs will be around 77 degrees with light winds. Tomorrow though, the chance of rain increases to 70 percent as a huge storm system enters the area for a few days. Be sure to bring your umbrella with you as these cloudy, wet conditions are expected to hang around for the next three days.

◎中譯

本希望今天的預報能為各位的週末假期帶來好消息，但從今天開始，天氣將轉為陰天且偶有大雷雨。高溫大約在華氏 77 度，有輕微陣風。這幾天因為有強烈鋒面系統進入本區域，明天降雨機率高達百分之七十。這樣多雲、潮濕的天氣情況預計將持續三天，外出請務必隨身攜帶雨具。

2.1

◎解答

b）It's a three-day weekend.
（這是三天的週末連假。）

◎中譯

為何這雨天來的不是時候？

a）這是返校期間。

b）這是三天的週末連假。

c）可能會淹水。

d）有許多戶外儀式。

◎解析

在關鍵句的第一句提到 holiday weekend forecast（週末假期的天氣預報），在最後一句又提到 ... these cloudy, wet conditions are expected to hang around for the next three days...（這樣多雲、潮濕的天氣情況預計將持續三天），故選 b）。

 2.2

◎解答

a）Carry an umbrella.

（攜帶雨具。）

◎中譯

氣象預報員的建議為何？

a）攜帶雨具。

b）待在室內。

c）穿著保暖。

d）不要出遠門。

◎解析

關鍵句為最後一句 ...Be sure to bring your umbrella with you...，可以知道氣象預報員提醒出門要攜帶雨具。be sure to + V. 是強烈建議的語氣，指「務必……；確保……」。

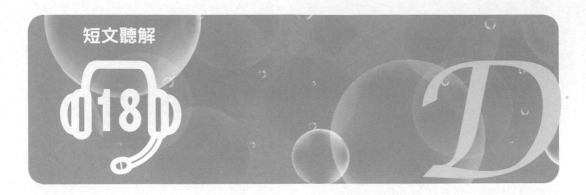

短文聽解

 學習重點

現代人的生活離不開廣告（advertisement），廣告傳遞各類訊息（delivering all kinds of messages），吸引消費者來購買產品或服務，例如以下這則廣告是藉著兩人同行一人免費（two tickets for the price of one），來增加火車的載客量。

 情境介紹及導引

Alice and her roommate are taking a weekend trip to the countryside to see the eastern coastline. A train ride seems an attractive way to travel because they will get to see the scenic mountain and river views not available from the highway. To save money, they plan to shop around to find a good deal.

範例 D-35

在以下資訊中，你會聽到一段的廣告，請注意廣告的內容。

What kind of advertisement is this?（這是則什麼廣告？）

_____

a）A car advertisement.（汽車廣告。）
b）A free ticket offer.（免費車票提供。）
c）Hotel advertisement.（飯店廣告。）
d）A bicycle riding competition.（自行車騎乘賽。）　　　答案：b）

（聽力原文請見詳解）

a. Information Focus

問題的重點是「廣告的內容」，從短文的 "...is currently offering 'Friends Ride Free.' "、"...a full-price, round-trip train ticket..." 得知是在促銷免費車票。

b. Language Skills

重點字彙：enjoyable（有樂趣的）、offer（提供）、full-price, round-trip train ticket（全價、來回火車票）、absolutely（完全地）

c. Tips for Listening

一般廣告的內容都是以吸引人的訴求做開場，如 "going somewhere is always more enjoyable with a friend"，接著是廠商滿足這項需求的產品或服務，如 "Friends Ride Free"，最後是獲得優惠的方法："Just buy a full-price, round-trip train ticket..."。

🎧 練習題　D-36

1 _____　承接範例題，請再聽一次並作答。

What restriction is placed on the offer?

a) It cannot be used with other offers.

b) Your friend is allowed to ride free.

c) It is valid only after November 30th.

d) It only applies to young people.

2.1 _____　請聽短文 **2**，回答以下 2 題。

What does "School to Work" do?

a) Allow adults to earn a high-school diploma.

b) Raise money for schools.

c) Teach physics.

d) Teach young people about work.

2.2 _____

How can you participate in the program?

a) Just make a call.　　　　　b) Go to the nearest office.

c) Find a training partner.　　d) Ask a high school teacher.

範例 & 1

◎聽力原文

Because going somewhere is always more enjoyable with a friend, North Coast Rail Lines is currently offering "Friends Ride Free." Just buy a full-price, round-trip train ticket between any two points in the four states we service, and one friend of yours can ride with you absolutely free. This offer lasts until November 30th and cannot be used in conjunction with any other offers or discounted ticket prices. Come down to any North Coast station today for more information.

◎中譯

和朋友一同出遊總是更加愉快有趣，北岸鐵路現正提供「好友共乘免費方案」。只要購買一張本公司所服務四大州內任兩個地點來回的火車全票，與您同行的好友便可免費共乘。這項優惠持續到 11 月 30 日止，但不能與其他優惠或折扣票價合併使用。今天就到北岸鐵路車站詢問詳情吧。

1

◎解答

a）It cannot be used with other offers.（不能與其他優惠併用。）

◎中譯

這項優惠有何限制條件？
a）不能與其他優惠併用。

b）您的朋友可以免費搭乘。
c）只能在十一月三十號之後使用。
d）只適用於年輕人。

◎解析

題目的 restriction 是問優惠方案的「限制」，由倒數第二句：This offer...cannot be used in conjunction with any other offers or discounted ticket prices... 可知應選 a）。in conjunction with 是指「連同、聯合」。

2

◎聽力原文

Remember what it was like to sit through a high school algebra or physics class and wonder how it related to real life? Well, the Castle Rock Independent School District is now offering students an opportunity to apply what they learn in school to real-life work experiences. It's called School to Work. It will better prepare students for college and careers by involving industry as training partners. School to Work is a positive project to improve education and provide direction for the area's youth. If you want to learn more about this program, please call 555-1815.

◎中譯

還記得以前在上高中代數課和物理課時，曾懷疑這些學科跟現實生活有何相關？堡岩獨立校區正提供學生一個機會，將學校所學應用到現實的工作經驗，名為「學以致用」計畫。此計畫會延攬企業成為合作訓練夥伴，幫助學員更能適應大學和工作職場。「學以致用」這項正面的計畫旨在提升教育並為本區的青年提供方向。如果您想更進一步瞭解這項計畫，請來電 555-1815。

about this program, please call 555-1815... 可知，欲知詳情可以打電話詢問，故選 a）。

2.1

◎解答

d）Teach young people about work.
（讓年輕人認識工作。）

◎中譯

「學以致用」計畫的作用是？
a）讓成年人獲得高中文憑。
b）替學校募款。
c）教物理學。
d）讓年輕人認識工作。

◎解析

第二句關鍵句提到 ...to apply what they learn in school to real-life work experiences... ，又說 ...better prepare students for college and careers... ，可知此計畫主要讓學生更能適應工作職場，故答案選 d）。

2.2

◎解答

a）Just make a call.
（只要打通電話。）

◎中譯

要如何參與該計畫？
a）只要打通電話。
b）到最近的辦公室。
c）找一個訓練夥伴。
d）詢問一位高中教師。

◎解析

由最後一句 ...If you want to learn more

短文聽解

介紹菜單

學習重點

去餐廳用餐時，服務人員（waiter / server /attendant）通常都會對客人介紹菜單（menu），尤其是餐廳的招牌菜色（special），或是較受歡迎的主菜（main course），還有當日推出的湯品（soup of the day）。

情境介紹及導引

Restaurant waiters have many responsibilities. Their main job is to take orders from customers for food or beverages. This includes presenting the menu, informing customers of daily specials, and making recommendations upon request. A waiter's good service makes customers' dining experience more enjoyable.

 範例 D-37

在以下資訊中，你會聽到一段介紹菜單的談話，請注意說話者的身分。

Who is speaking?（誰在說話？）

_____

a）A hotel clerk.（飯店人員。）
b）A chef.（主廚。）
c）A waiter.（服務生。）
d）A farmer.（農夫。）

答案：c）

（聽力原文請見詳解）

說明

a. Information Focus
問題重點是「誰在說話」，從短文的 "I'll be your server for this evening."，以及 dinner special, soup 等關鍵字彙得知是餐廳服務人員在說話。

b. Language Skills
其他字彙：grill（烤）、tuna（鮪魚）、salad（沙拉）、pumpkin（南瓜）、
take orders from customers（幫顧客點餐）。

c. Tips for Listening
本段的情境是在餐廳，聽力重點是熟悉在餐廳常用字彙的發音，如 server, waiter, dinner, fish, rice, soup。

練習題　D-38

1 _____　承接範例題，請再聽一次並作答。

What is the special treat for tonight?

a) A bingo game.

b) A live band performance.

c) A free cup of soup.

d) A salad coupon.

2 _____

What will the speaker probably do next?

a) Pay the bill.

b) Take a food order.

c) Cook for the guests.

d) Wash dishes.

3 _____

What is the purpose of the talk?

a) To promote a restaurant.

b) To teach people how to cook.

c) To teach people how to fish.

d) To vote for the best restaurant.

19 詳解

◎聽力原文

Good evening. My name is Winston, and I'll be your server for this evening. Tonight's dinner special is grilled tuna fish served with rice and a salad. Our soup of the day is creamy pumpkin soup. There is also a special treat tonight — a live jazz band will play for you while you have dinner with your family.

◎中譯

晚安，我是 Winston，今晚將擔任您的服務生。今晚的特餐是烤鮪魚搭配米飯及沙拉。本店的今日湯品是奶油南瓜湯。今晚還有一項特殊饗宴──您和家人用餐時將有現場爵士樂團為您演奏。

1

◎解答

b）A live band performance.
（現場樂團演奏。）

◎中譯

今晚的特殊招待是什麼？
a）賓果遊戲。
b）現場樂團演奏。
c）免費湯品。
d）沙拉優惠券。

◎解析

關鍵在文章最後一句 ...There is also a special treat tonight — a live jazz band will play for you...，可知正確答案

為 b）。選項 c）的濃湯和 d）的沙拉則是今日套餐的菜色。

2

◎解答

b）Take a food order.
（點餐。）

◎聽力原文

Hello, my name is Eliza. I'll be serving you tonight. Let me tell you about some of our specials. We have grilled steak with sautéed vegetables. We also have a nice fresh salmon dish that comes with rice. Our soup of the day is clam chowder. I'll be back in a minute to take your order.

◎中譯

您好，我叫 Eliza，今晚將由我為您服務。讓我先為您介紹幾道特餐。我們有烤牛排佐香煎蔬菜，還有美味的新鮮鮭魚搭配米飯。今日濃湯是蛤蠣濃湯。我一分鐘後會再回來為您點餐。

說話者接下來可能會做什麼？
a）付帳。
b）點餐。
c）替顧客烹調。
d）洗碗盤。

◎解析

由最後一句 ... I'll be back in a minute to take your order... 可知，說話的服務生稍後會為客人點餐，故選 b）。 take an / your order 通常指「（為客人）點餐」。

3

◎解答

a) To promote a restaurant.

（為餐廳宣傳。）

◎聽力原文

Rose Garden is a casual restaurant offering fresh food with terrific value and was recently voted one of the most popular restaurants in the north shore region. Please come and experience our fine dining atmosphere.

◎中譯

玫瑰園是提供超值新鮮美食的休閒餐廳，近來被票選為北海岸地區最受歡迎的餐廳之一。歡迎您蒞臨本餐廳感受絕佳的用餐氣氛。

這段談話的目的為何？

a) 為餐廳宣傳。

b) 教人們如何烹調。

c) 教人們如何釣魚。

d) 票選最佳餐館。

◎解析

本段內容在強調餐廳的特色與評價，最後一句 ...Please come and experience our fine dining atmosphere... 則歡迎大家前來體驗，可以知道是在宣傳這間餐廳，答案選 a)。

短文聽解

20

路況報導

 學習重點

當人們在開車時常會收聽路況報導（road condition reports），傾聽的重點是尖峰時間（rush/ peak hours）的交通，或是某個特殊事件（an unusual incident），例如輸水幹管破裂（a water main breaks）造成道路淹水。

 情境介紹及導引

Jason is on his way to work. For some reason, the traffic is congested and his car is moving slowly. He then hears on the radio that the roads are flooded due to a breakage. He hopes that the problem is fixed soon so he can get to work on time.

範例 D-39

在以下資訊中，你會聽到一段路況報導，請注意路況發生的原因。

According to the passage, what caused flooding?
（根據上文，是什麼造成淹水？）

_____

a) Heavy rain.（大雨。）
b) A broken water pipe.（水管破裂。）
c) A large sinkhole.（大坑洞。）
d) A gas explosion.（瓦斯爆炸。）

答案：b）

（聽力原文請見詳解）

說明

a. Information Focus

問題的重點是「淹水的原因」，從短文的第一句 "A water main break early yesterday..." 得知是因為水管破裂造成淹水。

b. Language Skills

重點字彙：main（自來水的總管線）、sinkhole（地表凹陷造成的坑洞）、shut off（關閉）。

c. Tips for Listening

路況報導都會先提到發生原因（A water main break）、時間（early yesterday）、導致的路況（a large sinkhole）、地點（Ogden Avenue），接著說明細節及後續處理狀況。

練習題　D-40

1 ＿＿＿＿＿＿＿　承接範例題，請再聽一次並作答。

What does the Councilman suggest people do?

a) Take alternative routes.

b) Help restore water service.

c) Visit the government website.

d) Stay at home.

2.1 ＿＿＿＿＿＿＿　請聽短文 **2**，回答以下 2 題。

What caused the problem on Highway 12?

a) Road construction.

b) A collapsed building.

c) Heavy rain.

d) A car accident.

2.2 ＿＿＿＿＿＿＿

What is true about the present situation?

a) Heavy traffic is building up southbound.

b) One lane has been closed.

c) The road has returned to normal conditions.

d) The traffic is still slow in both directions.

詳解

範例 & ❶

◎聽力原文

A water main break early yesterday in South Park left a large sinkhole in Ogden Avenue and damaged several homes. A 30-inch main broke about 4:30 a.m. on Ogden Avenue between Royal and George streets, and flooded roads before the water was shut off about 8 a.m. Workers replaced a section of the 30-inch pipe to restore water service last night. City Councilman Todd Gloria encouraged residents with damaged property to visit the official city website for information about compensation.

◎中譯

昨天稍早在南方公園的主要供水管線破裂，導致奧登大道路面下陷，並造成數間住宅受損。位於皇家街和喬治街之間的奧登大道路段，有一個 30 吋主管線於清晨四點半破裂，導致積水淹沒道路，直到上午八點才關上水閥。工人更換了部份路段的 30 吋管線，使昨晚能恢復供水。市議員 Todd Gloria 提醒受到財產損害的居民前往市政府的官方網站以了解相關賠償資訊。

❶

◎解答

c）Visit the government website.
（上政府機關網頁。）

◎中譯

市議員建議民眾採取什麼行動？

a）改道而行。
b）協助恢復供水。
c）上政府機關網頁。
d）留在家裡。

◎解析

關鍵句為最後一句 ...City Councilman Todd Gloria encouraged residents ...to visit the official city website for information...，故答案選 c）。visit the official website for + N.「上官方網站查詢（資訊等）」。

❷

◎聽力原文

Heavy traffic built up on both carriageways after a car overturned on Highway 12 this morning. The accident occurred southbound between Eight Mile Road and Highway 12, causing traffic to run slowly in both directions down to Weston. The road has now been cleared, and all lanes have been re-opened.

◎中譯

今晨一輛汽車在 12 號高速路翻覆，造成雙邊車道車流量大增的狀況。這場意外發生在八里路和 12 號高速路間的南下路段，造成往 Weston 的雙向交通行進緩慢。該路段目前已經清理完畢，所有車道均已恢復暢通。

❷.1

◎解答

d）A car accident.
（車禍事件。）

◎中譯

是什麼造成 12 號高速公路的狀況？

a）道路施工。

b）一棟倒塌的建築。

c）大雨。

d）車禍事件。

◎解析

關鍵句是第一句 ...Heavy traffic built up on both carriageways after a car overturned on Highway 12...，可知是因為有車輛翻覆而導致車流量大增，故選 d）。overturn 為動詞「翻覆」，car accident 則指「車禍」。

 2.2

◎解答

c）The road has returned to normal conditions.

（道路已經回復正常情況。）

◎中譯

關於目前的狀況，何者為正確描述？

a）南下路段的車流量大增。

b）有一條車道被封閉。

c）道路已經回復正常情況。

d）雙向車道仍車行緩慢。

◎解析

由最後一句 ...The road has now been cleared, and all lanes have been re-opened... 可知，目前道路已經回復正常情況，故選 c）。return to normal conditions 是形容「恢復正常運作」。

Linking English
大考英文聽力搶分秘笈

2012年1月初版 　　　　　　　　　　　　　　定價：新臺幣399元
有著作權・翻印必究
Printed in Taiwan.

主　　　編	陳　超　明			
編　　著	TOEIC 900 工作團隊			
發 行 人	林　載　爵			

出 　版 　者	聯經出版事業股份有限公司	叢書編輯	李　　　芃
地　　　　址	台北市基隆路一段180號4樓	文字整理	李　靜　儀
編輯部地址	台北市基隆路一段180號4樓	校　　對	謝一秀、李靜儀
叢書主編電話	（02）87876242轉226		徐采薇、張雅芳
台北聯經書房	台北市新生南路三段94號	封面設計	江　宜　蔚
電　　　　話	（02）23620308	內文排版	江　宜　蔚
台中分公司	台中市健行路321號	錄音後製	純粹錄音後製公司
暨門市電話	（04）22371234ext.5	插　　圖	黃　靜　書
郵政劃撥帳戶第0100559-3號			
郵 撥 電 話	（02）23620308		
印 　刷 　者	文聯彩色製版印刷有限公司		
總 　經 　銷	聯合發行股份有限公司		
發 　行 　所	台北縣新店市寶橋路235巷6弄6號2樓		
電　　　　話	（02）29178022		

行政院新聞局出版事業登記證局版臺業字第0130號

本書如有缺頁，破損，倒裝請寄回聯經忠孝門市更換。　　ISBN　978-957-08-3940-1 (平裝)
聯經網址：www.linkingbooks.com.tw
電子信箱：linking@udngroup.com

國家圖書館出版品預行編目資料

大考英文聽力搶分秘笈/陳超明主編．
TOEIC 900 工作團隊編著．初版．臺北市．
聯經．2012年1月（民101年）．336面．
18×26公分（Linking English）
ISBN　978-957-08-3940-1（平裝附光碟）

1.多益測驗

805.1895　　　　　　　　　　　　　100026435